"I don't know what I wish!" Eliza cried.

"Then let me tell you what my wish is." Gardner's rough whisper so close to her ear made her shiver. "I wish I'd met you in another time, in another place, where I wouldn't have to talk to you in riddles."

"Tell me who or what you're running from!"

"I can't," he said wearily

"The same as every Yankee shipmaster worth his name."

"Nay, Eliza, I'm not the same. I've enemies with memories running back to Adam and Eve, and someday they'll catch up with me."

"So what you're saying is that you care too much to let me care for you," she said bitterly. "That's a powerfully weak argument from a man who claims to live by his wits."

"It is, isn't it?" he admitted. "But it's all I have."

Dear Reader,

This month, Harlequin Historicals celebrates the arrival of spring with stories by four fabulous newcomers.

In *Steal the Stars* by Miranda Jarrett, the author uses her firsthand knowledge of the Rhode Island coast to weave a passionate tale set against the backdrop of America's struggle for independence.

Ana Seymour's delightful heroine finds herself the unwilling guest of an American *bandido* in the camp of the infamous Pancho Villa in *The Bandit's Bride*.

Arabesque by Kit Gardner, for those of you who like a touch of mystery, is the story of star-crossed lovers who discover the seamier side of London's upper class.

Set in medieval Wales, *A Warrior's Heart* by Margaret Moore is an unforgettable story of a soldier, wounded during the Crusades, and the spirited gentlewoman who turns his bitterness to love.

We hope you enjoy our March titles. And please be sure to look for more books by these four talented authors in the coming year.

Sincerely,
The Editors

Steal the Stars

Miranda Jarrett

Harlequin Books

TORONTO • NEW YORK • LONDON
AMSTERDAM • PARIS • SYDNEY • HAMBURG
STOCKHOLM • ATHENS • TOKYO • MILAN
MADRID • WARSAW • BUDAPEST • AUCKLAND

Harlequin Historicals first edition March 1992

ISBN 0-373-28715-1

STEAL THE STARS

MIRANDA JARRETT

is an award-winning designer and art director whose writing combines her love of history and reading. Her travels always include visits to old houses and historical restorations.

Miranda and her husband, a musician, live near Philadelphia with their two small children and two large cats. She is still trying to figure out how to juggle writing, working and refereeing disputes among preschoolers in the sandbox.

Printed in the U.S.A.

For Jake, with much love:
Of course, the first one's for you!

Chapter One

*Colony of Rhode Island
and Providence Plantations
June, 1772*

With a satisfied smile, Eliza Raeburn watched the dockmen load the final keg of rum into the hatch of the *Peacock*. Closing the leather-bound ledger in her lap, she slipped down from the crate that served as her informal desk and walked to the ship's rail. It had been a long day. She'd been here at six, and now it was late afternoon, the shadows of the masts lengthening across the water. The kegs of rum marked the last of her father's cargo for this voyage, and soon, probably next week, she would be sailing with him again for Saint Kitts. As much as she loved their home port of Providence, Eliza was eager to be off. Two, sometimes three, times a year she and Captain Raeburn made the long run along the coast to the West Indies, and the *Peacock* was as much her home as the yellow clapboard house on Angell Street.

Eliza untied the ribbons on her wide-brimmed hat and pulled it off, letting the breeze from the water play across her face and through her hair. She knew well how fortunate she was to have James Raeburn as her father. When she was seven, her mother had died in childbirth, and, grief stricken, James had chosen to take Eliza with him when he sailed, instead of leaving her with relatives. He had raised her more like a ship's boy than a young lady, giving her both a boy's freedoms and a boy's responsibilities. When she had proved quick with figures, James had handed her his account books to keep, and soon she assumed his correspondence with other merchants, as well. She shared his gambler's instincts for trade, a game where the wagers were called profits and the dice were ships and cargos, and as her skill grew he began to listen to her recommendations for new markets and investments. Together they had prospered, and along with the *Peacock,* which they owned, they held shares in a half-dozen other vessels.

Hers was a good life, she knew well, and yet as much as she tried to ignore it, there was something missing, an elusive emptiness that she couldn't define. It was only because they'd been in Providence so long, she reasoned. Once they were back at sea, the doubts would vanish.

Her father would be pleased their cargo was complete, for though he said little, Eliza sensed that he, too, was anxious to be gone. He was becoming more cautious as he grew older, and the *Gaspee,* the British naval schooner that had been sent to enforce the revenue laws in Narragansett Bay, worried him more than he would admit. He had even spoken of abandoning the rum trade in favor of cargos less lucrative but also of less interest to the customs officials in Newport.

Eliza didn't agree. None of the merchants in the colony had ever been overly concerned with paying the inflated duties on their goods that Parliament demanded. What did a group of pompous lords in London know about trading in Rhode Island? But she had found her position harder to defend ever since the *Gaspee* had seized the sloop captained by her cousin, Captain Nathaniel Chase, two months before, charging him with smuggling and taking him to Boston to wait for trial.

Absently Eliza swung her hat by its ribbons as she thought about Nathaniel. They had grown up together, sharing secrets and skinned knees, and for Eliza, Nathaniel was cousin, brother and best friend combined into one bluff, oversized package. She always pictured him laughing, his eyes curved merrily, his grin wide. She couldn't bear the thought of him in a prison in Boston, a creature of sunlight confined to a dark and airless cell.

She had written dozens of letters on his behalf, to Admiral Montagu and Governor Hutchinson and a slew of lesser officials, but the few who had bothered to reply knew—or pretended to know—nothing of her cousin's case. Nathaniel had simply vanished into the hostile bureaucracy of the British colonial government, and each day he was missing, Eliza's fear and suspicion of the system that had stolen him away grew a little deeper.

"You've done a good day's work, child," said James Raeburn, startling his daughter from her thoughts. Despite the years that had rounded his shoulders and faded his red hair with gray, the resemblance between the two was striking, and the affection they held for each other obvious. "That last delivery from Parker all stowed away?"

Eliza nodded, happy to bask in his approval. "All that's left are our own provisions. Tomorrow's market day, so I'll see to them then."

"More onions, fewer potatoes this time."

"And check the pork from Amos Wright to make sure he gives us quality to match his price," she completed neatly, teasing. "I know what you like, Father. You might recall I've been doing this for some time now, with no complaints from captain or crew."

He smiled and patted her shoulder. "I have noticed that, aye. And quite an able quartermaster you are, too."

"Name another who would see your house tidied and shuttered for you before you sailed."

His smile disappeared. "That task, at least, I won't ask you to do this time."

Surprised, Eliza waited for an explanation. Closing up their house was an obligatory if tedious part of leaving Providence, just as opening it up for airing was part of coming home. Something was not quite right. Her father was avoiding her eyes, fiddling instead with a loose button on his coat.

"There's something you and I must discuss, Eliza," he began, "and I fear it won't be easy for either of us."

James cocked his hat back with his thumb and let out a long sigh. He had already postponed this conversation too long. He looked down at his daughter's upturned face, and the innocent trust he saw in her dark eyes almost broke his heart. "When the *Peacock* sails next week, you won't be coming with us. I can't—I won't—risk taking you with me this time. Not now with the British so hot for our necks."

Eliza could only stare, just beginning to comprehend. He couldn't mean it. In fifteen years they had never been apart, not one day. He *couldn't* leave her behind. He needed her there with him on the *Peacock!*

"It's all settled," he continued uncomfortably. "You'll see, the time will pass quickly, and you'll scarcely know I'm gone. You won't be alone, after all. Your Aunt Anne is but two houses away, and there's Beckah Nye and all your other friends, too."

"But we've always outrun the revenue coasters before," she protested. "Why should it be different now?"

"Because the times are different, Eliza," said James bitterly. "These navy men have orders to teach us a lesson, and they're trying a good deal harder to catch us. And when they do, it's not just a fine and a talking-to, the way it used to be. Now they haul a man off to prison if his hat's on crooked, and with their cannon trained on your sides, you'd best go without a fight. Look at what happened to Nathaniel. I'd be out of my wits to take you into that."

She raised her chin defiantly, hands on her hips, her red hair tossed back. "I'm not afraid of a fight. You know I can shoot as true as any man, pistols or rifles. You taught me yourself. I'm not afraid of the *Gaspee*."

"Eliza, it's not a question of that."

"Then why, why won't you take me with you?"

As she stood there before him, her cheeks rosy from the argument and her eyes flashing, James thought the reasons were painfully clear. Somehow his daughter had changed from a leggy, sunburned girl into a beautiful woman, and while he wasn't sure just when the transformation had occurred, he was positive that no decent father would willingly put such a daughter in the path of the British navy. The Rhode Island men the *Gaspee*'s commander arrested had been beaten, abused and humiliated before they were sent to prison. He did not want to consider what would happen to a woman.

Not for the first time, James wished she was married and settled with a life of her own beyond him and the *Peacock*. There was a restlessness in his daughter that was rare in women, and it would take a strong man to anchor her. But Eliza had always been sensible about her suitors. Too sensible, in his opinion. Her mother had been seventeen when she wed, but Eliza would be twenty-two on her next birthday. Plenty of young men, both here and in the West Indies, had come calling, but to his dismay none had captured her interest. Perhaps he had been selfish, trailing her along with him on the *Peacock,* instead of settling her in one place so she had the ties that other women seemed to need. He would miss her desperately, but maybe this time without him in Providence would give her the opportunity to form some sort of connections on her own.

But all this he left unsaid. "Because, child, it is too dangerous," he answered. "You're staying here where I know you'll be safe, and there's an end to it."

"Father, I still don't see—"

"Eliza, no," he said curtly, the irritable edge in his voice a warning that silenced her. Like the crewmen who served him on the *Peacock,* Eliza was quick to recognize the set of his jaw, and she knew to swallow her frustration for now or risk the full fire of his temper. Instead she tied her hat loosely back on her head, gathered her ledger and followed her father down the gangplank.

"Good evening, Raeburn!" Standing at the end of the wharf was James's friend and counselor, Philip Deane. The little lawyer was waving excitedly, the late afternoon sun glinting off his steel-rimmed spectacles. "Heading for John Brown's house, are you?"

"Brown's? No. Why should we?" asked James as he and Eliza joined Philip.

The lawyer's smile split his fat-cheeked face, the news he carried fairly bursting from his lips. "Then you haven't heard! You must be the last two people in Providence who haven't. One of Brown's shipmasters has had the bold-faced good fortune to trap the *Gaspee* on the shoals off Namquit Point, and we're all invited to his house to decide what's to be done next."

Eliza's spirits soared higher than the gulls over-head. The *Gaspee* run aground! If it were true, then her father would have no reason to leave her behind. She could have danced a jig around Philip Deane from pure joy.

Chapter Two

The rebellion would break out soon, thought Gardner Griffin as he absently looked out the open window at the harbor below. Perhaps even tonight. He watched the men arriving for the meeting, climbing the marble steps alone and in small groups. They were a prosperous lot, these Rhode Island merchants. Their dark coats glittered with buttons of polished brass and cut steel, their white ruffled shirt fronts were starched and pressed and their three-cornered hats neatly brushed. Successful men, proud of the wealth they'd brought to this little town at the top of Narragansett Bay.

The evening air was sweet with honeysuckle, and the breeze from the river brushed the damask curtain across Gardner's hand. He was acutely aware of how out of place he looked in this elegant parlor. He had come straight from the deck of the little sloop *Hannah* with his news, still wearing salt-stained sea boots and his faded homespun greatcoat, and two days' growth of beard darkened his jaw.

But he knew well that the differences ran deeper than appearances. Most Yankee seamen were stocky and compact, while he stood well over six feet, with broad shoulders and a lean, sinewy frame. In a face that had been tanned and weathered by a life at sea, his eyes were a startling, intense shade of blue that made many reluctant to return his gaze. When he had first begun to sail for John Brown last year, town gossip had attributed his appearance to Indian blood, mistaking the sharp cheekbones and thick black hair he'd inherited from his Welsh mother Gwyneth. He hadn't bothered to correct the gossip, for the truth—that Gwyn had been Thomas Gardner's indentured servant, not his wife—was something he preferred to keep to himself.

Besides, he had not come to Providence to share confidences and companionship, nor was it his habit to do so. Long ago he had learned to trust no one beyond himself, a philosophy that had served him well, and one that he owed to Abigail Jenkes. She had sworn she loved him, promised nothing mattered more than becoming his wife, and young fool that he'd been, he'd listened and believed and trusted her, even as she betrayed him to his majesty's press-gang in exchange for another, more suitable, lover.

For the sin of being born in the colony of Massachusetts rather than in Great Britain, Gardner had been treated worse than most sailors in the Royal Navy, his life on the man-o'-war *Intrepid* marked by hardship and sudden, unpredictable cruelty from the officers. They had tried hard to break his spirit, and he would carry to his grave the scars of their discipline across his back. But he had survived, and while his bitterness had grown, so had his seamanship. When he was at last able to jump ship, he had no difficulty finding a berth on a Boston brigantine, and within two years he was sailing as a captain for the merchant John Hancock.

In Hancock Gardner found an ally, and through him an outlet for his hatred of the British in the undercurrent of radical politics that sought to separate the colonies from Great Britain. He joined the Sons of Liberty and quickly rose to become the confidant of powerful men like Hancock and Samuel Adams, his intelligence and abilities respected and his loyalties unquestioned. Gardner was the kind of man the Boston leaders cherished most: one who would risk everything because he had so little of his own to lose.

They sent him to Providence to work with John Brown, a sympathizer to the cause of liberty and the most prominent merchant in the colony. Together they made the most of Rhode Island's notorious "free trade," a situation referred to elsewhere more simply as "smuggling." And what an accomplished smuggler Gardner had become! Behind the false manifests he registered at the customs house were very different cargos in the hold of the *Three Brothers:* guns and muskets, lead for bullets and broadcloth for uniforms, everything necessary to outfit a rebel army when the time came.

Not even John Brown realized the extent of Gardner's success, nor did he know that the captain of his brig was also a trader in information that benefitted the rebels as much as did the muskets. Sometimes

Gardner amused himself by counting the reasons King George had for seeing him hung. Desertion, treason, spying and smuggling arms made quite a list. And tonight, if the raid went as he planned, piracy, as well.

Two servants dressed in gray moved along the walls, lighting the candles in the pewter sconces, and the flames flickered and jumped in the breeze from the open windows. John Brown was indeed a wealthy man, observed Gardner wryly, if he could afford to burn two score candles before sunset, and ignore the splatters of wax that were blistering his fine French wallpaper.

It was then, by the candles' light, that he first saw the girl. Her presence among the men was enough to catch his attention, but it was her beauty that held it. Her face was framed in profile against the brim of her chip hat: a straight nose, a generous mouth and a chin that erred towards stubbornness. Beneath the hat's brim her hair was a mass of coppery curls, a few loose tendrils curling around her throat. The white batiste kerchief she wore tucked into her bodice did little to disguise her high, round breasts, and with an experienced eye, Gardner was sure her waist was as narrow without stays as with them.

A beauty, he decided, but no coquette. Her blue-and-white-striped gown was simply cut, the linen mussed and wrinkled at the end of a long day, just as her hat was a little askew, the blue satin ribbons trailing untied across her shoulders. This girl's artlessness was unusual, but what intrigued Gardner more was her expression as she listened to the two men beside her. Whatever their conversation, she was listening carefully, her brows drawn together in a slight frown.

Eliza had lived her life among sailors and shipmasters, had travelled much in the world, and yet she had never seen a man quite like the one near the window. There was an easy masculine grace in how he held his body, a self-assurance that made his well-worn clothing more distinctive than any gentleman's velvet. The twilight and the candles threw his features into a bold pattern of shadow and light, accentuating the planes of his cheekbones and the strong line of his jaw. He wore his blue-black hair tied back, although a few locks, dark and shining like a raven's wing, had escaped to fall boyishly across his forehead. But it was his eyes that captured her, forcing her to stare back, eyes of a rare blue made startling by contrast to his sun-browned skin. In confusion, she felt a tell-tale blush creeping across her breasts and up her throat to her cheeks.

"What is it, Eliza?" James asked. "Are you unwell?"

"Oh, no, Father, I'm fine." With an effort she tried to return her attention to the conversation, but not before she saw the corners of the stranger's mouth twitch and curl with amusement at her reaction. Damn him, she thought angrily. I'm no green serving girl to have my head turned by some handsome rogue who doesn't even have the decency to come clean-shaven to Mr. Brown's parlor.

James touched his daughter's forehead lightly. "You're warm, lass. Come, I'll take you out on the steps for air."

"Really, Father, it's nothing." She tucked her hand into the crook of his arm and smiled up at him. "I was only seeing who else was here tonight."

"Anyone and everyone," said Philip cheerfully.

James's sigh was more pessimistic. "No one with any interest in trade could afford to miss what Brown says. This interference by the Crown must stop before we're all bankrupt. I'm no firebrand, but whatever Brown proposes, I'll back him."

"Desperate times, desperate measures, eh?"

"Something like that, yes," agreed James. "I hear Brown sent Griffin out expressly to lure the *Gaspee* onto the shoals. He'd be the man with the nerve for that kind of game, too, if Sam Brook can be believed. Sam shipped back with Griffin on the *Three Brothers* and says he's never seen sharper sailing. Martinique to Newport in fourteen days, and he's got every seaman in Providence clamoring to sign on with him."

In spite of her best intentions, Eliza's eyes crept back to the tall stranger, now in conversation with Josiah Buck, Mr. Brown's shipping agent. He had to bend slightly to hear Josiah, and with an impatient gesture he raked his fingers back through his black hair. He must be at least a shipmaster to be invited here tonight, but he didn't look prosperous enough to be a captain who owned his own vessel, like her father. He wasn't from Providence, that was certain. She would have remembered him.

A murmur ran through the crowded room as, at last, John Brown appeared. He was a heavyset man with powdered hair above a full chin and an imperious nose, and his manner was that of one who expected to be obeyed in all things. Gingerly he stepped onto the footstool a servant provided, and at once his audience fell respectfully silent. Behind him stood Josiah Buck, and three of his shipmasters currently in port.

Lined up like so much rich man's property, thought Gardner cynically. He knew he was expected to be there, too, standing obediently, but he waited until he saw the disapproval flicker across Brown's face before he sauntered across the room. The man's self-importance irritated him, especially tonight. He wanted no credit, no fanfare, for trapping the *Gaspee*, such things were best told to as few witnesses as possible for the Crown to later press into court. Let Brown's name be the one written large on the warrant for treason. He could weather a storm like that a great deal better than he, Griffin, could.

Eliza watched with surprise as the stranger took his place beside Josiah. "Tell me, Mr. Deane," she whispered. "Who is that tall man—there, with the black hair—with Mr. Brown?"

"That's the shipmaster that's brought us all here, Eliza," he replied. "That's Captain Griffin himself."

Eliza's eyes widened. When she'd heard about the new captain Mr. Brown had hired from Massachusetts, she'd pictured an older man, someone more respectable. Certainly someone less attractive.

James looked sharply at his daughter, noting the change in her expression. As much as he hoped she would fall in love and marry, it wouldn't happen with a man like Gardner Griffin if he had anything to say in the matter. He studied her face, praying he was mistaken.

John Brown cleared his throat. "This afternoon my sloop the *Hannah* was chased by his majesty's schooner, the *Gaspee,* persecuted and hounded, the same as has happened to so many of you."

Men nodded and muttered soft oaths under breaths, and Eliza thought sadly of Nathaniel. In the past three months, almost every merchant house had lost ships and cargos to the *Gaspee,* and there was little respect for the king or his navy in the room.

"But this time," Brown continued, "the tables are reversed. The hunter is now the prey, and Lieutenant Dudingston has fallen to Captain Griffin. Not only did Captain Griffin refuse to surrender when challenged, but he then led that scoundrel Dudingston neatly across Namquit Shoals." Brown cleared his throat again, savoring the moment and the expectant faces before him.

Get on with it, thought Gardner impatiently. The tide will turn in the river before you've told them why they're here.

"Gentlemen," said Brown at last, "I have the great pleasure to announce that the *Gaspee* is now aground, and tonight I intend to send a message to King George and his Parliament that cannot be ignored. Tonight, so help me, I'll see the *Gaspee* burned and Dudingston denied the future plunder of Providence shipping. How many of you will be there with me?"

At once the room echoed with a wild chorus of agreement, and Eliza was certain not a single man dissented. She saw her father and Philip exchange conspiratorial glances, and all around her, men were grinning like boys plotting mischief. Mischief that she herself had every intention of participating in. She had just as much reason to hate the British schooner, and she owed it to Nathaniel to be there for its destruction.

She knew, of course, that there would be no chance of going with her father's permission, but in the dark, dressed like a boy, it would be easy to slip into a boat among the others, and then she could trust her experience on the *Peacock* to carry her through. As long as she kept clear of her father, and was home before him, there would be no chance of being caught. It would all be so very easy....

Gardner, too, was planning. He had much to do within the next two hours, checking and rechecking the details of the raid, leaving as little to chance as he dared. He had always believed in luck, but he believed more in himself. Luck, and his own restlessness, had made him volunteer to sail the Newport packet when her regular captain had come down with the measles, and luck had sent the *Gaspee* in pursuit when he'd been sailing the small and agile *Hannah* instead of the larger and less maneuverable *Three Brothers*. But it had been his skill and experience that had trapped the British schooner, and he was now eager to finish what luck had begun.

Chapter Three

Eliza walked swiftly towards the river, enjoying the freedom of breeches in place of petticoats. She wore one of Nathaniel's outgrown jackets with the sleeves rolled up, her long hair wrapped and pinned under an old three-corner hat. As long as she kept the hat pulled low over her face and the jacket buttoned, she was sure no one would suspect. Tucked into her belt was one of the pair of Spanish pistols her father had given her years ago, the extra bullets and powder in a little pouch strung around her neck. She headed towards the sound of the drummer mustering more recruits for the raid, and as her feet fell into step with the ruffling drumbeats, she began to whistle along in a decidedly unladylike fashion. Aunt Anne, she thought, would be quite appalled.

Although it was nearly midnight, in the streets there was an excitement in the air that was nearly palpable, the sense of adventure contagious. Word of the *Gaspee*'s plight had travelled fast from one clapboard house to the next, for few families had been untouched by the *Gaspee*'s interference.

Eight longboats, borrowed from as many merchants, were tied alongside the dock where the crowd of men and boys was gathered. At the far end of the wharf, Eliza caught sight of her father's familiar profile, and in haste she ducked into the nearest boat, already filled with nearly a dozen men. She recognized most of them, but none seemed to recognize her in turn. Standing in the stern, she hesitated as the men settled around her.

"What's the matter, laddie, fearful you'll soil your dainty hands?" called out a barrel-chested man with a crest of turkey feathers in his hatband. "Stay a moment, and I'll lay my lace handkerchief here to keep your bottom dry."

"Watch your mouth, Ned Turner," Eliza fired back without thinking, "or the *Gaspee*'s watch will smell the rum on your breath before we're out of sight of Providence!"

At once she regretted her words as the others in the boat guffawed. While her voice was deep for a woman's, its pitch would never pass for a man's, and she hung her head in shame at her own stupidity. Any moment she would be hauled out of the boat in disgrace.

"No names, boy, no names," said a deep voice with a raspy edge, "unless you want to see them on a warrant from the king."

Eliza felt a heavy hand rest on her shoulder, and at once the boat fell quiet. "No harm meant, Cap'n," said Ned contritely, tugging on the front of his hat. "Just a bit of fun."

"This isn't supposed to be a picnic, damn it. Six miles of rowing should convince you of that," said Gardner sharply. "Here, boy, sit next to me where I can keep you out of mischief."

Not daring to look up, Eliza squeezed herself beside Gardner. She hadn't counted on being in this, the leader's boat, for it would make it doubly difficult to avoid her father's notice. Nor had she planned to sit next to Captain Griffin. She hadn't forgotten the way his eyes had raked over her earlier. What would he think if he knew she were beside him now, their legs pressed together in the narrow space?

With a shudder the boat was pushed off from the wharf. The men rowing immediately slipped into rhythm, their muffled oars barely marking the water's surface. Eliza looked back at the town: the neat houses ranging up the hillside, the tall masts of the ships like leafless trees, the ghostly spire of the meeting house. Above them the moon was only a silvery crescent, the sky a patchwork of stars.

It was chilly on the river, and Eliza pulled her coat a little closer. Left to their own thoughts, no one spoke, the earlier bravado changing to a tense quiet as they rowed closer to Namquit Point. Eliza watched the man in front of her compulsively check and recheck his rifle, and for the first time she wondered why she had come. The danger of the raid had seemed slight in the safety of Brown's parlor. Here on the river she realized it was very real indeed. What were the odds of rifles and pistols against an armed naval schooner?

She stole a glance at Captain Griffin beside her. He sat with his long legs sprawled before him, his face hidden in the shadow of his hat's brim. She could see the butt of a pistol jutting from the front of his coat, and the faint moonlight gleamed on the cutlass he wore at his waist. Unlike the others, he seemed calm and at ease as he gazed at the coastline slipping past them, and Eliza sensed he'd done things like this before. It seemed strange to her that, while he'd looked so out of place at Brown's house, here his cockiness struck her as the mark of hard-won experience, and she was suddenly glad to have ended up in his boat.

Gardner watched for the dark silhouettes of landmarks on the shore, waiting and hoping his faith in the Rhode Islanders wasn't misplaced. Many of them had, like himself, seen action in the last war, and the others were at least accustomed to taking orders.

With a few exceptions, he thought, remembering the boy beside him. From the look of his uncallused, ink-stained hands, the boy had yet to leave the security of his master's counting-house. But he'd showed nerve enough to stand up to Ned Turner's teasing. A little adventure like this would help season him, stretch his mama's apron-strings. That is, if he doesn't get himself killed in the process, thought Gardner drily.

Eliza's heart beat faster as the boats rounded the point and she caught sight of the *Gaspee*. The schooner's deck listed sideways where her hull had been caught on the shoals and she showed only two small lanterns, fore and aft. With as little noise as possible the small flotilla of longboats drew closer.

"Pull there to starboard," Gardner said softly, and the men at the oars obeyed. "We can't give them the chance to get the guns to the bow ports."

With each muted oar stroke they came closer, until their boat was nearly under the *Gaspee*'s bow. All around Eliza the men not rowing held their rifles ready, and she too gripped her pistol. Her hands shook with fear and excitement, and she took a deep breath, trying to steady the shaking that would ruin her aim.

Then, far too late, came the cry of the sentinels, and with the moment of surprise past, the rowers quickened their strokes. Suddenly a stocky figure appeared at the rail, hastily half-dressed in shirt and cocked hat.

"Who comes there?" he challenged, peering into the darkness. He climbed the starboard gunwale, his sword poised. "Who comes there?"

To Eliza's surprise, Gardner sprang to his feet beside her. "I'm the sheriff of the County of Kent," he replied, his raspy voice echoing across the water, "and I have a warrant for your arrest. Surrender now, God damn you!"

But before the British officer could answer, a rifle shot rang out and the man jerked back like a broken puppet and crumpled from view. Their leader fallen, the rest of the crew rushed about the deck in confusion.

"Who in blazes did that?" said Gardner angrily. "There'll be the devil to pay if we've killed Dudingston outright." Dropping back to his seat, he ordered the boat to the schooner's side. He grabbed a rope from the bows and was up and over the rail in one swift motion, his cutlass swinging.

Her heart beat wildly, and Eliza knew the time to test her courage had come. The British had begun to fire at them now, the bullets plopping dully in the water around the boat. Jamming the pistol into her waistband to free her hands, she clambered up the rope with the others.

The scene on the deck was more like a tavern brawl than a sea battle. As the attackers swarmed over the schooner, the outnumbered British sailors foundered helplessly. She saw one seaman raise a sword to defend himself only to be struck from behind. Another fumbled with a rifle as two Providence men with cudgels pulled him down and disarmed him. The majority dropped their weapons and fled below, for all the world like frightened rabbits. In ten minutes' time, forty men had swept over the rail and neatly captured an armed vessel of his majesty's navy, and it had seemed such child's play that Eliza found herself a little disappointed. In her inexperience, she had no concept of how perfectly the raid had been planned and executed.

She scanned the deck nervously for her father, but he was nowhere to be found, and she guessed his boat must be one of the ones left manned in case of retreat. One by one the British sailors were bound with black-tarred cords, pinioned like chickens for market and herded roughly into the waiting longboats. They would be taken to the shore and released, left with their lives and little else, but for them Eliza felt small pity. They would be back in Newport in less than a day if they had any wits at all, which was more courtesy than they'd shown to Nathaniel.

Eliza made her way to the front of the little crowd of Rhode Islanders gathered around Lieutenant Dudingston. Supported by his midshipman, the wounded officer was deathly pale, his face beaded with sweat, his left arm and the lower half of his white uniform soaked red. Sickened, she looked away. He had lost so much blood it seemed unlikely to her that he'd live.

John Brown stood over him with his arms crossed, staring sternly down his long nose. "We have you now, don't we, Dudingston?" he said. "And you look no better than the rascally pirate you are, damn your hide. You've broken most every law in this colony, and now you must pay."

Dudingston tried to stand, but fell back against the midshipman's shoulder. "I have been most grievously wounded," he said unsteadily. "If you will only permit my men to tend to me—"

Brown snorted derisively. "If you've been shot, it was likely by your own people, not ours." He beckoned to Eliza. "Find the sheriff, boy, and tell him we're ready to accept this scoundrel's surrender." He motioned towards the companionway to the cabin, and Eliza hurried down it, glad to leave the scene on the deck. She stumbled in the dark passage, feeling her way along as she headed towards a faint light outlining the closed door to what she guessed was the lieutenant's cabin. Fumbling a bit with the latch, she pushed the door open, and gasped. There stood Captain Griffin, bold as the devil himself, the long barrel of his pistol levelled at her forehead, the hammer drawn back and ready to fire.

"You shouldn't creep up on me like that, boy," he said, grinning as he relaxed and lowered the gun. "I don't take well to surprises."

"You could have killed me!" cried Eliza.

"Aye, but I didn't, did I?" he replied levelly. He cocked his head towards the deck. "Have they given up yet?"

Eliza swallowed hard, still struggling to recover. "Uh—yes, almost. I mean, aye, sir," she stammered. "Mr. Br—I mean, your friend says to tell you they're ready to surrender."

"I'm surprised it's taken this long." He returned to the task she'd interrupted, ransacking the lieutenant's desk and sea chest. He read the papers rapidly, discarding most of them, but a few he folded and placed carefully inside his shirt. He seemed to have forgotten her, and, unwilling to return to Mr. Brown without him, Eliza waited.

"Lieutenant Dudingston seems badly hurt," she began at last. "I doubt he'll live much longer."

"Oh, the surgeon will patch him together well enough to go with the others," he answered. "All men think their own wounds are mortal."

"But you can't mean to leave him on the beach, too! What if he dies?" Eliza faltered, realizing her error. A shipmaster's daughter, how could she forget that a captain's word is always law?

"Don't question me, boy." Gardner wheeled to face her, his face dark. "If he dies, he'll go straight to hell as he deserves."

"Aye, aye, sir," she agreed with little conviction.

Gardner slammed the desk shut. "Fortunes of war. It could just as easily been you or I. Do you think Dudingston would have stopped to think of us in his place?"

Suddenly Gardner took her by the arm and pulled her closer to the swinging lamp. He stared hard at her face, frowning. With his fingers he took her chin and gently turned her face towards the light.

Her heart pounding, Eliza forced herself to return his scrutiny without flinching. With a sinking feeling, she realized her masquerade was over. She watched the line of his lips curl up at the corners, as they had earlier, but now there was no humor in his smile.

"Why in the sweet name of God are you here?" Gardner asked, his tone deceptively mild. There were many things he'd hoped to find in Dudingston's cabin, but the red-haired girl hadn't been one of them. "Why aren't you home with your mother, where you belong?"

"My mother is dead." Eliza tried to raise her chin defiantly, but his grasp still held her face rigid before his.

"So is mine. But I have a good reason to be here, and you, young woman, do not."

"I have more reason than you!" she retorted, her temper flaring. It was bad enough to be held here against her will, but she refused to be treated insolently, as well. "At least I'm from this colony, and it's my property that's in danger. But you're just one of Mr. Brown's captains for hire, and you have only to worry that he pays you promptly, and there's an end to your concern for the colony of Rhode Island!"

His fingers tightened on her jaw, and there was a new edge in his voice. "Then if you value your stout Rhode Islanders so highly, why did you put their lives at risk for the sake of your silly playacting? You're

welcome to do whatever you wish with your own neck,
but what if one of them—your father, say—had been
killed on account of your foolishness?''

Eliza hadn't considered that. The fallen officer
suddenly had her father's face, and it was his blood
that stained the deck. Her anger slipped away before
the realization of her selfishness. What would she have
done if her father had been killed?

Gardner was surprised by how quickly the fight
went out of the girl. Mentioning her father had only
been a lucky guess, but it had left her vulnerable and
frightened.

Eliza tried to remember her reasons for coming.
''My cousin Nathaniel—''

''Hush now, no names, no names,'' he reminded
her again, and lightly slid his fingers from her chin to
her lips to silence her. Her presence might have jeop-
ardized all his careful plans, but he was finding it increasingly difficult to remain angry with her.

His fingers lingered on her lips, enjoying their softness, and he wondered idly how she'd react if he kissed
her. He had no hold on her now, and she could have
fled, but instead she chose to stay, her breath warm
and shallow on his fingertips. How had he ever mistaken her for a boy? The rough jacket and hat seemed
only to accentuate the delicacy of her features, her
dark lashes shadowing the curve of her cheek. He
hadn't noticed the freckles before, either, dusted like
cinnamon across the bridge of her nose.

Eliza was unable to pull herself away as his forefin-
ger traced the outline of her lips. The gentleness of his
touch startled her, yet at the same time, how it burned

her like hot coals! She closed her eyes, trying to shake the power his presence held over her. The confusion she was feeling made no sense and she felt frightened, not of him, but of herself.

He lifted her face upwards, and on their own she felt her lips part as her head tipped back. Instinctively she reached upwards, searching for his mouth, her hands resting lightly on his chest. Intrigued by her unexpected response, he circled his arm around her and pulled her close, lowering his face to meet hers.

They both heard the footsteps in the passageway at the same time. In one instant, Eliza jerked away from Gardner and rushed across the cabin, while his arm flew upwards with the pistol, again aimed at the door. It wasn't the greeting that Dr. Mawney had expected, and he froze, his hands raised and his mouth gaping.

"Forgive me, sir," said Gardner as he lowered the pistol, "but this seems to be a night for surprises."

"It's Lieutenant Dudingston," the doctor began nervously. "I've been told to tend to him. If I may have the use of the cabin..."

Gardner waved him in as he tucked the pistol back into his belt. "I want him ready to move as soon as possible. Ten minutes at most."

"I can't assure you that will be sufficient. The lieutenant is quite—"

"Ten minutes, and no more," said Gardner. "We've been here too long as it is."

Two men brought the lieutenant into the cabin, balancing him awkwardly across their shoulders. Eliza watched as they laid the man across a locker and Dr. Mawney began to examine his wounds. Although obviously in pain, the lieutenant remained conscious, his eyes still open. Gardner had been wise to insist no true names be used. The wounded man's gaze found Eliza and halted, curiosity and disbelief mixed on his pale face.

Gardner grabbed Eliza by the shoulder. "Come along, *boy*," he said roughly, pulling her with him out of the cabin and out of earshot. What devil had taken his reason where this girl was concerned? He was furious with himself for what had almost happened and furious with her for being too innocent to blame him.

"Is your father on board?" He was half dragging her through the passageway.

"Oh, please, don't tell him!" she cried. Too much had happened in the last minutes for her to comprehend, but she didn't want her father's wrath on top of it.

"Why shouldn't I? Someone should be looking out for you."

Eliza pulled free. She wasn't sure what had overcome her, but the weakness had passed, and as she began to think clearly again, her temper rose. "I've taken care of myself up till now, thank you," she answered tartly.

Gardner sighed with exasperation. "And a damn sorry job you've done of it, too!"

He climbed through the hatch and Eliza followed, determined not to be left behind. The slanting deck that had been so crowded earlier was now almost deserted. Most of the longboats had already pulled clear of the *Gaspee,* their silhouettes skimming the water like black bugs with oars for legs. Two men stood by

the mainmast with smouldering torches, waiting
Gardner's signal to set fire to the schooner.

"Get into the boat," Gardner ordered her.

"I'm not going until you do. I want to see what
happens."

"What, to see what it's like to be blown to Boston
if a spark hits the powder magazine before you're
away?"

Eliza shook her head. "I'm not your responsibility,
remember? I'll leave when you do."

"Then suit yourself, *boy*," said Gardner pointedly.
"You're no worry of mine."

Dr. Mawney appeared with Lieutenant Dudingston
carried on a makeshift pallet, his uniform greatcoat
draped across him, and Gardner motioned for him to
be lowered into one of the remaining boats. From its
stern, John Brown saluted Gardner triumphantly as
they pushed off, no doubt convinced, thought Eliza,
that he had executed the entire raid himself.

The only sounds on the deserted schooner were
those of the *Gaspee* herself: the water lapping against
her sides, her timbers creaking, the breeze slapping her
furled sails against the spars. The slope of the deck
had diminished as the tide had shifted, and in another hour the schooner would have floated free of the
shoals.

Gardner and the others worked quickly now, setting fires below decks where they would cause the
greatest damage. Wood and hemp, canvas, tar and
turpentine; there were few things on a ship that
wouldn't burn, and already Eliza could see bright
flares through the grates as the flames caught hold.

"Now over the side with you!" called Gardner, running towards her, and this time Eliza was swift to obey. Their boat pulled away as the flames shot through the main hatch, lighting the rigging like giant wicks. They were scarcely clear when, with a thunderous explosion and a brilliant flash, the flames reached the store of gunpowder. The *Gaspee*'s masts were gone now, and most of her deck was ripped away. The flames shot high into the night. Thick gray smoke billowed upwards, carrying the acrid smell of gunpowder and burning tar.

"They'll see that from Newport to Providence," said Ned Turner proudly as they paused to watch the burning schooner.

"It's what they see in London that I care about," said Gardner, and the other men laughed and cheered. They had done a good night's work, and a bottle of rum appeared and was passed around in celebration.

Fascinated, Eliza watched the fire in awe, her eyes stinging from the smoke. She had never seen anything so large destroyed so quickly and completely. She glanced up at Gardner's face, illuminated by the flames. Despite their success, he seemed only tired and preoccupied, his broad shoulders hunched with fatigue as he stared, unseeing, across the water. He ran one hand along his unshaven jaw, and Eliza recalled how those same fingers had touched her lips. Her face warmed from the memory. If so little had confused her so much, what would it be like to kiss him, to feel his arms around her, her body pressed close to his?

She wondered what, if anything, he'd felt in return. He was a man, and a worldly one at that, and perhaps to him she was no more than an amusing diversion. Since they'd been interrupted by the doctor, he had been only cold and quarrelsome with her, and especially careful not to touch her as they sat side by side in the boat. Yet she could have sworn that there had been something between them in the cabin, something that had made them both forget all else around them for those few moments.

"Tomorrow, or today, rather, you'll have the whole town thanking you," she said shyly.

His reverie interrupted, Gardner frowned. "Thanking me? For what?"

"Well, I know this—" she gestured towards the burning schooner "—wasn't Mr. Brown's idea, as much as he'll want us to believe so. He's a merchant, not a sailor. It's you who's made it safe to sail from Providence again."

She thought it was a pretty way of thanking him, but his expression only grew darker. "I hope you don't truly believe that."

"You've destroyed the *Gaspee*, haven't you?" she said uncertainly. "That's what we all wanted. Dudingston won't be bothering our ships for a good long time."

"And you think the *Gaspee* is the only ship in King George's navy, and Dudingston the only commander?" His voice sounded bitter even to himself. "This has only been the beginning, not the end."

"The beginning of what?"

"Let's just call it the beginning," he said cautiously. "No one gives up what's theirs without a fight. I doubt his majesty will take kindly to what we've done to his schooner and his servants tonight.''

Eliza shivered, tugging her coat sleeves over her hands. She had been a child during the last war, the one when France was the enemy, but she hadn't forgotten the three uncles—tall, good-natured and red haired, like her father—who'd never returned home to Providence, and the empty places they'd left in her family. She remembered, too, the terrible fear her mother had tried to disguise each time her father had sailed in wartime, how she'd always been convinced she was losing him forever.

"Another war, then," she repeated sadly, softly.

With an unexpected sharpness, Gardner felt her loneliness echo his own mood. She had no business discussing things she didn't understand, things he understood too well. He reminded himself he knew nothing about the girl, and cared less. She could change from a sweet-faced innocent to a hot-tempered little witch and back again with no warning at all, and his life was complicated enough without her blundering into it. He wished he'd never seen her at Brown's house—God, was it really less than twelve hours before?—and he wished he could forget how much he regretted not kissing her.

Slowly the boats had begun the long trip up the river to Providence, leaving the smouldering hulk of the *Gaspee* behind. It would be dawn before they returned, and Eliza hoped she'd be able to reach the house before her father. She yawned, struggling to stay awake, and wished she was already home in bed. She caught herself longing drowsily to rest her head against

Captain Griffin's shoulder, to feel warm and safe in the shelter of his arms. The image was so strong she could almost feel the rough wool of his coat beneath her cheek.

But Gardner was lost in his own thoughts. "Aye, it's true," he murmured softly. "After tonight, nothing will ever be quite the same."

Chapter Four

Eliza's irritation grew as the shop-girl chattered on, and without commenting, she paid for her purchases and fled into the bright afternoon sunlight. Automatically she glanced up and down the street, the way she had each time she'd ventured outdoors these past two days. She couldn't decide whether she hoped to see Gardner Griffin's tall figure approaching, or not. Either way, he had made her uncomfortable in her own town, and she was disgusted with herself for letting it happen. The man meant nothing to her, and the sooner that shameful moment on the *Gaspee* was forgotten, the better. No decent man would have taken advantage of her like that, and handsome as he was, Gardner Griffin was no decent man.

She walked quickly, kicking her skirts before her through the dusty street. By the time Beckah Nye caught up with her, the smaller girl was nearly out of breath.

"You might have waited for me," she said reproachfully. "You knew I had to buy thread for Mama. For two entire days, Eliza Raeburn, you've been prickly as a wet porcupine." Eliza was her oldest friend, and although Beckah was accustomed to the sudden twists and turns Eliza's moods could take, she didn't really mind. There was a wildness to the Raeburns' lives that Beckah found romantic and exciting, an adventurous streak that was sadly lacking in the Nye household. The greatest adventure Beckah faced was helping her harried mother feed dinner to seven younger brothers and sisters each night.

Eliza sighed restlessly. "Oh, Beckah, I'm sorry. But I am tired of people acting so almighty proud of capturing a ship that was stranded anyway, without a watch or guard to speak of, and boasting like it was some great sea battle. There were so many more of us than them that it was no battle at all. I've half a mind to tell Mr. Brown so, and skip his foolish party tonight."

Beckah cocked her neat blond head to one side. "So you did go with the men, didn't you? Don't pretend you didn't, because it's exactly the kind of trick you and Nathaniel would play if he were here."

Eliza sighed again. There was little use denying it. "Father doesn't know, and I'd rather he didn't, thank you."

"Oh, your secret's safe enough with me. You know that," said Beckah. "But tell everything! Was the British captain no better than a bloodthirsty pirate like they say? Is it true that his whole crew were pirates, too?"

"They were king's men, not pirates, and they looked the same as any other sailors, except for being a sight more cowardly," said Eliza, wishing Beckah would change the subject.

"Then the Providence men fought courageously?" Beckah persisted.

"I swear, Beckah, you've seen more exciting fights on market day. We surprised the British, somebody shot their commander—"

Beckah squealed. "No doubt he deserved it, the thieving cur!"

"Deserved it or not, I expect he's dead by now, and past caring." It was a thought Eliza preferred not to dwell upon. "Then the rest of the crew surrendered and we burned their schooner. Truly, that was all."

"Oh." The single syllable conveyed so much disappointment that Eliza almost laughed. She knew too well how much Beckah envied her what she thought was a much more exciting life. Her friend would never understand that she in turn envied her her family, the good humor and warmth that filled the crowded Nye house. "No one was a hero, then?"

"Not really."

"But it did help Nathaniel, didn't it?"

"I don't know," said Eliza softly. It was this very question that worried her most. If the British decided to retaliate, they might choose to use Nathaniel as a hostage, or worst of all, to hang him. No wonder the town's celebrations seemed premature to her.

But as she began to explain her worries to Beckah, something in her friend's expression stopped her. There was an uncharacteristic anxiety in her eyes, and unconsciously Beckah's plump fingers were twisting the corner of her apron. Eliza had suspected before that Beckah's interest in Nathaniel might run deeper than simply sharing her concern, and the way she now sought Eliza's reassurance seemed confirmation enough.

"He'll be all right, won't he?" Beckah asked again tentatively. "It's been three months since he was taken, but I'm sure Governor Hutchinson will see to his case now, after this."

Eliza was certain Rhode Island would be prominent in the Massachusetts governor's mind, but not in the manner Beckah wished. With a sinking feeling, she realized she couldn't confide her fears to Beckah.

"Oh, I'm certain Nathaniel's fine," she said instead, forcing her voice to be cheerful. "It's like him not to write and let us know how he is. Likely he'll surprise us all one morning, sailing up the river as if nothing had happened."

She slipped her arm protectively around Beckah's shoulders and hugged her. *If anything happens to Nathaniel,* she thought grimly, *Gardner Griffin will have a great deal to answer for.*

The musicians were beginning to tune their instruments as Eliza and her father arrived at Sabine's Tavern. The assembly room—the largest in Providence—ran the length of the building's third floor, the high ceiling sloping beneath the pitched roof, and four dormer windows were spaced across the long walls. At one end was a small balcony for the musicians, and at the other a separate room for the refreshments. Rum, ale, spiced lemon punch and cider would be followed later by a full supper. The candlelight from the pewter chandeliers gleamed on the wide-planked floors and softened the faces of the guests already gathered.

In the doorway, Eliza clung to her father's arm, smoothing her hair nervously. She was seldom comfortable at large parties like this. She had spent too much time away from society to perfect the flirtatious small talk that the men expected, and she knew that because of her life on the *Peacock,* the other women regarded her as an oddity. At times like this, she sorely missed the advice her mother could have given her. She took a deep breath to calm herself, wondering for the thousandth time if Captain Griffin would be here tonight, too.

"I've never seen you look more lovely, Eliza," said James proudly. "I'd say so even if you weren't my daughter."

Eliza smiled gratefully. At least tonight no one would mistake her for a boy. She wore her one fancy gown, the one that reminded her of Martinique, for that was where, at James's insistence, she had had it made. The silk was neither green nor blue but a brilliant color in between that also reminded her of the Caribbean. The pointed bodice fit snugly around her narrow waist, and the French dressmaker had cut the square neckline fashionably low. Curving borders of pleated ruffles trimmed the neckline and the sleeves, and the skirt was looped up *à la polonaise* over a flounced petticoat. She had brushed her hair until it shone like copper, and pinned it back simply in a twist.

"You'll see I'm right, Eliza. There won't be a young man here who won't share my opinion," continued

James happily. "You'll have every dance spoken for in an instant!"

Eliza laughed. "Stuff and nonsense, Father!" she scoffed. "You're busy husband-hunting for me again, and it's clouded your judgment."

"Miss Raeburn, Captain Raeburn, good evening!" called Josiah Buck, waving as he came across the room to meet them. As always he leaned heavily on a brass-headed cane, limping with his left leg stiff. "Now the festivities can truly begin."

Eliza dipped awkwardly in the formal curtsy that Aunt Anne had tried to teach her, and then, safely upright again, reached out to take the man's hand. "Please, Josey, don't call me 'Miss Raeburn.' Certainly we've known each other long enough for given names."

"It's easy to forget the little girl I knew when blinded by the beauty of the lady she has become." No one except Eliza Raeburn shortened his name to Josey, a nickname she'd adopted when, years ago, he had taught her the mysteries of bookkeeping and percentages. Then he had been merely a clerk in John Brown's counting-house, and now he managed most of Brown's shipping interests and could claim his employer's confidence, as well. He could afford silver buckles on his shoes and lace to trim his shirts. He had come far from his father's rocky farm in Warwick, far enough to aspire to a beauty like Eliza Raeburn.

Eliza giggled as he bent over her hand. Although Josiah was barely thirty, she thought of him as much older, more a contemporary of her father's, and his gallantry struck her as incongruous. During the last war a stray French bullet had shattered his knee and ended his career as a soldier. Perhaps, she thought, that was what had made him so serious. There was often a smile on his pockmarked face, but Eliza could not recall ever hearing him laugh.

Ruefully he tapped his cane against one buckled shoe. "While I can't promise you the capers of a dancing master, Eliza, I do hope you'll sacrifice one dance for conversation with me."

Eliza smiled, nodding. For all his airs, she felt at ease with him. "I haven't much experience with dancing masters either, Josey. If Father would let me, I wouldn't dance a step tonight."

"Nothing would give me greater pleasure." As he bowed again, Josiah's pulse raced. She was breathtaking in that dress, the loveliest woman in the room.

Over Josiah's back, Eliza glanced around swiftly. The party was growing crowded, with more people still arriving, but the one guest she sought was not there. Could it be that Captain Griffin would risk his employer's displeasure and stay away? The possibility hit her with a sharpness she hadn't expected, and stubbornly she reminded herself that what he did was no concern of hers.

"I hope, Eliza, that your frown isn't meant for me," Josiah was saying as he offered her his arm. Eliza forced herself to smile. She refused to let the evening be spoiled by some man she scarcely knew.

Gardner had not intended to come to Sabine's tonight. He never so much as shared a tankard of ale with these Providence men. Why should tonight be different? And even the idea of this party rankled him. A celebration like this was madness, flaunting the town's role in the *Gaspee*'s destruction. Was he the only one to realize the danger in their actions? Then there was that blasted red-haired girl, who'd almost muddled the whole raid with her presence. She'd most certainly be here. He couldn't think about her without growing angry at her foolishness all over again.

Not that Gardner wasn't proud of how well the raid had gone. He was probably the only one in the colony to appreciate that, too. But the real reward had come when he had sorted through Lieutenant Dudingston's papers. There he had found the detailed record of a local ship's detention on grounds so weak that Gardner had laughed out loud as he read the lieutenant's slanting handwriting. The incident was tailor-made for Sam Adams's pen. Gardner could already imagine the results: a dash of patriotism, a measure of rhetoric and, knowing Sam, a little exaggeration, all combined in a cheaply printed pamphlet or an article in the *Gazette* that would send Boston to seething once again. Soon the Sons of Liberty and other firebrands would have a new cause to champion in the streets, just as Governor Hutchinson would have a new thorn in his side. Perhaps the luckless shipmaster would even be freed, though Gardner wasn't overly concerned about that.

Until, that is, he'd learned from a barkeep that the shipmaster had a cousin who knew more about his case than anyone, and that that cousin was none other than the interfering, red-haired wench. If he wanted to give Sam all the information he needed, Gardner realized that, like it or not, he'd have to talk to her again.

And so here he was, washed and shaved and wearing his one shirt without darns, standing in an overheated, overcrowded room, watching Miss Eliza Raeburn talk with that fawning weasel Josiah Buck.

She had been tempting enough that night in the *Gaspee*'s cabin, but the sight of her now took his breath clear away. Her cheeks were flushed, her golden eyes wide and sparkling with excitement. A few loose curls had escaped from her bow to cling moistly to her forehead and neck. Her breasts rose round and tantalizing from the blue-green silk—God, he'd never seen a dress like that on a New England lady!—and her skin glowed rosily in the candlelight. He imagined how velvety soft that skin would be to touch, how there in the hollow of her throat his lips might taste the saltiness.

The music stopped and Josiah sighed. "Much as I cherish your company, Eliza, I must free you now to dance and break other hearts."

"Oh, Josey, you're as full of nonsense as my father," scoffed Eliza, laughing. "I'd rather die than dance all night with gentlemen I scarcely know."

"I'd wager it would take a good deal more than dancing to finish you off, Miss Raeburn," said Gardner's unmistakable voice behind her. "I'd like to be the one to prove it to you, if Buck here will let me."

Eliza whirled to face him, her heart pounding. She had only wondered whether they would meet, not what would follow when they did.

Josiah's mouth was compressed into a tight line of displeasure as he looked from Eliza to Gardner and back again. To his knowledge they had never met, yet the tension between the two was undeniable. "If that is what the lady wishes," he said stiffly.

Before Eliza could answer, Gardner's arm circled her waist and he swept her away from Josiah. Soon the faces of the other guests became a blur. She had forgotten how much taller he was, how she had to tip back her head to meet his eyes, and the irritation she had kept simmering these past days finally bubbled over.

"That," she said heatedly, "was very rude. Josiah Buck was my partner, not you."

"That wasn't the way I heard it," he answered, noting with amusement the sparks that lit her eyes. "But then I should remember that what you say and what you do—or even who you are—aren't always one and the same."

"You *are* rude," Eliza snapped indignantly. "You have no right to speak to me so. As I recall, we haven't even been introduced."

"Oh, I think we're well past that obstacle, Miss Eliza," he drawled suggestively. His arm tightened around her waist, reminding her of how close they'd been on the *Gaspee*, and he chuckled as her cheeks flushed from embarrassment. "Any young woman who runs about in breeches as freely as you do has scant right to put on ladylike airs."

Eliza raised her chin a little higher. Why did he enjoy taunting her so much, she wondered angrily. "If your memory is so perfect, then you'll also recall that you first aimed a pistol at my forehead, and then took unfair advantage of me in my shock.''

He laughed again, deep and full. ''I remember the pistol, aye, but as for the rest of it—sweet Jesus, you have the wrong man.''

''Well, you did,'' repeated Eliza stubbornly, wishing she didn't feel so foolish, ''and I've no intention of letting anything like that happen again.''

''And neither do I, sweetheart, though how you look tonight is a considerable temptation. All I want from you now is a chance to talk.''

She studied him suspiciously. ''Talk? What could I possibly have to talk about with you?''

''Your cousin, Captain Chase.''

He was amazed by how swiftly her expression changed, the wariness replaced by an eager hope. ''Have you heard from Nathaniel?''

''No, but I may be able to help him if you can help me first,'' he said uneasily. Her excitement was too obvious and was sure to be noticed by others. She knew he'd searched Dudingston's cabin, but no one else did, and he preferred to keep it that way. He had to get her away from this crowd before he'd feel comfortable enough to speak freely. ''Come outside with me. There are too many ears in here for what we have to say. Five minutes, maybe ten, and you can be back with mealy-mouthed Buck.''

Eliza hesitated only a moment. The man might actually be able to help. He was, after all, from Boston himself. ''Ten minutes, then.''

Without waiting for the music to stop, she slipped free of his arms and dodged between the other couples, leaving him to follow her down the stairs and out into the street. She stopped beside the tavern's doorway.

"Well?" she asked impatiently. "What do you know?"

"Not so fast. I'd like to put more distance between us and the others." He took her by the arm to guide her down the street.

"I don't need your help, thank you," she said as she jerked her arm free. Ten minutes, no more, she reminded herself. Nothing can happen in ten minutes.

They stopped when they reached the waterfront, the gray silhouettes of the ships in port looming before them. Tonight the moon was nearly full, but the breeze from the ocean was rising and pale wisps of clouds skittered across the silvery disk. Eliza waited with her arms folded defensively across her chest, the very picture, she hoped, of defiance. Yet inside she felt oddly unsure of herself.

Gardner had left his hat behind, and the breeze ruffled his straight black hair across his forehead. In the moonlight his shirt front gleamed almost blue white, as did his teeth when he finally smiled.

"Now, Miss Eliza, now you can tell me whatever you wish about how this cousin of yours ran afoul of Lieutenant Dudingston."

"You said you had news for me, not the other way around!" Disappointment swept over her. "I swear, if you dragged me out here for no reason—"

"Stop it," he said curtly, and his tone startled her into silence as surely as if he'd slapped her. He took one, two, three steps towards her, until only inches remained between them. "I said we would talk about your cousin. I promised you nothing, and I won't, not until you first tell me whatever you know."

Eliza swallowed. "It happened in March. Nathaniel had scarcely cleared Newport when the *Gaspee* surprised him. Dudingston said he'd fire his guns if he couldn't come on board the *Speedwell* to check Nathaniel's papers. When he did, he arrested Nathaniel and his crew and confiscated the *Speedwell*."

"Was your cousin smuggling?"

Eliza's chin shot upward. "Nathaniel believes in free trade, same as the rest of us. Why should we let those greedy customs men in Newport help themselves to the profits we've earned?"

"So guilty he was, in Dudingston's eyes," mused Gardner. "I guessed as much from the entries."

"What entries?"

"In Dudingston's log. Or have you conveniently forgotten that gentleman entertained us the other night?"

"The papers you took from his desk were about Nathaniel?" Eliza asked excitedly.

"Aye, it's all there, just like you've said. But I couldn't figure out why they packed him off to Boston while everyone else the *Gaspee* nicked only lost their goods. I couldn't, that is, until I heard he was your cousin."

Eliza frowned. "Why should that matter?"

"If he packs only half the temper you do, then likely he expressed his unhappiness more forcefully than was proper with one of his majesty's officers. Not that I blame him."

"Of course you can't blame him," said Eliza. Nathaniel's temper was certainly short, she couldn't deny that. "But what the British did was still against the law."

"No doubt. But it's hard to prove, seeing that they *are* the law in the colonies," he said thoughtfully.

Eliza rubbed her bare forearms, wishing she'd paused long enough for her shawl. The evening was cool for June. "And what do you know about my cousin, Captain Griffin?" she asked. Talking about Nathaniel like this made her realize all over again how much she missed him, and unwittingly her unhappiness crept into her voice. "I've heard you still have Boston friends. Can they tell you where Nathaniel's held, or what the British will do with him?"

She raised her hands with the fingers widespread, then let them drop to her sides in a gesture of helplessness. When she looked up at him, her eyes seemed too big for her face. "Not one thing I've done has helped bring him back."

Gardner felt oddly unsteady, as if the street were shifting beneath his feet. It wasn't her nearness, or the sweet fragrance that rose from her skin and hair to tease him, or how the moonlight cast tantalizing shadows across her breasts. If he was only responding to her physically, he would have kissed her and more, if she'd let him, and left when the amusement was done. His relationships with women had always been pleasurably uncomplicated, and over when he sailed again. But this was different. *She* was different. No one in his rough life had cared for him as much as she so obviously cared for this cousin of hers. She'd

turned quiet like this on the *Gaspee* when he'd reminded her of her father, too. What was it like, wondered Gardner with an unfamiliar pang, to be loved by
someone that much?

"With a little prodding, the British might release
your cousin soon," he said carefully. "Now that the
Gaspee is lost, Lieutenant Dudingston will have to
answer to a court martial. He won't fare well."

"He's still alive?" Eliza remembered the limp,
blood-stained figure in the longboat.

Gardner nodded. "Likely wishing he weren't. His
majesty doesn't take kindly to officers who lose their
commands. They'll have to cut him down and ship
him back to England on half pay and tidy up the
messes he left behind, including your cousin."

"What about what you said the other night? Do
you think the British will try to punish us for burning
the schooner?"

He noticed grimly how she included herself among
the raiders, and prayed she'd had the sense to keep her
involvement to herself. She'd be safe enough if no one
else knew.

"Aye, they'll try." He wouldn't lie to her. "But
nothing will happen until Parliament and the king
learn of it. That gives you at least two months to get
your cousin home."

"Truly?" Eliza wanted so much to believe him that
she didn't stop to question how a colonial merchant
shipmaster could be so knowledgeable.

"If someone were to pay a visit to Governor
Hutchinson, most polite and civil, of course, it could
happen." He was already planning what he'd say at

the governor's office, most of it decidedly uncivil. He had a few favors owed that he could collect, and a little silver should do the rest. Eliza would never learn the truth, but that was for the best.

But Eliza's thoughts were also running ahead. No one knew Nathaniel's case better than she did. She herself would go to Boston and tell Governor Hutchinson exactly why he had to free Nathaniel. The image of her returning triumphantly to Providence with her cousin was a pleasing one, and she smiled at the prospect.

"There, that's better," said Gardner softly. It was not his habit to do favors with no hope towards repayment, but this one, like the girl herself, was different. He wondered idly how willing she'd be to show her gratitude, remembering once again how she'd felt in his arms.

Eliza was suddenly aware of how close he stood to her, their bodies almost touching. The wind blew her skirts across his boots and against his legs with a soft rustle of silk, and skittishly she turned away from him to face the wind.

"Wind's freshening, north nor'east," she said as she shook her hair back from her eyes. "There's an end to the fair weather."

He looked at her curiously. "That's not the way most ladies would say it."

She shrugged. "I've spent more time with sailors than ladies."

"Aye, so I've heard. You sail with your father."

"Not any longer," she said shortly. She'd confided enough of her troubles tonight. The ten minutes she'd promised herself with him were stretching into thirty, but she didn't want to return to the party. Her mind was too busy planning the trip to Boston, and her body echoed the restlessness of her thoughts. She turned impulsively again to Gardner. "Our schooner's the *Peacock*. I'll show her to you, if you wish."

Gardner watched her skip on ahead as lightly as if she were still on the dance floor. The wind was moulding her skirts against her hips and legs and outlining her slim figure in a way that was bewitching. She didn't take mincing, ladylike steps when she walked, but there was nothing masculine in her movements.

"What does your father trade?" he asked.

"Rum and molasses mostly. A few fancy goods if we can get them."

"And he, too, believes in free trade?" he teased. "No visits to the customs house for the Raeburns?"

She smiled impishly. "And how much of your cargos on the *Three Brothers* do you declare, Captain Griffin?"

He only gave her half a smile in return. With luck she'd never know what the *Three Brothers* trafficked in. His cargos made untaxed rum seem like the farm wife's eggs on market day.

"There she is," said Eliza, pointing proudly. She loved the *Peacock* almost like a living thing, not only for her clean lines and speed, but also for what the schooner represented: the life she shared with James, their devotion to each other merging with their love of the sea's freedom.

"Your father is a fortunate man," said Gardner. The vessel was handsome enough, but it was Eliza, her straight back before him, that held his attention, and he thought he'd never seen anything as compelling as the soft curves of her bare neck and shoulders. With one hand he reached to twist his fingers around the wayward tendrils curling over her nape.

To her own surprise, Eliza didn't pull away. Part of her realized she'd been expecting this since they'd left the party. Her conscience urged her to run, to return to the others, but it faltered as his fingers began to stroke the back of her neck. Involuntarily she arched her neck back beneath his touch.

"You're cold," he whispered lazily. "You're shivering."

How could she explain that no mere chill could make her shiver the way he was doing right now? Don't be weak, she tried to order herself. Don't let this happen again. With a little cry of frustration, she twisted away from his hand to face him.

For one split second Eliza saw his face in the moonlight—the sharp, clean lines of his features crossed by the dark brows, the blue eyes now like the midnight sky—until his mouth was on hers, and she saw nothing more. In her short life, she had never been kissed like this. Skillfully he led her from a delicious tenderness to the dark intensity of a tempest, spurring her emotions to a level she never knew was within her. His arms pulled her closer, lifting her up to join him more completely. Her breasts crushed against his shirt, and beneath the rough linen she felt the hard strength of his chest.

Gardner felt no wish to protect her now as he freely plundered her eager innocence. Her beauty hadn't been an empty promise. He had guessed that the pleasure she was capable of would match his own, and so far he wasn't mistaken. How much he would enjoy teaching her more! He let his hands stray further across her skin, his desire quickening.

Yet lost as Gardner was in her, he still was able to sense the danger around them before he heard or saw it. They were no longer alone on the dock; of that he was certain. There was someone else in the moonlight, watching and waiting for him to let down his guard. Inwardly he cursed himself. What was it about the girl that made him forget everything else? He'd been a fool to dally with her so long, but he refused to pay for his foolishness with his life, or hers.

Abruptly Eliza felt him pull away. Still dazed from the sensations he'd roused, she reached out to bring him back, but instead he roughly took her by the arm and tried to lead her from the dock.

"Where are we going?" she stammered in confusion.

"Quiet now." His reply was low and terse. "I'm taking you back to the party."

His eyes darted everywhere but on her, and to her shock she saw, beneath his coat, the same pistol he'd had on the *Gaspee*. What kind of man carried a gun to a party?

"I don't understand." She stumbled in the dark and he pulled her back to her feet. "What are you doing?"

"What I should have done in the first place, if I'd had my wits about me," he said bitterly.

"But I—"

"Listen to me," he whispered with a hoarse urgency. "You'll go back to your precious party, and you'll forget me, and what has passed between us. It's meant nothing to either one of us, and you'll forget it completely, mind? Completely! Do as I say and we'll neither of us have anything to regret."

Gardner saw the anger and hurt in Eliza's eyes, and the fear, too, and he swore at himself again. She was precisely the kind of weakness his enemies would be quick to use against him. He couldn't afford to become involved. There was, he reminded himself harshly, no place in his life for Miss Eliza Raeburn.

Chapter Five

The gray, wet days that followed more than matched Eliza's spirits. The rain was heavy and constant, turning the usually bright days of early summer into a dripping twilight world where river and sky merged on the horizon in the same flat shade of pewter. The unpaved streets were muddy swamps that trapped wagons and horses and sucked at the feet of unhappy pedestrians. Each night Eliza hung the clothes that she and James had worn to dry before the kitchen fire, and their house perpetually smelled of damp wool and linen. In the tiny garden behind the house, the rosebushes that had been her mother's pride bowed into the mud, and even after Eliza cut all the sodden pink blossoms and buds to bring indoors, the petals turned brown and fell overnight. Much, thought Eliza sadly, like her own hopes for happiness.

In the morning the *Peacock* would sail, and for the first time in fifteen years, Eliza would be left behind. These past days she and her father had quarrelled more bitterly than she could ever remember, but James had remained unyielding. The only concessions Eliza had won were the right to stay in their house alone instead of moving in with Aunt Anne and the promise from her father that he would reconsider his decision before the next voyage. Neither offered much comfort. Even now, with James's trunk packed and waiting to be carried aboard in the morning, she found it almost impossible to believe he wouldn't change his mind.

She stared up at the ceiling, digging her nails into her palms as she fought back the tears. She could still remember the sickly smell of her mother's last illness as it filled her parents' bedchamber, the leeches in the jar beside the bed and the midwife's gnarled hand passing across her mother's face as she closed her eyes for the last time. Eliza had watched as her father cut one long lock of his dead wife's hair with the embroidery scissors from her workbasket. How the golden strands had gleamed in the firelight as he had wrapped them around and around his finger. There had been other people in the room, neighbors and grieving relatives whose faces Eliza had long forgotten. But she remembered every detail of how her father had taken her away from the house, and how they walked hand in hand to the top of Prospect Hill. They'd picked wild strawberries and sat on a fallen tree together to watch the sun set. Since then they had not parted, not one day, not one night. Until now.

Eliza counted as the church bell rang the hour. Three o'clock. James would rise at half past. She might as well get up herself, for there was little hope of sleep. She could at least send her father off with hot corn bread beside his chop and apple pudding for breakfast.

She watched her father eat, her own place empty save for a cup of untouched cocoa. In the silence between them, she was acutely aware of the clatter his knife and fork made against the pewter plate.

Although he had little real appetite, either, James realized how much effort she'd put into the breakfast, and forced himself to eat heartily for her sake, washing the corn bread down with gulps of black coffee. She looked so unhappy, her face pale and her bright hair drawn severely back in a single tight braid. "You know, Eliza, this is as hard for me as it is for you," he said at last. "Harder, maybe."

"I know because you've told me it's so." Eliza stared down into her cocoa.

"Damn it, you should know because you are my daughter," he said gruffly, "and because you're the most precious creature under the sun to me."

Eliza didn't trust herself to reply. Her mother had always sent her father off to sea with a great show of cheerfulness, however much her heart was breaking, and she was determined to do the same. She took a deep breath to steady herself. "I'll have much to occupy me here, Father, and then there's Beckah and Josiah—"

"Aye, Josiah." James couldn't help from smiling hopefully. "There's a fellow who's made something of himself."

Eliza shook her head. "No, Father. Josiah's only a friend, and that is all."

James tried to look surprised. "You don't hear me calling you Mistress Buck, do you? All I said was that Josiah was a fine gentleman." And you'd do well to consider him, he added mentally. Josiah was a hard worker, and Brown thought the world of him. Better him than that other man—Griffin, his name was—whom she'd gone off with at the party. Though from the black look on Eliza's face when she returned alone, James suspected that Griffin had gotten more than he'd bargained for. Eliza was quite capable, as she so often reminded him, of looking after herself.

"Well, you choose your company to please yourself, not me." His eyes twinkled. Even with separation looming before them, he couldn't resist teasing her. "Likely I'll come home this fall to find you wed and stitching baby things."

"Father!" exclaimed Eliza, scandalized but laughing nonetheless.

This was better, thought James. He wanted to remember her laughing. His face softened. "Marry for love, lass, and you'll be happy. That's all your mother and I could've wanted for you."

A loud pounding on the kitchen door interrupted them, and Eliza hurried to let Sam Hopkins, one of the *Peacock*'s seamen, in from the rain. Sam would carry her father's trunk to the dock for him. Eliza settled Sam at the table with what she guessed was at least his second breakfast, and then ran upstairs to watch her father pack his last few belongings. He was almost done. On top of the shirts she'd sewn and the socks she'd knitted went his razor and Bible, and last of all, the framed crayon portrait of his wife that travelled everywhere with him. With a thump he shut the lid on the battered chest and snapped the iron padlock through the ring.

The night was fading to a pale dawn as they walked towards the dock. Without thinking, Eliza had taken her father's hand as they left the house, clinging to the familiar callused fingers as she had when a child.

"I might as well be sailing the blasted ark," muttered James as they reached the *Peacock*. The rain collected in the upturned brim of his hat to drip from the corner beyond his nose like a rainspout. "Come on board, Eliza, until we're ready to cast off."

Eliza hung back and shook her head. "No, father, I can't. We'll say goodbye here."

"Very well." James cleared his throat. Farewells were one of the reasons he'd begun taking Eliza with him in the first place. "Turn to your aunt if you're in need. I know you two are often at odds, but she's your kin, and you don't have so much family that you can scorn her. All the business you know as well as I. Better, maybe. But if anything should happen to me, go to Philip Deane. All my papers rest with him."

"But nothing will happen to you, Father," said Eliza, her voice squeaking high with emotion. "You always come back. Always!"

James held his arms out to her, and she flung herself at him, her hands wrapped tight around his waist. Would she ever feel so safe again?

"Oh, child," he murmured as he cradled her protectively. "Come now. It's not for an eternity."

With a great effort Eliza loosened her embrace and stood upright. She reminded herself that she was

Captain Raeburn's daughter, that she should let him sail with dignity. "You'd best be gone," she said gamely, "or you'll miss the tide."

James regarded her this last time almost as a stranger would. The dark hood of her cloak framed a face that was uncharacteristically pale, the freckles across her nose in startling contrast to her white cheeks. She held her chin up, determined to be stoic, though her red-rimmed eyes betrayed how slight was her grip on her emotions. She looked to him both very young, and already very alone.

She kissed him quickly on the cheek. "Goodbye, Father, and may God keep you safe."

"And you as well, Miss Monkey." He chucked her under the chin, his smile forced, and left her for the schooner.

As if in a dream, Eliza watched the dark, rain-soaked mainsail catch the breeze. Slowly the *Peacock* began to move through the water. Her father raised his hand to her, and she silently waved in return. Although her mother had remained on the dock long after her father's ship was out of sight, Eliza had no desire to linger, nor, strangely, did she now succumb to the tears that had threatened to overflow all morning. Her father was gone, and there was no help for it. Weeping would only make her feel worse. As the *Peacock* skipped across the choppy water, she turned her back on the river and started towards John Brown's counting-house.

The tow-headed boy who approached her as she stepped through the door at Brown's eyed her curiously, for women seldom ventured into the offices.

"Please tell Mr. Buck that Miss Raeburn would be much obliged if she might speak with him," said Eliza as she untied her cloak.

The boy hesitated. Mr. Buck did not like to be interrupted and was quick to cuff the messenger who did so without a good reason. But when the woman smiled, the boy gallantly decided it was worth facing Mr. Buck's displeasure and scurried up the stairs.

Eliza smoothed her rain-streaked skirts and wished she'd taken more care dressing before she'd come here. Josiah had an eye for finery. Rapidly she ran her fingers across her hair, neatening her braid as best she could.

"Eliza! What a charming surprise!" Awkwardly Josiah limped down the stairs. "Come, I'll take you where you'll be more comfortable. Mrs. Berk's coffeehouse is—"

"You forget, Josey, that I'll be more at home here than at any coffeehouse," she said, smiling shyly. It was pleasant to be considered too ladylike for a warehouse. "It's business that's brought me here. Or rather, a proposition. Your office will do just fine. If that's agreeable to you, of course."

"Certainly, Eliza, whatever pleases you." Intrigued, Josiah wondered what "proposition" would bring her to him. With her father away, who knows what guidance she might be seeking, and he liked the fact that she had come to him. Casually he let his hand brush her arm and shoulder as he ushered her into his office.

Eliza glanced around the office, noting the framed engravings and maps, the case full of ledgers and books, the Turkey carpet on the floor. The room was small, but the mere fact that Josiah had an office of his own, with a fine view of the river, showed how far he had risen.

"It's more of a favor, actually," Eliza began. She leaned her elbows on the arms of the carved chair and touched her fingertips together. "I need to book passage on the packet to Boston, and Captain Rawson won't even look sideways at me because I'm an unmarried female."

She bristled at the memory. Rawson had treated her like some strumpet because she wished to travel alone. "But if you asked him, Josey, and were willing to vouch for my good name, he'd have to take me."

Josiah suppressed an indulgent smile. "Perhaps, Eliza, you misjudge my ability to influence Captain Rawson."

Eliza grinned triumphantly. "Oh, your word would do the trick. Especially when Captain Rawson is reminded that Mr. Brown still holds the lien on his sloop, and that he has two sons that sail in Brown vessels. Then, too, Rawson was in Mr. Brown's longboat when we—I mean they—attacked the *Gaspee*. So if you, with your place here and all, were to ask him, then he couldn't possibly turn me away."

Josiah drummed his fingers on his knee. He must remember not to underestimate her. "I'm afraid I'd have to agree with Captain Rawson, Eliza. The Boston packet is no place for an unescorted young lady."

"Oh, stuff and nonsense, Josey!" she scoffed. "I've been lots worse places than the deck of the *Polly!*"

"Captain Rawson will be the least of your concerns. Do you have friends waiting to greet you when you arrive? Boston is a far different place than Providence, and now especially, with the recent unpleasantness, it can be an unhappy, even dangerous, town."

Eliza frowned, perplexed, as she saw her dream of freeing Nathaniel fading even before the *Peacock* had reached deep water.

"And yet I might be able to arrange a solution," added Josiah thoughtfully. He was pleased to see her face light up. Even on this gray day, her copper-haired beauty warmed his office like a fire. Captain Raeburn had raised his daughter with entirely too much freedom, in Josiah's opinion, but he'd welcome the challenge of taming her. "Might I ask what your business is in Boston? Surely your father would not send you on such an errand."

"Oh, no, he knows nothing of this. I'm going to rescue Nathaniel." Briefly she outlined her plan to call on Governor Hutchinson, taking care not to mention that she'd come by the idea from Captain Griffin. "But you understand why I must go now, before news of the *Gaspee* reaches London."

Josiah nodded, his expression stern. "There will, I fear, be plenty of hotheads in this town who'll wish they'd kept to their beds instead that night. There's nothing honorable about vandalism, piracy and cold-blooded murder—which is, of course, how Parliament will view it."

While she hadn't realized it before, Eliza couldn't recall seeing Josiah in any of the boats around the *Gaspee* that night, although Mr. Brown had been the leader. But as she began to question Josiah, he absently knocked his shoe with his cane, and the gesture silenced her. No doubt he'd longed to join the others, but his crippled leg would have held him back.

"There might be a way, however," he was saying. "If Mr. Brown can spare me the time, I might contrive to accompany you on your journey myself. Though of course I offer my services with only the purest, most respectful intentions behind them."

Eliza looked at him curiously. She guessed that, in his roundabout manner, Josiah was promising to behave like a gentleman while they travelled together. How odd, she thought, for she'd never pictured him any other way. She studied him with fresh eyes: his high forehead and regular features, his brown wavy hair neatly curled and tied with a black silk bow, the rust-colored suit tailored to show himself to best advantage. Besides his lameness, his only flaws were the smallpox scars that peppered his cheeks, though even those could be regarded as adding character to his face. Most women would call Josiah a comely man, even handsome, but Eliza had known him too long to view him as anything other than a friend. If she must travel with an escort, then she could not ask for a better one than Josiah.

She rose to leave and took his hand. "I accept your offer, Mr. Buck," she said gaily. "Won't Nathaniel be surprised to see the two of us!"

"Indeed he will." That is, thought Josiah, if such a reunion ever came to pass, and it wouldn't through any assistance of his. That great red-haired oaf had lumbered into this disaster on his own, and he could just as well get himself out of it, as far as Josiah was concerned. But for Eliza's sake, he would pretend to make inquiries while he patiently used their time together to win her. In his experience, women loved a show of sympathy even more than flattery. But try to free Nathaniel Chase—never.

"I don't know how to thank you," Eliza said happily as he walked her down the stairs. In the hallway below them she overheard Mr. Brown bidding farewell to some visitor. "Nathaniel, too, will be—"

She froze in midsentence at the bottom of the stairs. The last step gave her just enough height to be face-to-face with Gardner Griffin. His eyes were like cold blue ice, his mouth an unyielding slash, and it was clear he intended to make no sign that they'd ever met. He had promised it would be so between them, and he was a man who kept his word.

Damn him, Eliza thought bitterly as she gripped the railing. She had once seen warmth and kindness in those chilly eyes, and desire, too, when he'd let that mouth soften against her own. She had almost liked him then, until he'd shown his true colors.

Gardner watched the emotions flickering across her face. Two bright patches appeared on her cheeks, and her whole body almost vibrated with repressed anger. Aye, she was good and mad at him, he thought. He vaguely recalled an old saying about the fury of a scorned woman, and surely the damage he'd done to this one's pride appeared considerable.

But how could her wounded pride compare with the unrest she'd caused him? Awake and asleep, her vibrant figure danced across his memory. No amount of rum had been able to wash the taste of her mouth from his, nor banish from his consciousness the impossibly delicate touch of her skin beneath his fingers. It was, he realized, high time he left Rhode Island. He'd lingered here far too long if he'd let himself become entranced by a freckle-faced witch like this one.

Eliza watched the muscles twitch across his square jaw as he jammed his hat onto his head. Without a word he turned on his boot heel and left, slamming the heavy door hard enough to rattle the glass panes on each side. Even then she found it impossible to let her anger go.

"I thought that you and Captain Griffin were acquainted," said Josiah with, for once, more curiosity than tact.

"Then you're just as mistaken as he is," said Eliza tartly. "The man's an ill-mannered scoundrel who thinks he owns Providence because he got Mr. Brown to burn the *Gaspee!*"

"Indeed?" Josiah covered his surprise with the single word. He had been convinced that his employer had acted alone.

"Indeed yes! Come now, Josey, you work here, and Griffin's one of Mr. Brown's men. You likely know all manner of black deeds he's done, but you're too much the gentleman to tell me."

"Discretion is a useful virtue, Eliza," he replied thoughtfully. The details of Captain Griffin's appearance last year and his subsequent voyages were among the few matters of business that John Brown did not confide in him. Of course, Josiah had his own suspicions. Griffin was no ordinary shipmaster. He was too observant in the same ways that Josiah had cultivated himself, and if the man kept apart from the others, it was from choice, not because he had nothing to offer. Josiah didn't trust him, and it rankled that John Brown did, and with the firm's top vessel, too.

"You would do well to avoid Griffin, Eliza," he said seriously. "We're all judged by the acquaintance we choose to keep. Let your name be linked with his, and you may find yourself sharing the blame for his misdeeds."

"Oh, Josey, only a liar or a fool could possibly blame me for any of Captain Griffin's mischief. I've done absolutely nothing in his company, good or bad," Eliza said defensively, but her conscience pricked her. Well, she'd done nothing anyone else knew about, and that was almost the same thing.

Josiah leaned closer, lowering his voice. "There's a great deal of wickedness in our world, Eliza, and I fear that man has more than his share."

Eliza gazed after the tall figure disappearing down the street and wondered how she could still doubt the truth in Josiah's words. And why did she care?

Chapter Six

Eliza leaned over the taffrail of the *Polly*, the wind tossing her hair as the green Rhode Island hills slipped by. Or maybe it was Massachusetts by now: she didn't recognize this northern coastline well enough to know landmarks. She was content to watch lazily as the gulls wheeled overhead in the cloudless summer sky. The *Polly* wasn't the *Peacock*, but she was so glad to be under sail again that she almost forgot to miss her father.

"Shouldn't you consider going below for a while, Eliza?" asked Josiah at her side. "You've been out here on deck since dawn, and I wouldn't want you taken sunsick."

"Sunsick is nothing compared to how I'd feel if I stayed below in that stuffy cabin with that poor Mrs. Gates we collected in Newport. Both she and her maidservant have been ill since they boarded, moaning and praying for a deliverance from their misery." Eliza wrinkled her nose. "You wouldn't wish me in the middle of that, would you?"

"Whatever you want, Eliza," said Josiah stiffly, wishing she hadn't discussed the other passengers' seasickness quite so graphically. He dabbed at his upper lip with his handkerchief and resettled his hat before carefully setting off across the deck to the starboard rail.

Eliza watched him sympathetically. There was a distinctly greenish tinge to his cheeks, and had he been less determined, she suspected he would be below in much the same condition as Mrs. Gates. For Eliza, who had weathered gales and hurricanes on the *Peacock* with nary a twinge of seasickness, the easy progress of the *Polly* was a pleasant rocking, no more. But she hoped for Josiah's sake that the fair weather held. Even then it could take the sloop several days more to circle the long arm of Cape Cod and cut back across the bay to Boston.

She turned back to the taffrail, wondering what her father would say if he saw her now. Certainly her aunt's reaction had been surprising when she had told her what she was planning to do last Sunday as they'd walked home from church.

"So Mr. Buck's taken an interest in your affairs, has he?" Aunt Anne had fingered the prayer book in her hands. "I would not have thought it, myself, but if a sober man like Mr. Buck is willing to take on a wild creature like you, I won't stand in his path."

Startled, Eliza had only stared at her aunt. She was sailing with Josiah, not marrying him. But then it had seemed easier to say nothing. Once Nathaniel was home, there would be plenty of time for explanations.

Eliza looked back across the *Polly*'s deck at Josiah, struggling manfully to appear at ease. Poor Josey! He was making more of a sacrifice than she'd realized to accompany her. She would remember to offer him a little of the cold tea she'd brought for supper and considerately keep the fried chicken and sweet rhubarb pickles out of his sight.

"Boston's a much grander place than Providence, isn't it?" said Eliza as the *Polly* made her way through the crowded port, dodging one-man fishing skiffs and the three-masted ships bound for Europe. Eagerly Eliza studied the town, spread out for her inspection like children's blocks and toys. This place was Captain Griffin's home. He must have sailed from the long wharfs that jutted out into the water, and he could have told her the names of the merchants who owned the dozens of warehouses that lined the harbor. The twisting streets so closely lined with brick and clapboard houses and shops, meetinghouses and markets, would be as familiar to him as Providence was to her.

"Grand, perhaps, but filled with ne'er-do-wells breeding smallpox, anarchy and more godless little brats to inhabit their unhealthy island," sniffed Josiah.

"I can count five church steeples at least," Eliza teased. "How godless does that make the people of Boston?"

"Any town that lets itself be ruled by lawless, rioting rascals deserves to be called godless. I wouldn't want my destiny determined by ignorant apprentices and mechanics, nor would any gentleman. Empty heads shouldn't be primed with dangerous ideas they can't possibly understand. You scratch any of these self-proclaimed Sons of Liberty, and you'll find only sons of—'' Josiah, in his excitement, barely saved himself ''—sons of the wicked.''

"You sound like the Tory newspapers that make Father so angry he can't read them through."

"Tory and Whig are meaningless titles, Eliza. Whatever you may hear, remember that no honest man need fear a fair master."

There was a patronizing tone to Josiah's voice that Eliza didn't care for, any more than she liked the way he appeared to be gazing down his nose at her with distinct disapproval. "And what's that honest man to do when his master isn't fair?"

The disapproval became layered with smugness. "Better one tyrant three thousand miles away than three thousand tyrants in the same town."

"And I say the best is no tyrant at all." Emphatically Eliza retied the ribbons on her hat, plucking at the bow beneath her chin to make the silk knot fuller. "I wonder what Mr. Brown would think of all your theories of fair masters and tyrants."

"In matters of trade and commerce, my thoughts and John Brown's are one and the same—to make an honest profit," Josiah answered. Smiling, he reached out to place his hand over hers on the railing. "But enough sour talk of politics. Have I told you today how fortunate I am to have such a lovely lady as my companion?"

Eliza wanted none of his compliments now. She tried to withdraw her hand from his, but Josiah only increased the pressure on her fingers.

"We'll take rooms at the Red Ox, if that pleases you," he continued. "The landlady there is quite genial, and she sets a decent table, too."

"I trust, Josiah, your arrangements have included separate rooms and reckonings."

He had been willing to overlook how she pulled back her hand from his, but now she'd abandoned his nickname, as well. He'd seen her be free enough with herself that night with Griffin on the dock, but she was unwilling to grant him the smallest favor. With an effort he swallowed his annoyance. "I fear I've offended you, Eliza."

"Not yet." Purposefully she looked again across the water to avoid his eyes. Likely he'd meant no harm, and she was overreacting. But when he'd touched her, her only desire had been to escape.

Angry with himself, Josiah struck at the rail with his cane. Thank God he'd be off this stinking little sloop soon and able to think of more than the heaving of his stomach. He'd have to go slowly with Eliza. If he lost her trust, he'd lose her as well. He was tired of sharing her beauty, tired of watching men like the *Polly*'s crew, even old Rawson, fall over themselves to earn the honor of her laughter. He wanted her to smile for him alone, and he wanted to be the only one with the right to touch her.

It was afternoon by the time the *Polly* was tied to the dock. Off the water, the summer heat rested on the town as heavily as a wet woolen cloak. The men slowly

loading wagons from the warehouses worked without
their shirts, the sweat streaming from their bare backs
and chests, while the dray horses in their traces listlessly hung their heads and swept away the flies with
their tails. Every window in every house was thrown
open wide to catch whatever breeze might rise from
the bay and the heavy doors to shops and taverns were
propped open with bricks.

After the brief ride to the inn in the hired chaise,
Eliza's skirts were filmed with gray dust and her back
was damp with perspiration. The front room of the
Red Ox seemed mercifully cool and dark after the heat
of the street as the innkeeper came bustling forward to
greet them.

"It's a pleasure to see you again, Mr. Buck, always
a pleasure," said Mrs. McKenna. She had come directly from the kitchen, still wearing her apron, her
broad-cheeked face flushed from the heat of her
cooking fires and daubed here and there with white
patches of flour. "I trust your journey was a pleasant
one?"

"Tolerable, ma'am, tolerable." Josiah drew Eliza
forward. "Miss Raeburn is the daughter of a shipmaster, and found our brief cruise not taxing in the
least."

"Oh, yes, the cousin you wrote about in your letter!" Eagerly the older woman bobbed a curtsy before Eliza. "A warm welcome to you, miss. I pray
you'll find our ladies' accommodations acceptable."

As her ample figure led the way up the stairs, Eliza
caught Josiah's sleeve. "What's this nonsense about
being cousins?"

"Forgive me, I should have mentioned it earlier, but the thing slipped my mind," he said contritely. "I thought it best to call us kin so as not to give rise to talk. There's nothing like an inn for gossip and half-truths. But if you wish, I can explain it all to Mrs. McKenna."

"No, no, Josey, I'm sure you're right," said Eliza slowly, and this time when he took her hand, she let him.

The room Mrs. McKenna unlocked for her was small but clean, with bed sheets whiter than could be expected in most lodgings. Eliza lay her hat on the bed as a boy brought up her trunk while Josiah waited at the doorway.

"You rest now, Eliza, and I'll tell you what I've learned at supper," he said over his shoulder as he began to close the door.

"Wait, Josey, wait! Wherever you're going, I'm coming with you!" She grabbed her hat and hurried to join him.

Josiah shook his head. "My dear, that's out of the question. Boston isn't Providence. If I'm to do my best for Nathaniel, I must make inquiries in neighborhoods where a lady doesn't belong."

"There's no place you'll go that I can't go, too," she replied staunchly.

"Eliza, I cannot in good faith allow you to come with me."

Mrs. McKenna chimed in from the hallway. "Oh, miss, there's many a neighborhood to this town where no decent folk go. It's the soldiers, miss, scores of the infernal lobsterbacks, acting like they're lords of the streets. The papers are full of tales of how they fight and steal and shoot poor, innocent children for the sport of it, and what they do to women—faith, I hope you'll never know!''

Josiah smiled sadly. "You see how it is, Eliza. I promise to tell you all at supper."

"But Josey!" she wailed.

"Until supper." He bowed his head and saluted her, then gently closed the door.

First Eliza threw her hat on the floor, muttering the choicest of sailor's oaths with Josiah's name attached, and then in frustration threw herself across the bed, as well. She thought she and Josiah would be finding Nathaniel together, but this way she might as well have stayed in Providence.

Angrily she kicked her feet against the coverlet. Josiah had no imagination. If he needed to go where ladies weren't welcome, she could have dressed like a boy again. That hadn't bothered Captain Griffin. He'd been able to treat her like any capable lad. Suddenly the memory of what had passed between them in the cabin came racing back, strong enough to make her blush. Well, she amended, he'd treated her like a boy in the ways that mattered. And petticoats or not, Eliza intended to make a few inquiries of her own. While Josiah was searching for Nathaniel in dark and dangerous places, she would begin higher, at the colony house. She'd certainly have no trouble finding that, even in a town as large as Boston.

She slipped down the back stairs, taking care to avoid Mrs. McKenna. Warm as the afternoon was, it felt good to be stretching her legs after the narrow confines of the *Polly*'s deck. And, she thought smugly, free of Josiah's confines as well.

She stopped to ask directions from an elderly man perched on his doorstep, a white clay pipe clenched in his toothless jaws.

"Colony house?" He squinted up at her. "Boston don't have no such article."

"Well, then, whatever place you have for your governor's business."

The old man spat scornfully in the street. "Governor's mischief be truer to the mark." He removed the pipe from his mouth and used its long stem to point out the way. "Follow your nose, lass, down Fish Street, to Anne, through Dock Square to King, and there sits the Town House."

Eliza thanked him and went on, repeating his directions like a litany under her breath. Providence was an easy town to travel, with streets laid neat and straight along the river or up the hill. Boston's streets ran every which way, curving here around this inlet, or stopping dead before that church. The houses all began to look alike, and as she walked Eliza wondered if she'd lost her way and unwittingly circled back towards the inn.

There was more traffic here, too, more wagons and horses and carriages to dodge in the street. Even the sidewalks were crowded, and Eliza found herself bumped by black house slaves with market baskets full of chickens and fresh peaches and jostled by apprentices in leather aprons, dawdling on their masters' errands. Sailors in checkered shirts and farmboys in homemade boots had come to see the highlights of

New England's largest city, and Eliza was uncomfortably aware of how, unescorted as she was, she figured among the sights to be ogled. She wished now that she had changed her gown to one less eye-catching, and modestly she tugged the lawn kerchief a little higher across her bodice.

She was hot and tired and thirsty, and close to admitting that Josiah had been right to suggest she wait for him. A small stone had worked its way into her shoe and she paused to lean against a silversmith's shop as, hopping on one foot, she freed the pebble from the other.

"Now 'ere's a fair lassie in need of a gallant friend," said a man's London-bred voice beside her.

"Speak for yerself, Ned, for I'll be damned before I'm gallant," replied his companion, the stale smell of rum another accent on his words. "Come, darlin', give us another sight of your pretty leg."

Eliza caught her breath. Reflected in the shop window, she saw her own startled face flanked by two figures in the unmistakable red-and-white uniforms of the British army. Their collar bands were greasy and the buff facings of their uniforms grimy with last week's gravy, but the long rifles each carried across their shoulders were spotless, the bayonets gleaming like polished sliver. At once she turned to flee, but the first private had already hooked his arm around her shoulders.

"Let me pass," she demanded, struggling. "Let me go! I have friends who are expecting me. They'll come looking for me, too, if I'm not there right away."

"Ah, my pretty poppet, time is one thing we've plenty of 'ere in the colonies," said the blond one as his hand crept across her breast. "If your friends are loyal to good King George, then they won't begrudge you givin' cheer to his lads so far from home. And if they're traitors, the less time you waste with them the better for you, sweet."

Eliza tried to slip free, but the other soldier laughed and shoved her back closer to his companion.

"Come now, love, give us a kiss for your king an' country," he leered. He tore off her hat and grabbed her jaw, twisting her face to meet his lips.

With a little cry of revulsion Eliza wrenched away, and with the flat of her hand slapped his cheek as hard as she could. "You're pigs, both of you!" she hissed. "Dirty, stinking, Tory, lobsterback pigs!"

The blond soldier's expression hardened as, across his face, the imprint of her hand bloomed red as his uniform. His friend sniggered. "Bloody 'ell, Ned, but she's a spicy one, ain't she?"

"The little harlot needs to be taught to respect his majesty, same as all these rebel bastards." Roughly he seized Eliza's wrists. He dug his fingers into the soft skin of her arm and shoved her back against the wall. The coarse wool and buttons of his coat pressed against her chest, and her back and arms scraped against the brick wall, but worst of all was the sickening stench of his breath in her face. That, and the way his unwashed body ground against hers, made her stomach turn.

"Let me go," she said again. Tears of fear and pain pricked behind her eyelids. "Oh, please, let me go!"

The man only laughed and pressed closer as Eliza tried to turn her face away. "Better, love, but you'll still need a lesson or two in minding your manners. What d'you say to a task like that, Davey, m'boy?"

Davey wiped his upper lip and pointed towards the narrow alley between two shops. "There be our schooling house, convenient for masters and pupil alike." He hiked the crotch of his breeches suggestively.

Eliza's heart pounded with terror as her eyes darted from the soldiers to the shadowy alley. The other pedestrians on the street had melted away; the few who remained deliberately crossed the street to avoid the two soldiers, or cast wary looks at their rifles and spared none for her. With rising panic, she realized that if she let herself be dragged into the alleyway, odds were that she'd never leave it alive.

With a grunt of eagerness, Ned released her wrists to free his own hands to lift her skirts, and gave Eliza the chance she needed. She jammed her knee upwards into the soldier's groin, and the man doubled over in agony as his rifle dropped, clattering to the pavement.

Eliza ran. Over her own ragged breath, she heard the heavy footsteps of the other soldier as she darted into the street, and knew he was close behind her—too close. Soon he would be able to reach her skirts, to grab her and pull her down. She felt her lungs would burst as she gasped from exhaustion. She stumbled and felt his hands close and tighten around her. But instead of dragging her down, the hands were lifting her upwards, away from the street and the startled face of the soldier and across the saddle of a chestnut horse.

"Why is it," asked Gardner Griffin as he scrambled back in the saddle behind her, "that I'm always finding you in the damnedest places?"

Chapter Seven

Gardner cradled Eliza in his arms as they rode west through the town, holding her as gently as he could against the horse's gait. The dry shudder of her breathing was fading to a few jerking sighs, but she was still huddled against him from shock.

"First the navy, and now the army. Faith, but his majesty's servants have their hands full with you." For her sake he managed to keep his banter light as he struggled to hold his anger in check. If he could, he would have showed her terrified face to every man who wavered towards loyalty to the Crown.

Unconsciously his arms tightened around her, and he wondered what fate had made their paths cross this afternoon. Sam would likely chide him for brawling in the street when he learned about the soldier's broken jaw, but then Sam hadn't felt the awful stab of recognition when Gardner had seen Eliza's copper-colored hair over the soldiers' scarlet backs. If he had let his anger run free, he probably would have killed them both, and when he gazed down at Eliza, he was sorry he hadn't.

Eliza did not question why Gardner was in Boston or how he had appeared from nowhere when she needed him most. She was safe. That was all that mattered now. She could forget the soldiers and Josiah and even Nathaniel, and let herself be lulled by the rhythm of the horse's ringing hoofbeats on the paving stones. She let her head fall back against his shoulder. She could ride like this forever and not care if they ever stopped.

The hoofbeats softened as the paving stones ended and dirt began. The houses on each side grew fewer and the road rose gently uphill. Before them lay open pastureland, with white-faced cows grazing in the shadows of a clump of maple trees.

Eliza had lost all sense of time and distance, but the changing landscape was enough to rouse her. "Where are we? This can't still be Boston, can it?"

"Aye, it is. That's Beacon Hill, there, past the Common." Gardner was thankful just to hear her speak. "I'm to meet friends there, and like it or not, you're coming with me."

She sighed. "I must be back for supper, or they'll worry," she said vaguely, thinking of Josiah and the McKennas.

"They'll have to wait. I haven't time to ferry you back now."

"Oh, no, I wouldn't ask you to." She liked the way his arms circled her. Tanned nearly as brown as the leather reins they loosely held, Gardner's hands seemed strong and capable, and beautiful, too, despite the innumerable calluses and scars that marked the fingers of every working sailor. "You've done so much for me already."

"No more than any man might," he said gruffly.

"Any man might, but you're the only one who did."

"Don't go making much of nothing." She had lost her kerchief in the scuffle, and the low, uncovered neckline to her gown offered him a heady view of her breasts that he'd have to be blind to ignore. Not an hour earlier he had saved her from those two rutting lobsterbacks, and now the discomfort he felt in his breeches proved his own desires weren't one whit more honorable. So much, Gardner thought wryly, for honor. He reined in the horse before the tall, white fence protecting John Hancock's mansion. He didn't have to look to know that Sam Adams would be waiting impatiently at the front parlor window, scowling between the parted curtains.

With a sinking feeling, Eliza realized they had reached their destination. The house before them was far grander than any in Providence, the first she'd seen built from neither brick nor wood but granite and freestone. It stood three stories high, with a delicate railing across the tiled gambrel roof from each pair of chimneys.

"Your friends are prosperous," she said awkwardly. The elegance of the house reminded her of her own dishevelled appearance. "I'll wait for you here, by the fence."

"Sweet Jesus, girl, I didn't bring you this far to let you wander with the cows on the Common. You'll come inside with me."

Her hands flew to her hair. "I can't. Look at me! What would your friends think? My sleeve is torn, I've lost half my hairpins and my hat—oh, my hat!" she wailed.

"You look fine without it." While he smiled at her vanity, he found it oddly touching that she cared how she looked to his friends. "But if you'd rather not come inside, there are always the gardens out back. John is uncommonly proud of them. Cato here can show you the way."

A black servant in bottle-green livery came running towards them to take the horse's bridle, and Gardner tossed him the reins. Effortlessly he swung himself from the saddle, then turned to help her down.

Eliza noticed how his hands continued to span her waist long after she was safely on the ground, and how she in turn kept her fingers resting lightly on his broad shoulders. She must speak now or not at all, and from sudden shyness her words tumbled over one another in an awkward rush.

"I've tried to thank you before and you've always turned me away, but this time, I'll have you hear me out. Thank you, Captain Griffin, for what you did for me. There, I've said it, and I meant it, too. Now if you still wish me to pretend we've never met, then I'll obey."

She stared at the ground to avoid seeing his reaction. She remembered how he'd shunned her and the angry hurt his rejection had caused her. The anger had long passed, but the hurt was still fresh. "I'll do as you wish," she ended lamely, "though how or why I've given offense to you, I cannot guess."

"Nay, Eliza, it's not as it seems," he said quickly. "You, of all women, should know otherwise."

Her heart leaped at the first sound of her given name on his tongue. Expectantly she lifted her face towards his. With one finger, Gardner brushed a loose curl back from her forehead, considering what, if anything, he should do next. He wished desperately that he could tell her what she wanted—what she deserved—to hear. But nothing had changed since Providence. She was still as much a danger to him as he was to her. If he had forgotten why, Sam Adams was waiting just beyond that carved doorway ready to remind him.

Sam Adams waiting—damnation! He was keeping the two most important men in Boston sitting idle while he mooned on like a green boy.

"I must go now," he said quickly, wincing inwardly as he saw the disappointment fill her eyes. "When I'm done, I'll see you home."

She nodded in silence and followed the waiting servant down the path that led to the garden. Late as he was, Gardner paused to watch the sunlight through the poplar trees catch the burnished copper in her hair as she disappeared around the house. What devil kept tossing this girl into his life? No good could come from it for either of them. He shook his head at his own weakness and turned his thoughts to the meeting ahead.

"You've done well in Rhode Island, Gardner. If this affair of the *Gaspee* doesn't rouse the sleepers from here to Virginia, then nothing will."

Steal the Stars

From Sam Adams this was extravagant praise, and Gardner knew it. In his shabby red suit and cheap brown wig, his hands shaking with palsy, Adams was not an imposing figure. But when he spoke, his blue eyes glinted with intelligence and his words carried a persuasive power that none in New England matched.

"I play the hands luck gives me, Sam," said Gardner. "I've learned that much from you."

Adams grunted. "Luck can take as readily as she gives. You did destroy the king's property and injure one of his officers. English law states that that merits your death. Hutchinson's already calling for public hangings, and Parliament will agree. You are, you know, in a good deal of trouble."

Gardner leaned back in his chair, his arms folded across his chest, and smiled lazily. "They have to know who I am before they catch me, and they have to catch me before they can hang me."

"Don't get cocky, lad," snapped Adams. "Your size and face will make you easy to recall, and the price they'll put on your head will serve to spur flagging memories."

Gardner's smile vanished. "Then the Tories will have to hang the whole blasted town, because there's not a family in Providence that wasn't bound to the raid by at least one man. I made sure of that with John Brown. We had four score men when half that would have served, just to spread the guilt, and they're too clannish to turn on themselves for gold."

"Where, then, does that place you? You know better than to trust your neck to the good humor of strangers. I'd given you more credit for judgment than to fall into a trap like that."

Gardner was on his feet instantly. "Damn it, Sam, I—"

"Gentlemen, gentlemen," interrupted John Hancock with soothing calmness. "I'll ask you please to control your passions in my home. Gardner, I'm certain Sam's concerns are only for your welfare. You're the best sailor my wharf ever launched, the only one of my captains never to bring home a loss, and you're uncommonly clever in the bargain. Besides, you're too tall already without the hangman stretching you further."

It was a slender joke at best, but it defused the tension in the room. Gardner slid back into his seat and grudgingly nodded in Hancock's direction. He respected Sam's vision and abilities, even admired him, but John Hancock he genuinely liked.

Adams cleared his throat, as much apology as he admitted, and shuffled through the sheaf of papers before him. "Clearly Dudingston erred by taking this Rhode Island Captain Chase from his own colony for trial. We can make good use of his example to justify the *Gaspee*'s destruction."

"No, Sam, we won't," said Gardner evenly as he met the surprise in the older man's eyes. "I've changed my mind. I want him free instead."

Adams rumbled impatiently. "Perhaps you'd care to tell us why?"

"Because of a promise I made to a friend. You don't need Chase, not really. If Hutchinson is out to avenge that fumbling English lieutenant, then he could be persuaded to release Chase now, and give Dudingston a clean account to take to his court-martial."

"As if I care what becomes of a British officer!"

Gardner leaned across the table. "In all the years I've known you, Sam, I've never once asked you for a favor. I've risked my skin for you more times than I'd want to tally, and I've set aside my own wishes because I believe in the same things you do. But I've asked for nothing for myself until now. Let me have Chase."

Adams sighed again, smoothing the papers before him with his unsteady hands. "Since Chase's fate seems so important to you, I'll do what I can for him. But you keep clear of Hutchinson yourself, understand? And back to Rhode Island with you. You're too well-known in these neighborhoods to suit me."

Gardner nodded, the tension leaving his shoulders as he realized he'd won.

"And you know, Gardner, I can guarantee nothing."

Gardner chuckled. "Your 'nothing,' Sam, is worth more in Boston than any other man's word of honor."

"Bravo, my friend, bravo!" Hancock applauded, his lace cuffs falling across his pale hands. "You've bargained and won with the devil himself. I only hope this special friend—Chase's sister, perhaps?—rewards you well!"

But as he left the room, Gardner's smile was, at best, half-hearted. He retrieved his horse from the stable and went around to the front to find Eliza sitting on the stone steps, her flowered skirts tucked neatly around her ankles. Across her lap was spread the latest issue of the *Boston Gazette* and in her hand was a half-eaten peach. The stallion nickered softly beside him and, startled, she looked up from the paper.

At once Eliza saw that Gardner was in one of his rare open moods. It made him look younger, almost boyish, with his dark hair falling across his forehead. His eyes, changeable as the weather, were now as blue as the summer sky above, and the suggestion of a smile played along the corners of his mouth. He stood with an easy nonchalance, his hands in his breeches pockets and the skirts of his faded blue coat flipped back, allowing himself the uncharacteristic liberty of rocking back in his boots. Above those boots she couldn't help but notice how snugly his breeches fit across his thighs, and higher, too, where the fabric was pulled even tighter by his hands in the pockets.

"What lies and tall tales has the *Gazette* printed this week?" he asked as he stroked the horse's long nose.

Eliza grinned and bit the last of the fruit from the pit. "What a tempest we raised by burning the *Gaspee!* There are some folks here who'd like to see every last Rhode Islander hunted down for treason, and others who think we stopped too short, that we should have murdered the lieutenant and all his crew."

"Ah, they're only jealous because they didn't get the chance to do it first," he said lightly, wishing again that she wouldn't include herself among the raiders. The horse nuzzled against his shoulder, eager to return to the livery stable and dinner. "Along with you now, Miss Raeburn. It's almost nightfall, and your friends have no notion of where you've been."

She was sorry to hear him go back to calling her Miss Raeburn, and she longed for an excuse to dawdle. Late as it was, she wasn't eager for the afternoon to end, or to return to the inn and face Josiah, either. She tossed the peach pit into the bushes and walked slowly down the steps towards Gardner, absentmindedly licking the last of the peach juice from her hand.

Gardner watched her pink tongue run the length of each finger in turn and almost groaned aloud. If she tried a lifetime, she couldn't have invented a gesture to tantalize him more. For a moment he considered telling her what he'd done on behalf of her cousin in the hope that she would be generous with her gratitude. And for that brief moment, he allowed himself to picture her as very generous indeed. How much he wished there were no Tory hangman to avoid, so that he could taste that peach juice on her lips.

Unhappily Eliza saw Gardner's expression change, his smile replaced by a bitter, blank look she could not comprehend. She realized he was closing her out again, and there was not one thing she could do about it.

As Gardner settled behind her on the horse, Eliza took care to sit stiffly apart from him. Earlier, when she had been too frightened and upset to care, she had focused only on the security she found with his arms around her. Now, calmer and having had time to think, she had no such excuse for relishing the warm proximity of his body.

Gardner noticed the change in her, and it puzzled him. While earlier she had been soft and yielding as they rode together, she now was stiff and aloof. Her laughter and conversation had been replaced by a cold silence. Perhaps, he thought with concern, she had been more shaken by the soldiers' violence than he had first thought.

"Where are we headed, lass?" he asked gently. "You haven't told me where these friends of yours live."

She glanced around at him curiously. "I'm staying at the Red Ox in Prince's Street. And it's business that's brought me to Boston, not friends. I'm trying to arrange for my cousin's release, the way you suggested."

"You mean you came clear up here by yourself on account of what I said?" He'd never dreamed she'd try to meet with Hutchinson herself.

"Oh no, I'm not alone," she answered blithely. "Josiah Buck agreed to come with me, and he's staying at the inn as well."

"Then it's a mighty poor guard he's set on you, sweetheart," he said roughly. Thank God he had shown enough sense not to tell her the details of his meeting. She would not have guessed what lay behind it, but Buck would, and the last thing Gardner wanted was to have his affairs discussed by Josiah Buck. "What made you trust yourself to a rogue like Buck?"

"I didn't 'trust myself,' as you call it." Her voice turned edgy and defensive. "I merely asked him to accompany me here, and he was good enough to agree."

"Buck won't take one step unless there's some reward in it for him. I'd keep well clear of him if I were you."

"You might be interested to know he says exactly the same thing about you," she retorted. "Josey is a decent, sober man who has worked hard to improve himself, and he's promised to help me get Nathaniel set free as quickly as possible."

"So 'Josey' it is, is it?" He hated hearing her speak so familiarly of Buck. "Your 'Josey' may have others dancing to his tune in Providence on account of John Brown, but I'd like to see what kind of favors he can collect in this town."

She tossed her hair back angrily. "Oh, and I suppose you could do so much better! At least Josiah was gentleman enough to offer to help me, which is more than you have ever done."

He sucked in his breath, biting back the truth. So this, he thought bitterly, is what comes of doing empty favors. "Then the next time you go walking in King Street, take care that *Master Josey* goes with you. I can't promise I'll be gentleman enough to save you again."

Before Eliza could reply, he pulled the horse up short before the open door of the inn. The shadowy forms of a half-dozen people spilled out into the dark street, and, with lantern in hand, it was Mrs. McKenna herself who sailed out to greet her.

"Merciful heavens, miss, here you be safe at last! We've been so worried, it's nearly eight o'clock with no word or sign. When you didn't come back for supper, we sent for the sheriff."

Self-consciously Eliza slipped from the saddle. This time, she noted, Captain Griffin made no move to help her. "I'm sorry to have caused you anxiety, Mrs. McKenna, but I'm perfectly well."

"Oh, miss, but you're not!" exclaimed the landlady. She held the lantern closer to Eliza, making a hasty inventory of her torn gown, missing hat and tousled hair. Frowning, she looked sharply up at Gardner.

"Nay, ma'am, this time I swear I'm innocent as the holy lamb," he said. "As I was passing, I saw this lady had run afoul of a pair of redcoats."

The woman's expression melted with concern. "You poor lass! How terrible for you! Come, let me take you inside."

Eliza spotted Josiah hustling around Mrs. McKenna's broad figure. "Dearest Eliza!" he cried. "At last you're back!"

To Eliza's surprise, he folded his arms around her in what she guessed he determined was a cousinly show of affection. Uncontrollably she stiffened in his arms, pushing back against his chest; the unexpected contact reminded her too strongly of the soldiers' attack. Clumsily she slipped free, stammering an apology, but from the look on Josiah's face, she knew he felt slighted by her repulsion.

"It's of no concern, Eliza," he said lightly, striving to be generous in spite of his displeasure. "We'll have plenty of time to talk later. What matters most is that no harm has come to you."

Mrs. McKenna gently took Eliza's arm. "Come, miss, let's get you tidied up, and then some supper into you."

As the woman shepherded her towards the door, Eliza hesitated, looking back at Gardner. A dozen phrases of apology and reconciliation were unspoken on her tongue, waiting only for him to speak first. But he stayed as silent and unyielding as a statue, his face hidden in the shadow of his hat brim. Eliza felt the sharp tears of frustration spring to her eyes, and with her head bent, she let herself be led indoors.

From the back of his horse, Gardner had not been able to see Eliza push away from Josiah, or the displeasure it caused him. To Gardner's eyes, she had gone freely to the comfort of the other man's arms just as she had earlier sought his own. With sudden vividness, he thought of Abby Jenkes. Abby, too, could charm like an angel when it suited her, and at eighteen he had been inexperienced enough to believe her guile. Had he learned nothing more about women since then?

As he watched Eliza go with Mrs. McKenna, he wondered if indeed this would be his last sight of her. She had not even bothered to say farewell to him. He intended to book passage on the next packet or ship to Providence, and then the *Three Brothers* would sail. There had been too little for him to do on land, he told himself, not enough to occupy his thoughts or time. That was the only reason she had beguiled him so. Once he was back at sea, he would have no problem forgetting her.

"I understand, Griffin, that I have you to thank for Eliza's deliverance," said Josiah. "I'll be sure to let Mr. Brown know of your service."

"Don't waste your breath," growled Gardner. "I make my own way without your kind of help." He looked down at the man's smug, satisfied face with no attempt to conceal his contempt. How could Eliza bear to be touched by those hands, as pale and white as a woman's? "You show damned little regard for Miss Raeburn."

Carefully Josiah noted the hostility in Gardner's voice, just as he had noticed the odd coincidence of Griffin appearing as Eliza's savior. He tapped his cane lightly on the paving stones. "On the contrary, Griffin. I hold Miss Raeburn in the highest regard. In fact, if I may be forgiven my eagerness, I believe she will soon do me the honor of becoming my wife."

Gardner jerked the reins sharply and the horse wheeled around beneath him. "I wish you well of the little witch," he said over his shoulder. "The pair of you deserve each other."

Yes, decided Josiah as Gardner galloped down the street, he had been right to speak to Griffin about his plans for Eliza. Even if his announcement was a bit premature, it would be just a matter of time before Eliza was his.

Chapter Eight

With a dull pop, Josiah pulled the stopper from the bottle of canary wine and poured the amber liquid into first Eliza's glass, then his own. "You are remarkable, Eliza. When I think of the hours you were trapped with those brutes—"

"If it had been hours, Josey, I don't think I'd be here now," she said truthfully. While across the hall the inn's taproom was busy, she and Josiah had the dining room to themselves. This was the first time since Eliza had returned the night before that Mrs. McKenna had let her out of her sight, and the first time, too, that she'd spoken to Josiah alone. "Captain Griffin rescued me right away."

Josiah didn't like that word, "rescue." Heroes performed rescues, and he didn't want Eliza thinking of Griffin in those terms. "But you didn't return until nightfall."

Eliza sipped the wine. "That was because Captain Griffin was on his way to meet friends, and since he didn't have time to bring me back, I went with him."

"He should have put your needs before his own concerns," said Josiah sternly.

"I didn't mind at all." Eliza recalled how much she had enjoyed riding with her head nestled against Gardner's chest. "I walked in the orchard behind the house while he was busy, and then we came straight back here."

"Whose house?" demanded Josiah.

"He didn't tell me, and I didn't ask, since it was none of my affair," she answered, wondering why it mattered so much to Josiah. "The house was very large and elegant and made of stone, with tall fences all around it. It was at a place called Beacon Hill, near the Common."

"Hancock's place. It couldn't be anyone else's," Josiah said excitedly. "A quarter of Boston depends on the man for their livelihoods, and when he meddles in politics, the rabble follows his whims. But why would he be entertaining Griffin?"

"I don't know and I don't care," said Eliza flatly. "Josey, if you don't mind, I'd rather not talk any more about Captain Griffin."

"Whatever you wish, of course. Besides, Eliza, I have a surprise for you."

Eliza caught her breath. "It's Nathaniel, isn't it? You've found him!"

Josiah sighed, dabbing his lips with his napkin. "No, my dear, I'm afraid I haven't, not quite yet. I've told you before that these things take time. Obtaining his release won't be easy."

From what Josiah had learned at the coffeehouse frequented by British officers and other loyalists, there wasn't the remotest chance Nathaniel Chase would ever again be a free man, though of course he had no intention of telling Eliza. "You must trust me to do all I can on your cousin's behalf. You have my word."

Eliza's anticipation crumbled. "I do trust you, Josey," she said plaintively. "You're the only one I can trust. I'm just discouraged. Sometimes I think I'll never see Nathaniel again."

"Then perhaps this will cheer you." Josiah reached behind his chair to produce a large pasteboard box, which he proudly presented to Eliza. This was his first gift to her, and he expected it to be perfect.

Slowly Eliza undid the cord around the box and lifted the lid. Inside lay a wide-brimmed lady's hat of golden leghorn straw. The ribbons were pale pink silk, and large silk roses were clustered to one side of the low crown.

"It's to replace the one you lost," explained Josiah. "The milliner assured me that this is a style favored by the most genteel ladies."

Eliza stared down at the hat. Instinctively she knew she must not accept such a gift from Josiah. It was more than that the hat was too personal and far too expensive to be a proper gift from a man. Did Josiah really believe she was so shallow that a new bonnet could make her forget Nathaniel's plight? She did not want the hat, nor even like it, and her first impulse was to toss it back in Josiah's face.

"Go ahead, my dear, try it on and show me how it looks," he urged, delighted by how his gift had left her speechless.

"Excuse me, miss, sir." Mrs. McKenna stood stiffly in the doorway. "Forgive me for interrupting, but there's a man here in the taproom claiming to be a cousin—*another* cousin—of Miss Raeburn's."

Without a moment's hesitation, Eliza flew from her chair and rushed past Mrs. McKenna. Crowding the taproom were men smoking, laughing, arguing and, most of all, drinking, but for Eliza there was only one. There, near the empty fireplace, twisting his hat in his oversized hands, stood her cousin Nathaniel.

"Eliza, Eliza, I should've known you'd come for me!" he murmured as he hugged her fiercely. His husky voice broke with emotion. "When they told me I could go, I should have known it was your doing, little cousin. Nothing ever stops you when you set your mind on it!"

Giggling happily, Eliza felt his familiar arms around her like some huge red-haired bear. Familiar, yes, but different somehow. She sensed the change, and stepped back to look at him. Nathaniel's eyes seemed haunted, his broad shoulders bent under some inner sorrow or defeat, and even the copper hair so like her own seemed to have dulled and lost its spark. She touched the ribs that, when he had hugged her, had been too evident in his barrel-shaped chest. "Didn't they feed you, Natty?" she asked softly.

"Enough to get by, no more." Self-consciously he tugged at his shirt. His coat and breeches hung on his broad frame like clothes begged from another man. Buttons were missing, his shirt poked through a tear in one sleeve, and everything he wore was grimy and soiled. Sorrowfully Eliza could understand why Mrs. McKenna had been suspicious.

"I'll see you eat your fill and more," promised Eliza. "Your mother will weep to see you like this."

"She's well, then? And Father, too?" he asked anxiously, and Eliza nodded. "And the *Speedwell*'s crew? Did they make Providence safe?"

"Jemmy and the others came home the day after you were captured," said Eliza, touched by his genuine concern for the men under him. "It's you alone we've had to worry over."

"Benjamin Childe most of all, I'll wager." Nathaniel's shoulders sagged even lower. "Jesus, but I've made a sorry mess of things for him, haven't I? I've lost his ship and his cargo, and likely brought him a heavy fine from the customs house, too. The old man has every right to expect my blood to make up for it."

"Oh, Nathaniel, I don't see how Mr. Childe could blame you for what happened." She put her hand on his shoulder to comfort him. "It was bad luck, pure and simple. And how can he fault you for standing up to the British like you did?" She drew him to an empty table and motioned for a tankard of ale.

Nathaniel shook his head and tried to stop her. "Nay, Eliza, don't. I haven't a penny to my name, and I won't be drinking what I can't pay for."

"But I can," Eliza answered firmly, "and between us such things don't matter. You'll stay here with us until Josiah finds us passage back home."

"Josiah? Where's Uncle James?"

Eliza sighed. "It's a long story. Father should have cleared Saint Eustatius by now, tides and winds being equal. I'm here in Boston with Josiah Buck, who came to help me free you. And he has, hasn't he?''

"Lawful heart, Eliza, what are you doing with Buck? Weren't there no one else more fit to ask?" Wearily he rubbed the back of his neck. "Well, no matter. I'm here, and he's to thank, it seems. But when the guard told me I had powerful friends in Boston working for me, I surely didn't think of Buck.''

"Faith, you're as hard on poor Josey as—" Eliza stopped short, realizing that, for now, she didn't want to explain Gardner to her cousin "—as you can be," she finished lamely. She noticed how Nathaniel's eyes were glazed with exhaustion and realized he had heard little of what she said. She took one of his pawlike hands in her own and stroked it gently, and was rewarded with the first glimmer of a smile.

"I should've known you'd come through for me, Eliza," he said again. "I should've known you'd be the one.''

Eliza sat perched on a pile of white oak timbers on the deck of the coaster *Marianne*, listening to the doleful tolling of the little ship's bell as they cautiously made their way out of Boston's fog-shrouded harbor. Uneasy, she pulled her shawl closer around her shoulders against the chill morning fog. Too many things could hide in the gray mists, especially since today she was trusting her life to a captain and crew she didn't know. The oak beneath the tarpaulin was destined for a shipyard in Newport, and Josiah had convinced Captain Pierce to take them that far as well. From Newport it would be simple to find a vessel to take them up Narragansett Bay to Providence. Although the *Marianne* was not accustomed to passengers, Eliza found the clean fragrance of the new lumber infinitely preferable to the stuffy quarters she had shared on the *Polly.*

Beside her on the lumber sprawled Nathaniel, lost in thought as the smoke from his pipe drifted around his face. A week of Mrs. McKenna's cooking had already done much to fill out the gauntness in his cheeks, and a visit to a tailor had transformed him from a scarecrow to a respectable mariner again. But the haunted look Eliza had noticed in his eyes remained, and he refused to confide in her, brushing aside her tentative inquiries without answers. To Eliza, his silence was both painful and disturbing, and she longed to find a way to reach him.

"Where's your friend Mr. Buck?" Nathaniel asked, relighting his pipe, and Eliza bristled. He had begun calling Josiah that almost from the first, and it wasn't done from respect. Although Nathaniel had acted grateful enough in the beginning, he had quickly made it clear he had no use for Josiah's company, and his rudeness was another source of unhappiness to Eliza.

"He went below. He had some papers to prepare for Mr. Brown."

Nathaniel snorted. "Now that's a pretty tale, isn't it? I saw the color of his gills. I'd say he's preparing to toss his breakfast into the scuppers."

Eliza remembered the trip on the *Polly* and couldn't disagree. "Poor Josey," she said. "I'm afraid he's not much of a sailor."

Nathaniel muttered something Eliza couldn't make out, but his scorn was clear enough. In their family, among Chases and Raeburns, seasickness was an unforgivable sin, but Eliza wished Nathaniel could be more charitable to Josiah if only for her sake. She settled the hat Josiah had given her more firmly on her head, retying the ribbons beneath her chin. It wasn't a very practical hat for sailing, but it was the only one she had, and when the sun finally burned through the fog, she would need the protection. Besides, it pleased Josiah to see her wear it.

Nathaniel climbed down from the pile of lumber, swinging his arms before him as he stretched. Imprisonment had made him perpetually restless, and he never stayed long in one place. "I believe I'll go back and talk to Pierce about how this sloop's handling. He could put more canvas on, and she wouldn't mind."

Eliza snorted, guessing how Captain Pierce would welcome Nathaniel's advice. As she heard her cousin greet the other captain, her ears caught a third voice, too, with a dry rasp to it that she recognized at once. No, she thought as her head whipped around, not here!

But there on the quarterdeck, shaking hands with her cousin as Pierce made the introductions, was Gardner. Even from here she could see his rare smile and the way his eyes crinkled at the corners. Quickly she ducked behind the shelter of the tarpaulin, her heart already beating faster.

Compose yourself, Eliza, she ordered sternly. Don't let him make you skulk about like you're afraid of your own shadow. You've never run from anything before, and you won't start now. She slid down from the lumber, and with her head held high, she headed aft to where the three captains stood in conversation, their backs to her. She stopped at the two steps that rose to the quarterdeck. Even on a poky little freighter like the *Marianne,* she knew well that the quarterdeck was the captain's inviolable domain, and she wouldn't dream of trespassing.

"Good morning, gentlemen," she called. "We've a fair breeze for Rhode Island, haven't we?"

Almost in unison the three turned around to face her, but she only saw Gardner. So this was how he looked at sea, she thought, her heart squeezing tight in her breast. Here he was at home. She could tell by the way he held his body against the wind, his face turned to meet the sky, and how he stood with his legs widespread against the roll of the deck. There was a sense of exhilaration in his whole posture that spoke of a kinship with the wildness of the wind and the ocean, a kinship that she recognized at once. Her eyes met his, and she felt herself drawn into their blue depths. She forgot everything else, almost forgot to breathe, as she swayed gently on her feet with the deck's roll.

"I knew, Miss Raeburn, with Captain Chase aboard, that you wouldn't be far behind," he said.

"You've said it yourself, Captain Griffin," she answered with an evenness she didn't feel. "I always turn up in the damnedest places."

"That you do, no mistake." He was finding it difficult to think, let alone speak, with her there on the deck below him. The wind had pulled her hat back so the slender ribbons crossed her bare throat, her copper-colored hair blowing like flames around her upturned face. Of all the vessels in Boston Harbor, why in God's name had he chosen this one?

Nathaniel shifted his gaze from his cousin to Captain Griffin and back again, baffled by what he saw. "Sounds like the other way around, Griffin, that you're the one following my cousin," he said uncomfortably. He thought that Eliza had set her sights on Josiah Buck, but here she and Griffin were staring at each other bold enough to shame every Raeburn ever born. He'd never seen her act like this, and he wasn't sure he liked it. "She didn't tell me you two were such friends."

"You never asked me, Nathaniel," answered Eliza breathlessly. What was it about the man that made her so instantly, ridiculously giddy like this?

"Aye, Captain Chase, your little cousin has taken a good deal of my time looking after her," agreed Gardner, not moving his eyes from Eliza's. He was behaving like a witless fool, but worse, he had no wish to do otherwise. Slowly he smiled and watched the blush creep across her face as finally she broke the spell and looked away. That weasel Buck was wrong. She couldn't care for Buck and still color like that when he did no more than smile at her, and the knowledge made Gardner absurdly happy.

Nathaniel cleared his throat uncomfortably. "You'd best go for'ard again, Eliza. I'll be back directly."

"Aye, miss," agreed Captain Pierce with obvious relief. "We just be talkin' men's talk. Ain't nothin' a lady like yourself might fancy hearin'."

Eliza laughed. "Oh, Captain Pierce, there's precious little men's talk that's new to me. My father's a shipmaster, too, and I've spent my whole life hearing men's talk without harm."

She waited for the invitation to join them, but Pierce stubbornly shook his head. "Nay, miss, I can't abide it. Best you go for'ard, like Captain Chase says."

Frowning, Eliza looked sharply at the faces of the three men. Gardner's had become a noncommittal mask, but Nathaniel and Captain Pierce avoided her scrutiny and fidgeted uneasily.

"Faith, but I've never seen men with guilt writ so bold across their faces," she said, testy at being excluded. "To look at you I'd swear your fine men's talk must be nothing short of high treason."

To Eliza's surprise, both Nathaniel and Captain Pierce grew red, the *Marianne*'s captain staring at the deck and shaking his head repeatedly. Only Gardner seemed unruffled.

Eliza gulped and hastily tried to repair the damage. "Of course I don't care if what you say is treason. These days it seems almost anything said in New England is treason to Parliament, isn't it?" Their stony faces didn't alter, and she rattled on desperately. "I mean, I can name only one Providence man who doesn't say how wrong and unfair King George and his lords in Parliament are, and that's Josiah." Instantly she realized her blunder as the warmth she'd found earlier in Gardner's eyes vanished and Nathaniel swore violently.

Her words sobered Gardner more quickly than a bucket of seawater. Eliza might not love Buck, but she trusted and confided in him, and that was infinitely worse. In his mind he tried to replay every conversation he had had with her, sifting his memory for careless words that could mean betrayal to his friends and associates. From long habit Gardner was always careful with names and places, but Buck was clever enough to be able to piece together any slips with other information he was being given. While Sam Adams's network was far-reaching, it had stopped short of identifying Buck, and Gardner blamed himself for not naming him sooner.

"Go back to your friend Mr. Buck, then, cousin," said Nathaniel roughly. "If he's the only man you can trust, then you'd best be with him."

Without answering Nathaniel, Eliza turned and stalked away with as much dignity as she could muster. She had pride enough not to stay where she wasn't wanted. They had no right to treat her like that, she decided furiously, dismissing her like a naughty child.

Moving as far forward as she could short of climbing out on the bowsprit, Eliza gulped at the salty air, trying to calm her temper long enough to think clearly. The way Nathaniel had thrown back Josiah's name at her had sounded like an accusation. She'd grant that Josiah was conservative in his politics, but she couldn't believe Josey was a Tory. How could he be, and work for John Brown, or even live with the rest of them in Providence? And Josiah had arranged for Nathaniel's release. No loyalist sympathizer would have done that. So why did her own reassurances have a hollow ring to them? She remembered the cold, hard expression that had come across Gardner's face. There was something unsettling about all three of them— Josiah, Nathaniel and Gardner, too—that she sensed rather than knew for certain. She felt as blind as the *Marianne* creeping through the fog, stealing her way through unseen dangers.

On the morning they expected to reach Newport, Eliza rose early and went on deck to watch the sunrise. So far dawn was no more than a pale gray band on the eastern horizon, and all the stars and a new moon still glittered overhead. This was Eliza's favorite time at sea, when she found it easy in the peaceful quiet of a new day to let her mind wander. She hadn't bothered to braid or pin back her hair, and she arched her head back languorously to let the breeze play through the waist-length curls and lift them gently from her neck and shoulders. They could be home tonight, yet while she was returning with Nathaniel as she had planned, somehow the triumph she had expected to feel wasn't there. But perhaps there would be a letter waiting for her from her father.

High above her, sitting with his legs curled around the main topgallant, Gardner lowered the polished brass spyglass and considered the significance of the tiny pinprick of white that he had spotted on the horizon. Soon the pinprick grew into a square, then another appeared below it, until the faint outline of another ship was at last recognizable. Like the sun rising behind her, she came from the east, which meant she was outbound from Europe, and from the number of sails, she was in a hurry.

Gazing again through the glass, he cursed the distance and the shining curve of the rising sun that made the vessel unidentifiable. Much as he trusted his own abilities, he needed another opinion, a second set of eyes. He scanned the deck for Pierce's hands. The two old men and one young boy who formed the morning watch were gathered at the helm, idly swapping yarns. With disgust Gardner turned away.

It was then that he saw Eliza, her figure tinted rosy red in the dawn's light. He had sworn to avoid her for the rest of their journey, but now he realized she was his only choice. He could wait, or he could ask her. Impatiently he looked once more at the approaching ship, then jabbed the spyglass into the waistband of his breeches. Hand over hand he lowered himself rapidly down the main shrouds, his feet skimming over the ratlines, dropping to the main deck below and into the middle of Eliza's reverie.

Chapter Nine

Startled, Eliza gasped. From the corner of her eye she had caught the final movements of Gardner's rapid descent, his motions agile and effortless like a great cat. He, too, had not expected company on deck this early, and, bareheaded and barefoot, he wore only his shirt and breeches. His shirt was open nearly to the waist, the sleeves carelessly pushed up over his elbows. In contrast his tanned skin seemed almost bronze, and the dark curls that patterned his bare chest were as black as the hair that now tossed back and forth across his forehead.

He thrust the spyglass into her hands. "Your cousin says you've a sharp pair of eyes," he said. "Use 'em, and tell me what you see."

"What am I looking for?" she asked curiously as she accepted the glass. She was intrigued by his excitement, a contagious energy that she hadn't seen since the night of the *Gaspee* raid.

"First tell me what's there," he ordered. He had never seen her with her hair loose before and his eyes kept returning to it, swirling wild and untamed around her shoulders.

With a confident smile, she swung the glass up to her eye and began to scan the sea around them. This was a task she often performed for her father, and she knew she did it well. But Gardner, impatient, couldn't wait. He stepped behind her and, with his hands on her shoulders, steered her gaze to the brig on the horizon. She felt his warm breath near her ear as he bent close to guide her, and her own hands shook slightly. It took all her concentration to steady the glass.

"I see a sail—three sails," she said slowly. "A ship, then."

"Come, lass," he whispered urgently in her ear. It seemed oddly important to him that she not disappoint him. "You can do better than that, or you're calling your cousin a liar."

"At least now I know what you two talked about," she grumbled, but trained her eye against the lens. "A three-masted brig with all sail on. Either her hold is more full than it ought to be—a greedy owner?—or she's taking water, for she sits low in the waves, and labors too much under all that canvas. Or maybe she's just a clumsy sailor. Dutch-built, maybe?"

"Dutch, eh? I hadn't thought of that," he said, impressed. "Friend or foe?"

Eliza shook her head, lowering the glass. "She's still too far to read her colors. But she'll be on us in no time." She turned slightly to return the glass to him and her body shifted closer into his, her arm brushing his bare chest. Although her reason for their nearness had passed, she did not draw away, nor did he step back.

"Aye, she'll be on us like a fox on a fat hen, if that's her game," he said with resignation. "The navy's taken queerer ships into her service."

Eliza looked up at his face, the sharp planes of his cheekbones burnished by the rising sun. "I'd wager she's no more than a Liverpool merchantman outward bound to Newport."

His eyes remained fixed on the horizon. He had already gauged the distance from the *Marianne* to the coast. The rocky beach wasn't a welcoming sight, and the water would be cold, but he could swim it, if it came to that. "Sweet Mary, but I hope you're right."

"And if I'm not? If she's a king's ship, one sent to replace the *Gaspee,* what of it? Captain Pierce trades nothing that would interest customs men, and besides, he has neither the speed nor the skill to outrun her. We'll reach Newport this day even if we are stopped. But you, you're nervous as a cat."

He answered levelly. "Any Yankee on the water these days should be cautious. It's only the careless ones like Pierce who aren't. Why d'you think your father left you home?"

"No, there's more to it than that," she said. Now that she'd begun, it was easy to put into words the vague misgivings and resentments that had plagued her this past week, and she spoke rapidly. "You, Nathaniel, and Josiah, too, you're all forgetting I have eyes and ears and a good mind. Not that it's taken me much to guess that something's not right. You're all dancing circles around me like I wouldn't notice, not one of you trusting me with the truth about whatever is happening.''

His answer was slow to come. "Maybe that's because we all, in our ways, care about you too much to drag you into our quarrels."

Eliza shook her head violently. "I don't believe that, not of you, anyway. Nathaniel and Josiah, perhaps, but not you." Defensiveness made her voice sharp. "I'm not worth a tinker's dam to you, and you can't deny it."

Something close to sorrow twisted his features even as he smiled. Gently he touched her face, letting the curve of her cheek fill his palm. She was so vibrant, so alive, and he longed to find comfort in her warmth, like a cold man seeks a fire on a winter's day. "Would you wish it otherwise, Eliza?"

"I don't know what I wish!" she cried. It was so hard to think with him this close.

"Then let me tell you what my wish is." His rough whisper so close to her ear made her shiver. "I wish I'd met you in another time, in another place, where I wouldn't have to talk to you in riddles like this one and pray you understand enough, but not too much."

"Tell me more, Gardner," she said eagerly. "Tell me what or who you're running from!"

He pulled his gaze away from hers and forced himself to remember Hancock and Adams and all the others who were depending on him. "I can't, Eliza," he said wearily. "My whole life is built on taking risks and trusting luck, and hoping the last sworn promise I heard doesn't turn false before I'm clear of it."

"Same as every Yankee shipmaster worth his name," she said stubbornly, placing her hands on his chest. "Same as my father, same as Nathaniel."

"Nay, Eliza, I am not the same. I can't tell you more than that. I've enemies with memories running back to Adam and Eve, and someday they'll catch me. Maybe not today—" he waved in the direction of the approaching ship "—but someday, for certain, they will. And I don't want you there when they do."

"So what you're saying is that you care too much about me to let me care for you?" she said bitterly. She jerked away from him, twisting her hands in the corners of her shawl as if they had betrayed her on their own. "That's a powerfully weak argument from a man who's claiming to live by his wits."

"It is, isn't it?" he admitted. "But it's all I have."

She looked away from him, out across the water. Where she would have once been angry, she now felt only empty and sad. Behind them one of the *Marianne*'s crew finally spotted the brig, bawling out his hail. Within minutes the rest of the crew would be gathered on deck to gawk at the other vessel as she bore down on them.

"No gunports or pirate flags that I can see," Eliza said to Gardner, without turning to face him. "You're safe enough from your enemies today."

She lifted her chin a little higher, hoping her voice did not betray the tears that were so perilously close to spilling over. "And you're safe from me as well," she added softly. She turned and walked away from him, concentrating on putting one foot before the other as she crossed the broad deck planks, filling her mind with anything to make her forget him standing there behind her.

As Gardner watched Eliza walk away, he felt the loss sweep over him like a wave. She was brave and strong, like no other woman he'd ever known. But she wasn't meant for him. She couldn't be. He reminded himself how little he had to offer her, not even his father's name. She deserved better than a wandering rebel, always two steps ahead of the hangman. He knew he was right to send her away, but the knowledge brought, at best, a bleak comfort that was no comfort at all.

He saw Josiah Buck take Eliza's arm, leaning close to speak to her with proprietary confidence. Her face blank, Eliza nodded woodenly, and to Josiah's obvious approval, she began to braid her hair, pulling the curls into a single severe plait. Gardner could watch no longer, and with an effort tried to interest himself in the English brig.

The brig's captain was ranging his vessel alongside the *Marianne* long enough to exchange brief civilities and news. As Eliza had predicted, the brig was a merchantman, the *Felicity,* thirty-two days out of Bristol and bound for Boston. Gardner watched the *Felicity*'s captain being rowed over in his boat to visit the *Marianne* and Captain Pierce's obvious pleasure and confusion at being so honored. It wasn't often that a coaster like the *Marianne* was the first to hear news from London. Gardner was heading below to avoid the inevitable introductions and finish dressing when he noticed the red-faced British captain brandishing a fat sheaf of printed handbills.

"I've half a mind to go to Newport myself, just for the joy of seeing their faces," the man was saying as he first pulled one of the handbills free for Captain Pierce and then began passing them around to the others. "Those blackguards will learn what comes of crossing his majesty, damn my eyes if they don't."

Outwardly calm, Gardner accepted one of the sheets. Printed at the top was the royal coat of arms, the lion and crown and unicorn, and below that, in bold letters, "GEORGE R. BY THE KING. A PROCLAMATION. For the discovering and apprehending of the persons who plundered and burnt the *Gaspee* schooner and barbarously wounded and ill-treated Lieutenant William Dudingston, commander of said schooner."

Gardner had been anticipating this moment since June; almost been looking forward to it, in fact, just to see how angry he had managed to make the king. But Gardner hadn't expected the shock he felt when he reached the fifth paragraph of stiff, formal wording.

TO THE INTENT that said outrageous and heinous offender who called himself, or was called by his said accomplices, the Head Sheriff, believed by us to be one Gardner Griffin of Providence Plantations, mariner; so that he may be apprehended and brought to punishment, such discoverer shall have and receive as a reward upon conviction, FIVE HUNDRED POUNDS.

Five hundred pounds! Five hundred pounds was more money than most colonial families saw in a year, and many in a lifetime. Five hundred pounds bought a handsome house in Providence, a good-sized farm in South County, a vessel the size of the *Marianne,* and now, thought Gardner with sickening clarity, it also bought his life. He had expected a reward, but nothing so large, and he had had no idea they would learn and print his name, too. Already he was aware of how the others on deck were eyeing him differently, backing away as if his fate were somehow contagious. Sweet Jesus, but five hundred pounds would tempt a saint to sin!

"This will drag the filthy rascals from their lairs," bragged the *Felicity*'s captain, unaware of the reaction his news was causing. "Then we'll send the lot of them to·London to meet Jack Ketch. By God, I'd like to be there to see 'em swing at Tyburn!"

Without thinking, Gardner looked for Eliza and found her beyond the Englishman. She might have been a statue, so still did she stand, and as Gardner's eyes met hers, the crumpled handbill dropped from her fingers to the deck.

"I tell you, Griffin, you're wrong about Buck," said John Brown evenly as he settled back in his armchair. "I don't believe there's any possibility that he gave your name to the British."

Furious, Gardner slammed his fist down on the table between them. "Then I'd like to know who the devil did! I've warned you before, and still you trust the damned Tory hypocrite!"

"You forget yourself, sir!" Brown motioned imperiously to the younger man to retake his seat, but

Gardner was too angry to sit. Instead he began pacing the length of the narrow office, his anger barely held in check. "I've known Josiah Buck since he was a boy, and, until your accusations, always had complete confidence in him."

Impatiently Gardner raked his fingers through his hair. "Sweet Mary, but I'd like to see the proof of his innocence!"

"I have more than you might think," answered Brown. "Against my own judgment, I took your advice and purposefully kept your involvement in the *Gaspee* raid secret from Josiah. I credited you with grounding the schooner, to be sure, but beyond that, I took full responsibility myself. If Josiah knew otherwise, then he was told by someone other than myself."

Abruptly Gardner stopped pacing. "Then one of the other men must have told him."

"Perhaps, but not likely. You're forgetting that they have prices on their heads as well. Though at five hundred pounds apiece, you and I seem to be the prize catches." Brown chuckled. Protected as he was by his position in the colony, he felt little threat of prosecution, and the picture of his highly respectable self as a heinous pirate amused him. "The men in our party were all hand-picked, and you won't find a turncoat in the lot. Nor, I think, will anyone in this town turn you in to collect the reward. They all knew the risks, same as you did."

The image of Eliza, dressed in boy's clothing for the raid, came suddenly to Gardner. Not everyone had realized the risks, and much of his anger now rose from the danger he had brought to her, and his inability now to protect her from capture and trial.

"Then who was it?" he demanded.

"Who, indeed." Brown's eyebrows pulled together over his bulbous nose. "I don't like it, Griffin, don't like it one bit. It's bad enough having a wanted man as the *Three Brothers*'s master when we're involved in such a dangerous trade. But it's worse still not knowing who that master's real enemies are."

His eyes flashing, Gardner wheeled around to face Brown. "What are you implying?"

"I'm implying nothing. I'm merely observing the facts as they stand." Brown would be sorry to lose Griffin. He was a clever man, and he would be hard to replace. "An unknown person has betrayed you to the British officials. I can't afford to lose my ship—or her cargo—if that person docs it again. You're no use to the cause like this, Griffin, at least not in Rhode Island. Even Hancock must see that."

"Nay, I don't believe he will. As loyal as he is to freedom and independence, he's more loyal still to his friends." Gardner plucked his hat from the table and headed for the door. "I'll keep my word and finish out this voyage. After that you can find yourself another captain for your precious *Three Brothers*."

"Good night, Mr. Buck, sir." The young clerk ducked his head as a final farewell and closed the door softly behind him. It was half past eight, and from the papers piled high on Mr. Buck's desk, it looked like the man meant to stay until midnight.

Josiah laid aside the manifest he had been reviewing and took out the small box that had arrived for him earlier that afternoon from the Newport bookseller. Without pausing to scan the titles, he removed the top two books from the box. It was the third one, with the red binding, that he wanted. He cracked the book's spine backwards, fanning the pages with his fingers until a folded slip of foolscap dropped to his desk. The note was very brief, the way all of Colonel Osborne's messages tended to be.

Yours of fifteenth instant regarding Griffin and Brown received and most welcome. We now seek a Providence female described by Lt. D. as Griffin's partner on *Gaspee:* a bold red-haired young hussey. All yr. advice requested in this for Admiralty wants to hang the pair as a Lesson.

> Our thanks & respects,
> Yr. obt. servt. —D.J.O.
> God save the King.

Eliza. It had to be Eliza. There wasn't another "red-haired young hussey" in Providence, not that knew Griffin. Josiah scowled, recalling all the times he had seen the two of them together. And so, apparently, had Dudingston.

He sighed, drumming his fingers on the desk. He couldn't very well marry a woman guilty of treason. The only way he could be certain that no one learned about this would be to make sure Griffin failed to return to Providence, and these days that was simple enough. With Griffin in their hands, the Admiralty would soon forget his "partner on the *Gaspee*."

He read the note one more time before tossing it into the fire, prodding the embers until he was satisfied that the paper was reduced to illegible ashes. Then he dipped his pen in the ink and began his response to Colonel Osborne. There were, he wrote, no red-haired young women in Providence known to be consorting with Griffin. Then he carefully copied out the sailing orders and destinations for the *Three Brothers*.

With the autumn sun warm on her back, Eliza tugged hard at one of the dandelions clogging the small garden behind her house. During these weeks since she had returned from Boston, her father's business had kept her at the warehouse, and she had neglected both the garden and her housekeeping. Now, with the *Peacock*'s last shipment of molasses finally sold off and the bills paid, she could turn her attention to home.

As the weed at last gave way, Eliza tossed it with the others into the willow basket on the walk and stood upright with her hands on her hips to survey her progress. Hemmed in by houses on all sides, the garden had raised beds outlined with white clamshells and neat paths that sloped downward as they followed the side of the hill. She liked the pungent fragrances of the herbs—red mint and sage, tansy and French thyme— and while most of the flowers had already begun to die back for the season, the marigolds and snapdragons were still brave, straggling patches of gold and pink in their last flowering before the first frost. It might come any night now; the trees up Prospect Hill were beginning to change, yellow oaks and red maples among the fading greens.

"What do you think, Beckah?" Eliza asked her friend, who sat knitting a sock for Nathaniel on the slate step by the kitchen door. "Should I cover the strawberry vines now, or let them have the sun for another week or so?"

Beckah looked over at the vines, her fingers continuing to rhythmically loop the gray yarn around her needles. "You'll have other tasks more pressing when your father comes home."

"I'm not sure when he's coming home, not now." Absently Eliza wiped her hands on her apron.

Surprised, Beckah's fingers paused. "You've had another letter, then?"

Eliza shrugged wearily. "The *Peacock* hit heavy seas off Saint Kitts, bad enough to dismast her. Praise God they're all safe on board, but Father says it's been a struggle to get her set to rights again to suit him." It wasn't like her father to blame bad weather for his misfortunes, nor, for that matter, was it like him to have misfortunes at all. "And Father says the whole Caribbean is chockablock full of British warships."

"Have you told Nathaniel?" asked Beckah anxiously. "He'll be bound for Surinam next month, and I don't think he could bear running into another British trap."

"He's heard me tell Uncle Enos, but Nathaniel has no interest in listening to me." Eliza kicked at the basket. "I don't know what's got into him. It's as if he blames me for bringing him home safe."

"It's not you, Eliza, not exactly." Nervously Beckah smoothed her neat blond hair. "It's Josiah. Nathaniel's afraid that you're in love with him. He doesn't know how to tell you he doesn't like it, so instead he just avoids you, hoping you'll change your mind on your own."

Eliza rolled her eyes to the sky with exasperation. "Oh, Beckah, not you and Nathaniel, too! Everyone, including Josiah himself, seems to think we're practically betrothed, and nothing I say or do seems to stop the talk. Faith, Beckah, what do I have to do to prove I don't love the man?"

"Then who are you in love with?" asked Beckah, with her head cocked quizzically to one side. "If it's not Josiah, it's surely someone else. You're stargazing, moonstruck, and lovesick, all at once. Unless, of course, it's from the extra weight of having a price on your head for being a pirate."

"Beckah, hush!" scolded Eliza, her eyes flashing. "You swore you wouldn't tell a soul about that, and I don't want word getting back to my father. He has troubles enough without worrying about me."

"Well then, it must be the other reason," teased Beckah. "Maybe it's that gentleman from Boston who sails for Mr. Brown."

"Captain Griffin is not so much a gentleman as a—a—"

"As what, Eliza?" prompted Beckah, giggling. "As what?"

"As you are a provoking, chattering magpie and the sorriest excuse for a friend I've ever seen!" snapped Eliza. As soon as the words were out she regretted them, and instantly hot tears of remorse burned in her eyes. Beckah was right, she wasn't herself, but it couldn't be from love. Love was supposed to be glorious and uplifting, the way it seemed to be for Beckah and Nathaniel, while Eliza had never been more miserable in her life.

"I'm nothing to Captain Griffin, and he's nothing to me, Beckah," she said unhappily. "You'll have to look elsewhere for your matchmaking."

Listlessly she swung the basket over her arm, her pleasure in the afternoon's tasks gone. She stepped through the beds to the farthest corner near the fence, to the rosebushes, and with her pruning knife began to cut back the woody branches. She knew that from this corner, if she stood on the crossbar of the fence, she could look between the clapboard houses and see the tip of the topgallant mast of the *Three Brothers*. But today, with Beckah there, she wouldn't let herself do it, even though tomorrow, the *Three Brothers* would sail and even that little bit of mast would be gone.

Yet when she heard the footsteps crunch on the crushed shells of the walk behind her and the squeak of the gate hinges she kept meaning to oil, she knew without looking who it was. Inexplicably she had known he would not be able to keep away, any more than she had been able to resist staring morning and night at the masts of the *Three Brothers*.

"Now I could surely use a fine pair o' socks like that," Gardner said to Beckah almost playfully. "Socks like those would be a comfort on a cold, wet night."

Beckah giggled. "And so they shall, on the feet of Captain Nathaniel Chase."

Eliza scrambled up from her knees and turned in time to see her Beckah proudly holding out the half-finished sock for Gardner's inspection. But his gaze had swept beyond Beckah and her sock to find Eliza, raking her hungrily from her head to her toes and back again. Under such scrutiny, Eliza thought with dismay how she must look to him: her feet in thick wooden pattens, her skirts hiked ankle-high through the strings of her grubby apron, dirt caked under her nails and a faded kerchief on her head. But she forgot it all when her eyes met his. Slowly she picked her way across the garden to him, only half-aware of Beckah gathering her yarn and knitting and hurrying towards the gate. She caught Eliza's hand and gave it a quick squeeze.

"You don't need me for matchmaking, Eliza," she whispered with a knowing grin. "You've done quite well on your own."

"Wait, Beckah, don't go!" Eliza said hastily, but the other girl was already scurrying down the narrow walk, her skirts swishing against the fence pickets.

"You needn't look so fearful, lass," said Gardner drily. "You're the one who's armed, not I."

Foolishly Eliza glanced down at the knife in her hand and set it on the fence post.

"The first time I was alone with you," he continued, "it was a pistol, I recall, and now this. You're a dangerous woman, Eliza."

She loved the way he drawled her name, lingering over the sound of it in his mouth. "No, the pistol was yours that night, and aimed straight for my heart, too."

"Nay, then you disremember. I was expecting a man, not you, and while I aimed for the intruder's breast, I found your face instead in my sight."

How could he be so calm, she wondered, standing there before her, swinging his hat in one hand as he bantered carelessly. He seemed too large somehow for her mother's garden, the scale of his broad shoulders and long limbs all wrong beside the low whitewashed fence.

"Why have you come?" she asked abruptly. "I thought there was nothing more to be said between us."

"Eliza, about that night," he began, his voice suddenly serious. "Have you told anyone, anyone at all, that you were there?"

She shook her head. "No, I haven't. Not Father, not Nathaniel. Not Josey, either, before you ask. Beckah guessed the truth, but she'll keep it to herself."

"Then you'll be safe," he said quietly. "I couldn't have cleared Providence tomorrow without knowing for sure. I couldn't forget your face when you saw that blasted proclamation. It was like you'd just read your own death warrant."

"Oh, no," she said swiftly. "Oh, no, that wasn't it at all. It wasn't my own life I feared for. It was yours."

He stared at her, uncomprehending at first, until the open truth of what she'd said hit him like a blow. She needed him, cared for him, more than her own life, and the realization left him shaky and unsure. He struggled against the feelings rising within him, afraid in a way he never was of physical danger.

"Gardner, be careful." Eliza stepped closer and gently took the revers of his coat in her hands. "I don't know what devils make you run, but the ones the king has sent after you now are real."

"I've weathered more than this before, and likely will see worse again," he said gruffly. What was it about her that made him feel so curiously off balance? "You needn't be worrying about me."

"I can't help it," she said simply. "I wish to God I could, but I can't."

"I must go now, Eliza," he said, more to remind himself than her. But even then his own hands were betraying him, reaching out to take her, to pull her closer. He tugged the kerchief from her head, and his fingers tangled in the soft curls.

"Swear you'll be careful, Gardner." Eliza's voice was husky with emotion as her hands crept up his chest, her eyes searching his for an answer. "Faith, I know I've no right to say so, but I could not bear a world without you in it!"

Almost against his will he bent towards her, and without resistance she offered her lips to his. The reality of her in his arms again went a thousand times beyond his dreams, and her mouth was almost unbearably sweet. His senses felt drunk with the taste of her, the fragrance of her skin and hair. She had so much to give him, and he felt himself lost in his need for her, lost and found and carried on her love to a place he'd never dreamed existed. For these moments, she could make him forget who and what he was, that tomorrow he would sail from her life forever, and that tomorrow all of this would be no more than a bittersweet memory.

Her head spinning, Eliza gave herself over to the rapture of his embrace. As his mouth explored hers, tenderly at first, and then with a growing fire, she felt unbelievably. alive, every sense quivering with new awareness. With shyness that soon changed to an unfamiliar urgency of her own, she answered him with her lips, her body, her whole being. In every corner of her soul and heart she knew she was his, and always would be, and her spirit sang with the boundless joy of her love. For her, for now, it was everything, and it was enough.

Chapter Ten

The winter's first snowfall began the afternoon that Beckah and Nathaniel were married in the Nyes' front room. Eliza had anticipated this wedding eagerly, but now she found the ache in her own heart too deep to share in such happiness. Gardner was a man of the world, and although Eliza knew she loved him, she also knew he had never promised her anything in return. She felt hot tears burn behind her eyes, and in the confused rush of congratulations to Beckah and Nathaniel, she slipped unnoticed from the room and through the kitchen. Today Mr. Nye's workshop was closed and empty, and she sat on the arm of an unfinished settee, snuffling back the tears.

"Eliza, my dear, are you unwell?" asked Josiah with concern. Gingerly he picked his way through the tools and benches, following her. "You left so abruptly."

"I'm fine." She brushed her sleeve across her eyes, ashamed to let him see her cry.

"Then I'll attribute it to the happy event we just witnessed, no more." He smiled crookedly. "In truth,

I'll admit I was affected, too. I've seen few unions that were as joyful, as blessed, as that one."

Eliza felt a little rush of affection for Josiah. Most men would be ashamed of such emotions. She smiled as he came to stand beside her.

"Still snowing, I see. Well, this early in the season, it won't amount to much." He studied her face in the cool afternoon light. He had guessed right, she had been crying. Her father should not have left her alone in that big house; she spent too much time by herself. She needed him, decided Josiah happily, just as much as he needed her. Almost without thinking he found himself speaking the words he'd been rehearsing inwardly for weeks. "Eliza, my dear, I had planned to wait until your father returned, but as he has been so long delayed—"

"He'll be home by Christmas." She couldn't remember ever seeing Josiah so flustered before. "He promised in his last letter, and he always keeps his promises to me."

"Nonetheless, I can silence my heart no longer. These last months, when you have graced me with your company, have been the happiest of my life, and I would dare to hope you have felt the same."

Eliza felt her heart beat faster, but not with love. How could he be so wrong about their friendship? He was going to ask her to marry him, and she did not love him, and never would. She stared at the cut-steel buttons on his coat, knowing how much her inevitable refusal was going to wound him, and wishing it wasn't so. When he lifted her face to briefly kiss her,

her lips might have been carved from ice, so little did she respond.

But to Josiah, her silence was caused by maidenly shyness, and his words came out with feverish emotion. "Eliza, my dearest, dearest Miss Raeburn, will you do me the honor—"

"No, Josiah, please, I beg you, stop!" Eliza cried with a little half sob. "I would not hurt you for the world, but if you go on, I must say things you do not want to hear!"

"If you would rather I waited to speak first with your father—"

"That won't make any difference." Already she could see the growing pain in his expression. "I cannot be the wife you deserve, Josiah."

Impulsively he seized her hands. "But I can think of no other woman I would rather wed!"

"Don't, Josiah, please!" Eliza pulled free and turned away towards the window. "I don't love you, Josiah."

"But where there is respect and friendship, love can grow, too."

"No, Josiah," she said sadly. "Not for me, not for you. You will always be my friend, and I will cherish that between us. But I know I will never be able to love you as a wife should love her husband." Behind her she heard him let out a long, low sigh and then the rhythmic tapping of his cane against a stool. She had not wanted to hurt him like this. Why had he pressed her until she had no choice?

Her rejection was worse than anything Josiah could have dreamed, for he had never dreamed she would refuse. All the long hours with John Brown, the wages earned and carefully invested had been for her. For her he had made himself over from a farm boy into a gentleman. For her he had learned to speak and dress and act so that he would be welcomed in any drawing room in the colony. He had even betrayed his employer and his neighbors to the British for a chance at a better life to offer. All for her, and her love, and yet, somehow, it was not enough.

His gaze dropped to his cane, the wooden limb that supported him where his own shattered bone and flesh would not. Perhaps that was it. She did not want him because he was a cripple. Perhaps if he still stood straight and sure like other men . . .

Like one other man. Suddenly Josiah remembered Griffin, and the complete physical confidence of the man. The hatred and bitterness that welled up within him almost overwhelmed his grief.

"It's someone else, isn't it," he said slowly, his voice taut. "I don't even need to ask his name. It's that bastard Griffin."

Eliza swung about to face him, and her expression was answer enough for Josiah. His voice shook with rage, and each word flicked across her like a whiplash. "He is a bastard, you know. Has he told you that? His mother was a drunken whore, his father God knows who. Has your fine Captain Griffin told you that?"

Eliza froze. She could not tell which was worse: Josiah's accusations, or the vehemence with which he spat them out.

"And how has he treated you, Eliza? Has he ever spoken to you of love and marriage and honor and respect?—ideas with which he has no experience, I'll wager," continued Josiah contemptuously. "Has he ever offered you more than a dance and a rough embrace on a dock at night, like some common, rum-soaked seaman with his wench?"

Eliza gasped, her eyes flashing. "You followed us that night! Gardner said there was someone, but I never thought it was you!" Her hand swung back to strike him. "How dare you spy on me like that!"

He caught her wrist before his face and held it so tightly she winced in pain. "Because, Eliza, I love you," he said grimly.

"Love! How can you talk of love and trust and then treat me like this?" She wrenched free and backed away from him, rubbing her wrist where his grasp had left deep red marks. "Are you so perfect that you can stand in judgment of Captain Griffin?"

"It's the truth I offer you, Eliza, not a judgment." Josiah had not intended to hurt her physically, but now that he had, he was surprised at how little regret he felt. "Gardner Griffin is a man with no past and no future. He has no possessions beyond what he can carry in his sea chest. He has quarrelled with John Brown, and this voyage will be his last as captain of the *Three Brothers*. Where he will drift after that I neither know nor care."

"That's not true, Josiah," she said defensively. There were still many things she didn't understand about Gardner, but because she loved him, she believed he was worthy of her trust. "He is respected and liked by every man who has sailed with him. He's one of the best shipmasters that this town's ever seen, and if he leaves it will be Mr. Brown's loss. Everyone on Main Street says so.''

Josiah's eyes glittered like the cut-steel buttons on his coat. ''Then you know what else everyone says as well? About the woman he keeps on Martinique? Or more correctly, she keeps him. She's French, they say, from Paris, with her own sugarcane plantation and an obligingly absent husband. Quite exquisite is Madame de Neuville, they say, and quite attached is she to your Captain Griffin. Everyone on Main Street says so.''

Eliza stared at him. It could not be true. Gardner could not have kissed her the way he had and then gone to another woman. What she felt for him was something she had no words to express, something rare that went beyond words, and she was sure he had felt it in return. What Josiah said could not be true.

''If you believe for a moment that such lies will make me change my mind towards you, Josiah Buck, then you are very, very wrong,'' she said with a quiet intensity that startled Josiah more than her anger had. ''That you could—''

The door to the shop was suddenly filled by the round, happy face of Beckah's father and behind him Uncle Enos, already flushed with too much rum punch.

''Lookee here, Chase, here's another pair of love-birds!'' exclaimed Mr. Nye gleefully. ''Seems we'll be having another wedding on our hands soon!''

With her head high, Eliza pushed past the two men and through the door, without another glance to spare for Josiah.

Josiah could only stare after her, at the last disdainful flick she gave her skirts as she left him behind, and he wondered how his precious offering of love had gone so devastatingly wrong.

Gardner walked slowly through the darkened streets of Fort Royal, enjoying the evening breeze that blew gently off the water. The house of Martinique's governor, the Marquis de Bouille, had been close and crowded, and he was glad to be free of the chattering Frenchmen who spilled out of the assembly rooms. Word of his role in the *Gaspee* incident had reached the Caribbean, and the French, with their perpetual hatred of the English, had tried to make a hero of him. Though better that, he thought wryly, than if they had tried to turn him in for the reward. Sam Adams was right. Too many people knew who he was. He'd best lie low for a while, maybe change his name, if he wanted to keep his freedom.

He walked with his hands deep in his coat pockets and filled his lungs with the heady mixture of thousands of tropical blossoms. In another day the rest of the *Three Brothers*'s cargo would be unloaded and accounted for, and he would sail up the coast, towards Saint Pierre, to the little cove that marked the plantation of Athenais de Neuville. There, with the help of her slaves, they would rapidly take on whatever contraband she had arranged for them and be back in Providence in time for Christmas.

"*M'sieur le Gentilhomme, m'sieur!* You are lonely, *m'sieur?*" The small mulatto girl darted out from between the whitewashed walls and tried to link her arm through his. "*M'sieur* would like to taste island love?"

"No, *ma petite,* not tonight," said Gardner gently as he disengaged himself from her clinging grasp. She was too young for this kind of trade, he thought sadly. Her eyes were enormous in her bronze-colored face, and her painfully sharp shoulders above the dingy gown betrayed how thin she was. He pressed a coin into the girl's hand. "There now, go buy yourself something to eat. And don't tell your papa, hear?"

But the girl persisted. "Oh *non, m'sieur,* I cannot take your money without—without—"

Gardner frowned. Even if the girl was inexperienced, there was more fear and nervousness in her face than there should be. Too late he felt the pistol's muzzle jammed into his ribs, heard the clicking of the trigger's catch and the little shriek as the girl darted back into the shadows.

"So sad, M'sieur Griffin," said a voice with a thick island accent. "You would have enjoyed the chit's invitation more than mine."

Gardner thought quickly. This was no simple robbery: the man knew his name and, perhaps, the reward connected with it. "Who are you, and what is your blasted invitation?"

"Fine questions, *m'sieur,* from a man with a price on his head!" The man cackled, while another searched for and found Gardner's own pistol. So there were at least two of them. Maybe more, in the dark, but he wouldn't wait to find out.

Gardner twisted sharply to one side, knocking the gun away into the street, before he slammed his shoulder into the first man's jaw. With a grunt the man fell heavily backwards. Regaining his own balance, Gardner saw the second man scrambling for the loaded pistol where it lay in the street. Gardner grabbed him by his coattails and jerked him upright by his collar. But as the man whimpered and thrashed in his grasp, Gardner felt a blow across the back of his own head and realized that the rush of air he heard was his own breath. Then he felt and saw no more but blackness.

Stars. A score of them, clustered together in the night sky overhead, and yet it was no constellation Gardner recognized. He leaned back to see them better and was rewarded with so sharp a throbbing in the back of his head that he quickly closed his eyes again to shut out the stars and the pain. He heard a woman's throaty laughter and opened his eyes cautiously again, this time shielding his brow with his arm.

"Athenais?" he asked tentatively. His own voice echoed oddly in his ears. "What in blazes are you doing here?"

The woman laughed again. "A fine question, *mon cher,* to ask a lady in her own boudoir!"

Carefully Gardner turned his head towards her. The stars overhead slowly resolved themselves into a chandelier, the candle flames reflecting a thousand times in the dangling crystal prisms. Beneath it, in a small gilt armchair, sat Athenais de Neuville, watching him with bemused sympathy as she languidly drew a carved ivory fan through the humid air. She was undressed for the night, though not for sleep, in a transparent linen gown heavy with drifting lace. Beneath the open gown she still wore a pink silk corset that displayed her breasts extravagantly above diamond-trimmed bows, and on her crossed feet were backless silk slippers with high lacquered heels.

If any woman could make him forget Eliza Raeburn, it would be Athenais. Or should have been. Yet even as his head still rang like an August thunderclap, he kept comparing the two women. He saw Athenais's elaborate sugar-water curls, and remembered how Eliza's russet mane tumbled freely down her shoulders. He watched how the candlelight played across Athenais's flawless complexion, perfected with powder and paint, and recalled the bright flush the wind brought to Eliza's cheeks on the deck of the *Marianne*. He admired the elegance of Athenais's lace and ribbons, her pearl choker and diamond rings, and thought of how Eliza was always a little dishevelled and how charming she'd looked in a boy's jacket.

"The last thing I recall," Gardner said slowly, "was grappling in the street with a pair of bounty-hunting rascals."

Athenais clicked her tongue in mock dismay. "Rascals! Jacques and Pepe would be most sad to hear you call them that! They are merely high-spirited, eager to please."

"Friends of yours, then?"

"*Mais oui,* such friends as a handful of *sous* can buy. They were only messengers." She pouted prettily, arching her wrist so the lace ruffles tumbled back towards her elbow. "You've been avoiding me, *mon ami*. I know how long you've been on my island, and not one moment to spare for poor Athenais."

"If that was only loneliness, then I'm damned glad you're not angry." Gingerly he kneaded the lump on the back of his head. "Was the girl in on it as well?"

"She was a test, a diversion, to see if you are as soft-hearted as ever. And you passed, *mon cher*. Or failed. A wanted man cannot afford such weaknesses."

He ignored the criticism. "You paid her, too, I hope?"

"What, Coco? Why should I pay her?" Athenais shrugged her powdered shoulders. "She is mine already, and scarcely worth her keep. Too weak for the fields or breeding, too simple for the house. I would sell her tomorrow if I could get a decent price for her."

"Perhaps," he said testily, "you should try feeding her." Carefully he sat upright on the daybed, and though the room swung wildly for a moment, it soon settled down to a reassuring levelness. On a chair beside him he saw his newly polished boots, along with his hat and pistol, and for the first time he noticed he was naked beneath the coverlet.

Athenais watched his discomfiture and laughed merrily. "I myself checked to make sure you were not injured, beyond that trifle on your head." She smiled wickedly. "Nothing important, it seems, was damaged."

With one swift motion she was beside him, and her fingertips circled lazily through the dark curling hair on his chest. The soft roundness of her breast pressed against his arm and her voice became no more than a throaty purr in his ear. "Most men are not worth five pounds, let along five hundred. But I know your value is much, much more."

Her hand traced the path of dark hair down his belly to the coverlet over his lap. Deftly her fingers began to ease the cloth downward, lower and lower, until she felt his hand tighten around her wrist to stop her.

"Athenais, no," Gardner said hoarsely. "We agreed last time that it was over between us."

"You decided, I agreed," she murmured. "If the rest of your memory is as faulty, *mon cher capitaine,* I shall have to strive to restore it."

She pressed closer, moulding her body against his. He couldn't deny the pleasure they had given each other, but now he longed for something more, something he still could not find a comfortable word for. Slowly he disentangled himself from her embrace and went to stand near the window, wrapping the blanket around his hips. It was almost dawn. The sky was gray as the moon and stars faded, and the chattering birds in the trees below were already awake. Behind him he heard Athenais sigh.

"I will not beg, you know," she said. "Not even for you."

He ran his fingers through his hair, wondering when he'd lost the ribbon that usually held it back. His head still throbbed, and he wanted no more than a bath and sleep. "I must go back to the *Three Brothers.* They must think the devil's taken me by now."

"*Mais non.* They know where you are." Athenais stretched out the length of the daybed, her ankles crossed and her head resting comfortably on her folded arms. "I sent word that you were visiting me, and for them to sail here to meet you this morning."

Gardner swore under his breath. She'd had no right to do that. The *Three Brothers* was his responsibility—crew, cargo and ship—and one he took most seriously.

"So who is she, *mon cher?* Don't try to deceive an old friend. Is she a Yankee miss, your new *amourette?*"

"She isn't my little love, old or new," answered Gardner irritably. "And she isn't any of your business."

"Ah, so she is a most foolish Yankee miss!" she said cheerfully. *"Quelle dommage pour vous!"* Athenais watched him hungrily, glad she'd sent his clothes to be washed in the kitchen. She had always loved the way his broad shoulders narrowed to his hips, the sinewy grace his muscles gave every move, the latticework of scars that crisscrossed his back, scars he wore as proudly as any general's medals. "Do the *Anglais* know you were in their navy?"

"Nay, and I've no intention of letting them know." Gardner turned back to face her. "This will be the last of me on Martinique for a good long while, Athenais. I need to put some distance between me and the hangman."

"Then come work for me, *mon cher.* My old offer is always open."

"What, to join your 'import trade'? Smuggling and slaving for a pile of gold Louis?" He smiled. "You know as well as I do that it would never last."

"Oh, I know, I know. I am nothing but a heartless mercenary, while you, my fine Yankee, you work only for principles." She wagged a finger at him. "There you are, your pretty scruples again, leading you astray! But you have breakfast now, while I dress. Coffee, brioche, whatever you please. Then I shall show you what *Père Noël* is sending you principled Yankees for Christmas."

Later that morning, Gardner followed Athenais down the path beneath the overhanging mangroves to a well-hidden warehouse not far from the beach. The low, whitewashed building was guarded by a wiry Frenchman and two muscular black slaves, who immediately flew to attention at Athenais's approach. She waved them aside and unlocked the barred door with a key from the ring she wore at her waist.

"You're quite fortunate this time," she told Gardner as she led him to the back of the building, past crates and barrels dimly outlined in the half-light. She unfastened the shutters on one window and the bright sunshine streamed across stacks of long, narrow crates. Gardner felt a rush of anticipation, for he could guess what the boxes contained. The lid on the top crate had already been pried open and, ripping it back, Athenais rummaged in the wood shavings. With a dramatic flourish, she pulled out a long-barrelled infantry rifle as tall as herself.

"Austrian," she said proudly. "You won't find finer craftsmanship, *mon ami.*"

Gardner took the rifle, running his fingers the length of the cool steel barrel before he held it to his shoulder. The weapon was beautifully balanced, the stock cleanly shaped of polished cherry, the barrel straight and true. Gently he squeezed the trigger, and the mechanism slipped back with an empty click.

Athenais handed him a little pouch with bullets, wadding and gunpowder. "I expected you would wish to try it. Though through the window only, *s'il vous plaît*. I would keep those three outside in ignorance."

Gardner put down the first gun, pried open another crate and pulled out a different rifle. Athenais had never switched her samples before, but perhaps that was always because he was careful to check what he bought. With practiced ease, he loaded the gun, ramming home the charge, and slipped the long barrel through the window's bars. Carefully he aimed at a coconut near the top fronds of a palm tree a hundred paces away and fired. As the gun's explosion reverberated through the closed space, he saw the nut split neatly and tumble into two halves to the ground. He grinned at Athenais through the fading puff of gunpowder.

Athenais arched one brow. "Your aim, *mon cher,* is, as always, excellent."

"So are your rifles. How did you come by them?"

"Oh, my usual ways." Athenais shrugged. "A certain subaltern in a certain regiment found himself embarrassed at the gaming table. You may have the lot, once payment is made to my agent's account in Fort Royal. My fee is quite fair, considering the quality of the merchandise this time. Unless you are having second thoughts about my part in your rebellion, hmm?"

"Nay, it's not that, Athenais," said Gardner thoughtfully. She had done well, very well, for him this time. "It's that these crates won't come close to filling the *Three Brothers*'s hold. I'll have to sail in ballast. I can't risk going beams up in a winter gale."

"Ah, but Gardner, since you are my *bon ami,* I have thought of that, too. You will find my people ready to fill your hold with my sugar—the very finest of my autumn crop—and in return I trust you to find a buyer for it in your Rhode Island. It is a pretty arrangement that will suit us both, *mais oui?*" Coolly she held our her little hand with the jeweled rings, to shake on the deal like a man.

Gardner paused, considering. John Brown would not like being bested by a French trader, especially one who was a woman, but Gardner could see no way out of her "arrangement" and still bring back the guns. Besides, though his conscience nagged him, the sugar would not be his problem.

With considerable reluctance he took her hand, and her narrowed eyes glittered triumphantly. "You see, *mon cher capitaine,*" she said, "you do not always get your own way."

Chapter Eleven

The week before Christmas Beckah asked Eliza to walk over Prospect Hill to the Hunters' farm, and Eliza jumped at the invitation. She had seen little of her friend since her marriage, and it would be good to be outdoors and away from her own worries. They left early in the morning, taking a basket of oranges to Mrs. Hunter from Beckah's mother. Though the morning was clear and warm for December, by mid-afternoon the breeze had grown much colder, and Beckah and Eliza pulled their woolen cloaks close around themselves as they walked. Their shoes crunched on the frozen corn stubble and their breath made little clouds in the chilly air around their faces.

Carefully Beckah climbed over a stone wall between two fields. "I'm thankful Nathaniel sailed last week, before this cold came back," she said. "I don't know how sailors can abide it, to be all wet and frozen clean through at the same time."

"It's not the cold so much as the wind," said Eliza as she clambered over the wall. "What we've had here as breeze fit for kites and laundry might be a gale out to sea, with waves and spray that toss a ship around like a walnut shell. But I expect it's all nothing to Nathaniel," she added hurriedly as she saw Beckah's eyes widen. "There's precious little that would frighten him."

"I expect not," agreed Beckah without conviction. "But just the same, I'll be glad when he's back safe at home."

Eliza glanced at her friend wistfully. "You do miss him, don't you?"

Beckah sighed. "More than I could tell you. But it's not so bad, in a way, this time. He's gone on his own free will to Charleston, and he'll be back as soon as he can. It's not as if he's a prisoner again. And besides," she said, her cheeks growing pink. "This time he didn't leave me alone."

"If you mean because you have to live with my aunt and uncle, why, that's scarce company I'd like to keep."

Beckah giggled into her mitten, enjoying for once knowing something Eliza didn't. "No, silly, a baby. I'm with child."

"Oh, Beckah! How wonderful!" Now it was Eliza's turn to blush. "But—but how do you know so soon? You've only been wed two weeks."

"Oh, Eliza," said Beckah archly. "The words that Mr. Hislop said over our heads didn't have much to do with it."

"Then you and Nathaniel—" Eliza stopped, too embarrassed to continue. She had still only vague notions of what passed between husbands and wives—it was not a subject her father chose to discuss—and now it seemed that Beckah and her cousin had been doing whatever it was for weeks, maybe even months.

Misinterpreting her friend's confusion, Beckah shyly put a hand on Eliza's arm. "Don't think the worse of us, Eliza," she said. "I love him, and he me. Where's the sin in that? The world is such an uncertain place. What if I had lost Nathaniel again before I'd had a chance to be truly his?"

"Faith, Beckah, you know I'd never judge you! You're just so lucky, you and Nathaniel both, to have each other." More sadness crept into her voice than she realized. "I hope someday I'll have someone, too."

"I think you already do, Eliza Raeburn, if you'd only mind your heart instead of your head," declared Beckah. "And I don't mean Josiah."

Eliza shrugged, trying to appear indifferent. She didn't want to discuss her jumbled emotions with anyone, not even Beckah. "Have you told your great news to Aunt Anne yet, or is it still a secret?"

"Of course it's a secret!" exclaimed Beckah indignantly. "I want Nathaniel back beside me before she starts counting off the months on her fingers. Lord, how she'll scowl and frown. I wouldn't face that alone for the world!"

Simultaneously the two friends exploded with laughter. Arms linked, they climbed the rest of the way to the crest of Prospect Hill. The town and river lay spread before them, gilded by the sinking sun of the short winter afternoon, and Eliza and Beckah paused to catch their breath.

"Look, Eliza!" exclaimed Beckah, pointing down the hill past the rooftops and chimneys. "While we were gone, someone's come home!"

It took only a second for Eliza to pick out the new set of masts, the sails still full and unfurled, and less time to identify the vessel. "It's the *Three Brothers*," she began happily. "I'd heard Gar—I mean, they weren't due for another—oh, dear God, no!"

Eliza's voice suddenly twisted with anguish, and Beckah watched the color drain from her friend's face. "What is it, Eliza? What's wrong?"

"The flag," whispered Eliza. "Look at the flag." She hugged her cloak tightly around her body, as if trying to protect herself from the shock of the brightly colored cloth fluttering from the *Three Brothers*'s stern. Please God, she prayed, let it be some mistake, a broken line or an inattentive seaman. For as she knew all too well, there was only one explanation for a vessel's homecoming with her flag at half-mast.

And that was the death of a captain.

Eliza ran down the hill towards the crowded wharf, dodging between people and wagons. Her hood fell back and her hair blew loose around her shoulders, but her only thought was to find John Brown, find him and learn what had happened.

Please let me be wrong, she prayed, her breath coming hard in her chest. Please let Gardner still be alive!

She turned the corner of the warehouse and finally could see the *Three Brothers*, and her heart almost stopped. There beside the gangplank stood Gardner himself, his familiar worn coat and hat dearer to her eyes than she ever could have imagined. He was talking angrily to Mr. Brown, his large hands cutting through the air, and there was no question that he was very much alive. She called his name and waved, and was rewarded by the way his anger vanished when his eyes found hers, his whole face warming with the pleasure of seeing her again. She had to reach him, now, to tell him how she felt, how she'd feared she'd been too late. So intent was she on reaching him that she didn't notice that the crowd had changed around her. Men stepped back to open a path for her, and almost every one removed his hat and stared uncomfortably at the ground as she passed.

Nearly dizzy with joy, Eliza let herself fall into Gardner's outstretched arms. She pressed her face close to his rough coat, relishing the haven of his embrace as he held her tight. He was so strong and tall, so vitally alive. How could she have ever thought him dead?

"Eliza, listen to me," he said softly. He took her by the shoulders and gently pulled her back so she could see his face. Her cheeks were flushed, her lips slightly parted in a smile of completely happiness. Happiness, he knew, he would shatter with a handful of words.

"You're here, and you're safe," she whispered. "When I saw the flag—"

"Eliza, the flag is for your father. He's gone—lost over the side in the gale Tuesday night." He was shocked by how quickly her face went rigid, white and stripped of emotion. Desperately he plunged on, knowing that the worst had already been said. "The *Peacock,* too. We couldn't save her, though God knows we tried. The rest of her crew came with me."

Her father was dead. Part of Eliza understood what Gardner was telling her, heard the words and accepted their meaning. But her heart and her soul refused to comprehend that her father would not be home for Christmas, would not take her back to the Caribbean on the *Peacock,* would never tease her or scold her or call her "Miss Monkey" again. *Her father was dead.*

She stood frozen, unmoving, her face an expressionless mask. Gardner had seen it before in men who'd lost a brother or friend in battle, the mute withdrawal of new grief, but he had never felt so helpless as he did now with Eliza.

A small, sandy-haired man carrying a canvas-wrapped bundle came forward and touched her arm. "Miss Raeburn, it's Jemmy, Jemmy White," he said. "I was there beside your pa at the end, miss, and it was like Cap'n Griffin says. Cap'n Raeburn didn't have no chance. He was took clean away in an instant."

Mechanically Eliza swiveled to face the man. He was—had been—the *Peacock*'s first mate, and she had known him since she was a little girl.

"The *Peacock,* she'd been taking on water since off Hatteras. We was two men working the pumps night an' day, but she still weren't no better for it. She never was put to rights again after that hurricane near Bermuda. It broke her spirit with her back, Cap'n Raeburn said."

"Go on, Jemmy," she said with unnatural calmness. "Go on."

"Well, we was nearly home just off Block Island, when your pa sees we're being chased. Two Britishers, from the cut of 'em, one from the nor'east an' one to the south, tearing down on us fit to burst. Almost like they was expectin' us, somehow. And Cap'n Raeburn, he says, 'Damn the navy bastards'—beggin' your pardon, miss, but you know your pa—'we'll give 'em a chase,' and we cut out across Nantucket Shoals. But 'tweren't no good. We headed straight into hell, we did, wind an' seas high as a house an' day turned black as night. All of us was prayin' for our souls with one breath an' damnin' the Britishers with the next. The poor *Peacock,* being all loggy with the water, she broached to and lost her mainmast. Your pa, and Will Bolton and Henry Greene, all went over in the same wave. There was nothing we could do, miss, nothing at all."

Eliza's imagination readily filled in the details that Jemmy omitted. She could picture it all with sickening clarity: the *Peacock* tossed like an eggshell by the storm, the great wave that sucked the sloop sideways into its curl before crashing down with all its force. Eliza realized her father's death must have been mercifully swift—no one would survive long in the icy Atlantic—yet she could still imagine him struggling amidst the tangled rigging, fighting to reach the air one last time before the waves closed over his head forever.

"If Cap'n Griffin hadn't come on us that afternoon, we would've all gone down, too. There weren't much left to save from the poor *Peacock*. She wouldn't go on without her master, and that's the truth." Eliza saw there were tears glistening in Jemmy's eyes and wondered that her own were still dry. Carefully he began to unwrap his canvas bundle. "Here, miss. I was able to save a few of your pa's things."

One by one, he placed the last of her father's possessions into her hands: the *Peacock*'s log, a blue silk neckerchief with his embroidered initials, the worn little Bible, a pocketknife with a silver clasp. Last of all was the portrait of her mother. Eliza stared at the painted face with the gentle smile and old-fashioned hair. James was with his Alice now, together again at last, and it was their daughter who was the one left behind. Alone.

With a choked little cry, she slipped down onto the dock and into the peaceful oblivion of unconsciousness.

Gardner was not a church-going man. Unlike most New Englanders, he had never acquired the habit as a child, and questioned the value of it as an adult. He believed in a God that was in nature, the water and in the air, not a clapboard meetinghouse, and though he always read Sabbath prayers to his crew at sea, he did it more for their expectations than his own soul. Yet as he sat to the back of North Main Meeting House, listening to the service for James Raeburn and the others lost with the *Peacock*, he found himself fervently praying, not only for the souls of the dead men, but for his own as well, and for forgiveness for the pain he had caused Eliza.

He could scarcely take his eyes from her this morning. She sat in a pew near the front, her copper hair luminous in the weak winter sunlight. Surrounded though she was by the Chases, she still seemed somehow alone and set apart from the others. She held her head high with her shoulders resolutely squared. Even her grief, thought Gardner, had a forlorn bravery to it. He had not seen her since she had fainted on the dock and he had carried her, senseless, to John Brown's office. While old Mr. Chase had thanked him, he had also made it quite clear that Gardner would not be welcome to call on his niece.

The old man need not have bothered. Gardner had sworn to himself he would never see Eliza alone again, and it was an oath he intended to keep. While everyone in Providence believed that the final meeting between the *Peacock* and the two coasters had been only a deadly coincidence, he knew better. The coasters had been waiting for the *Three Brothers*, and fate had traded his life for James Racburn's. Gardner had always feared some harm might come to Eliza because of him, but the death of her father—no, not even he had considered that. He remembered how, the night he had walked with her by the docks, she had been so eager to show him the *Peacock*, and how proudly she'd spoken of the sloop and her father. Both had been precious to her, and now both were irretrievably lost because of him.

Him, and one other. Gardner's gaze sought Josiah's back, sitting near the Chases, as if he were already a member of the family. Involuntarily Gardner's hands tightened on the pew before him until his knuckles turned white. He was certain it was Josiah who had betrayed him, and James Raeburn, to the British. No one else besides John Brown had known when the *Three Brothers* was due. The British had appeared from nowhere on the first of that week, chased the *Peacock* and vanished again, believing their mission complete. They had been there by invitation; it was as simple as that.

The score with Josiah Buck was growing: the man had ended Gardner's safe harbor in Providence, put a price on his head that made his own name a death warrant and tried to arrange his capture by the coasters. But worst of all, decided Gardner bitterly, Josiah had destroyed whatever chance of happiness Gardner might have found with Eliza Raeburn. Josiah would have to pay for that, and the price Gardner set would be very dear indeed.

In the front of the meetinghouse, Eliza only half listened to Mr. Hislop's eulogy for her father. She already knew her father had been a good man, a fair master, a devoted husband, father, brother and son. What she didn't know, and no one could tell her, was why, if her father had been all of these wonderful things, did he have to die?

She felt the tears welling up again and with an effort fought them back. Her father never liked to see her weep, and always tried to distract or tease her out of it. She struggled to forget how he had died and remember the happiness and satisfaction they had shared working side by side. The trade they had built up over the years, the network of buyers and sellers, sailors and merchants. That was, she felt sure, the final testimony to his life, and not the flowery words of Mr. Hislop. It was the one she was also determined to continue, though she wasn't quite sure how.

It wasn't a question of capital. She knew every penny of James's estate, and with the insurance money for the *Peacock*'s loss, she would be reckoned to be quite comfortable, if not actually wealthy. What worried her was whether she would still be accepted in a man's world of business without her father standing beside her. But she would find a way to do it, and she would succeed. Unconsciously she raised her chin a little higher, pleasing Mr. Hislop with her seeming attention to his conclusion.

Around her, people were beginning to stand, buttoning their coats to leave. Reluctantly Eliza rose, too. The worst part of the day still lay before her, when all of her father's friends would fill their—now her—house for one last chance to reminisce over rum punch, shake their heads over the unfairness of life and death and pat her hand as they each tried to comfort her. After the stress of this past week, her nerves and emotions were worn raw, and she wondered how she would ever survive the afternoon that would surely stretch into night.

With a sigh she took her aunt's arm and led her from the pew and down the aisle. James's death had drained the final bit of feistiness from his sister. She seemed to have grown frail and very old overnight, and, for the first time, Eliza felt an empathy for her aunt built on their shared loss.

Outside, her uncle Enos was waiting at the door of the rented carriage. But as Eliza and her aunt drew closer, she noticed beside him the ever-present figure of Josiah, and something inside her rebelled. He did not belong here, not today, and she resented how he had managed to ingratiate himself into her family.

"A sad time, Eliza," he murmured, but she ignored him and abruptly turned away.

"You go on without me, Uncle Enos," she said quickly. "I'll walk home and meet you there."

Surprised, her uncle frowned. "It will seem odd to the others for you to be absent, Eliza."

"I won't be long. I just need a little time by myself." She kissed him quickly on the cheek and, with her head down, walked swiftly towards the churchyard. Not even Josiah would dare follow her to stand beside her parents' headstones.

With her hood pulled forward, she did not notice Gardner standing beside the burying ground's fence until her hand was on the gate, but a little catch in her breath was all the surprise she registered. The shadows beneath her eyes told of sleepless nights, and grief had dulled the vibrancy of her expression. Even her freckles seemed somehow faded, subdued, and Gardner found it difficult to recall the joyful warmth with which this same face had greeted him a week earlier.

"I must see if the stone carver has done what I asked," she said, almost apologetically. She swung the gate open and he followed, unsure of why but unable to leave her just yet. She skirted through the headstones, some moss-covered and canting wildly, others still new and properly upright. Dry leaves skittered around their feet, and here and there the ground was cracked by frost. Uneasily Gardner tucked his hat under his arm and, bareheaded, traced her path.

Eliza halted before her parents' headstones. She had insisted her father's marker match her mother's exactly, the crisp new slate etched with the same design. She stared at the carved names and dates, wishing she felt closer to them here. But their spirits were no more in this churchyard than her father's body was beneath this stone, and she realized sadly she now had only herself to draw upon for strength.

"Will you come back to the house with me, Gardner?" she asked quietly. Unlike Josiah, Gardner belonged here. He had saved her father's crew and tried to save the *Peacock*. Little wisps of hair blew across her cheek and absently she swept them aside with her fingers. "I'd like you to be there."

What would she say if she knew the truth, thought Gardner bitterly. Would she thank him still if she knew the British had taken her father instead of him? He shook his head. "I'm leaving Providence day after tomorrow, and I've much to do before then." It sounded lame even to his own ears.

"Oh. So that's why you haven't come this week." Her disappointment was palpable, hanging in the air, but there was no reproach in her tone, and Gardner almost wished there were. "That's Christmas Day."

He shrugged his broad shoulders. "A horse doesn't know one day from the next."

Eliza easily pictured him on horseback, remembering how skillfully he'd handled the large chestnut in Boston. Most sailors were distrustful of horses, indif-

ferent riders at best, but he rode with the same skill
and ease with which he seemed to do everything. She
remembered sitting across the saddle, how his arms
encircled her, and the warmth she had felt where their
thighs had pressed together. Swiftly she jerked her
thoughts back to the present, but not before a blush
crept into her cheeks. "Then what they say about your
leaving is true?'

"If what they say is that I no longer sail for John
Brown, then aye, it's true," he replied cautiously. Lord
knows what gossip was flying around Providence. And
with her cheeks gone all rosy like that, he was likely to
babble whatever she wished to hear.

"Do you have another command waiting for you?
In Boston, perhaps?" She had a reason for asking.

"Nay, I'd best leave New England for a while. These
waters are so hot for me right now, they're near to
boiling." He grinned, and Eliza felt her face grow
warm all over again. His smile was perfect, and all the
more special for its rarity. "But I always end right side
up and spitting no matter which way I'm tossed. I've
a mind to head south. I've a friend there that always
has a welcome for me."

He meant Philadelphia, and a one-legged man who
ran a shipyard there. But Eliza heard south and
thought Martinique, and that the friend must be the
Frenchwoman Josiah had described. She did not want
to believe it, but the doubts Josiah had planted suddenly found support when she remembered how
Gardner had not once come to call since her father's
death. Only coincidence had brought them together
today. And now he had all but told her he was return-

ing to his mistress. How much clearer could he make it? She had mistaken Gardner's kindness for interest, his flirtation for love, and she felt like a foolish, empty-headed little girl.

Puzzled, Gardner watched Eliza's expression change. In an instant he caught the surprise, followed by pain, then as swiftly as if she'd stepped behind a curtain the moment was gone. So was the becoming flush and the smile he'd begun to coax once again from the corners of her mouth.

"I must go," she said hurriedly, and rushed past him.

He caught her arm, and Eliza felt his fingers burn through her sleeve like a brand. "Stay a moment longer, Eliza."

"No, I can't!" She pulled free, not trusting herself to look him in the face again. She was running now, dodging the headstones, and then she was through the gate and free. She heard him call her name again but only hurried onward. Here in the street, today, no one would question the tears that ran freely down her cheeks.

Chapter Twelve

Back at the house Eliza tried hard to concentrate on what each person said to her, the kind words and memories of her father they wished to share. Yet she still found them all blurring together, forgetting what one man had said as soon as the next had begun. The one man she wanted to be there wasn't.

When her uncle found her, she gratefully took the glass of Madeira he offered. "Here, lass, drink up," he said, his face stern as a doctor dispensing medicine. "You're bearing up well, but you'll need your strength."

Eliza smiled, as thankful for the respite from conversation as for the wine she sipped. Then, over the glass's flaring crystal rim, she saw Josiah.

"I've not had the opportunity before this to offer my condolences, Eliza," he said respectfully. "Your father's death is a great loss to us all."

Eliza fought back the desire to snap at him. Her father had always liked Josiah. For today, anyway, she could try to be pleasant to him. Besides, he wasn't likely to press his attentions with the whole town acting as chaperon.

When she smiled, Josiah allowed his hopes to rise. Perhaps Mr. Chase was right. She only needed a little time. She would need an advisor she could trust, too, if half the rumors he was hearing about her father's estate were true.

"You know, Eliza, you can always count on me to help you through this time of trial," he ventured delicately. "I'm here for you, however I can help."

Enos nodded his approval. He couldn't understand why Eliza had turned on poor Buck. If she wasn't careful, she'd drive him off for good, and his niece was getting a mite too old, to his mind, to scorn a bachelor as eligible as Josiah Buck. "You should listen to Josiah," he said. "To begin with, he could help you find a buyer for this place."

"A buyer, Uncle?" repeated Eliza, her voice rising with incredulity. "Why ever would I need a buyer when the house is not for sale? I intend to continue living here, in my father's home. *My* home."

Enos snorted. "Now you and I both know that's not proper, niece. Oh, James let you have your way, but it's not seemly for you to be rattling around in here alone. You'll come live with your aunt and me, and Beckah, too. That's as should be, with family."

"Mr. Chase is right, Eliza," agreed Josiah. "There's already been talk."

"If you're so concerned, Josiah, then why do you listen?" She drew herself up straight, her chin high, and crossed her arms over her chest. She had been half expecting this from her uncle for days, and tired as she was, she was ready. She hadn't really expected Josiah to be here beside her uncle, but perhaps it was just as well for him to hear her plans now, too. "You're forgetting, Uncle Enos, that my father made me his single heir. This house, and his trade, are mine to do with what I please."

Josiah cleared his throat uncomfortably. "That's common enough, Eliza. No doubt your father wished to spare you the legal difficulties of a more complicated settlement. But surely he didn't intend for you to assume all his responsibilities."

"I think that's exactly what he intended, Josiah," said Eliza so warmly that others around them paused in their own conversations to listen. "I know my father's trade as well as he did, and if he's left it to me, it's because I was his partner as well as his daughter."

Her voice quavered momentarily from emotion. Oh, how she was going to miss her father! "He would want me to stay here, in the house he built for my mother, just as he would expect me to replace the *Peacock* and continue trading under his name."

Enos snorted. "Don't be an obstinate girl, Eliza."

"I'm not a girl anymore, Uncle," she answered quietly. "I'm twenty-two years old, more than of age, and there's not a law in this colony that won't back up my father's will. Or me."

While Enos sputtered indignantly, Josiah chuckled. "And do you propose to take your father's place on the deck of this new *Peacock,* too? Perhaps the courts will let you handle your own affairs, but I'll stake my name that you won't find a crew of sailors eager to sail with a captain in petticoats."

"I don't pretend to be a mariner, Josiah," she said quietly. "That's why I mean to hire Gardner Griffin as my shipmaster."

"The fellow's not from Providence," Enos objected. "What do you know of his habits, his ways of running a ship or crew?"

"Providence born or not, I know Captain Griffin's the only one to sail from here sharp enough to outrun the British three times. We'd all still be plagued by the *Gaspee* if it weren't for him." Her chin rose a little higher. "And that's what I care most about in the captain I hire."

She sounded so confident that she could almost herself believe it was going to happen. Now all she had to do was convince Gardner.

Eliza left her house early the next morning, before the meetinghouse bell had rung seven and the sun was barely a lemon-yellow stripe beyond Prospect Hill. Nervously she smoothed her skirts again beneath the cloak. She had changed her gown three times before settling on the dark green linsey-woolsey, one of the plainest she owned, and modestly tied a white linen scarf over the neckline for good measure. She licked her lips and swallowed nervously. It was business that was bringing her to Gardner this morning, she reminded herself sternly. Business, and nothing more.

It had been easy enough to learn where he lodged, in the rooms above Hudson's Tavern. Hudson's wasn't the worst tavern in town, but it wasn't the one preferred by gentlemen, either, and with some reluctance Eliza swung open the heavy oak door and stepped inside. In the deserted hallway, a small boy took one look at her and ran off bawling for his father. To her right was the common room, its low ceiling beams blackened by countless pipes and cheap candles, and a half-hearted fire flickered in the large hearth at the far end. Huddled before it in mismatched chairs were the room's only occupants, two seamen Eliza didn't recognize. Neither noticed her arrival, and their conversation continued uninterrupted.

"So where you be figurin' the cap'n's heading, Eb?" asked the younger man. "I'd sign on with him in a shallop to hell, his luck's that good."

"He ain't be tellin' me his secrets, you chowderhead," said the second irritably. "But I heard Hudson say the cap'n's leaving tomorrow by horse, not sea."

"Go on with you!" exclaimed the first. "The cap'n wouldn't be goin' on no horse!"

Shamelessly Eliza eavesdropped. They had to be speaking of Gardner, and perhaps she'd learn something she could use to persuade him to join her.

Eb shrugged and relit his pipe with a wisp from the fire. "You believe as you please, Jonathan. Cap'n Griffin, he's too smart to be temptin' the king's men again. I 'spect he be headin' back to his fancy ladylove for a spell."

"Mother of Mary, can you blame him?" exclaimed Jonathan. "I'd heard of her, for sure, same as every man what sails with Cap'n Griffin, but when I saw her with him, the diamonds a-sparklin' like stars on her frock, I swore I'd seen the Queen o' France herself!"

"All I saw was the cut of that frock, settin' out the finest pair o' lovelies ever made to please a man. If I was the cap'n, I'd fair crawl back to Fort Royal to get my hands on 'em again, and the rest o' the candy she's got stowed below." They both laughed coarsely and jabbed each other in the ribs.

Eliza stood very still, her ears burning as her heart drew into a tight little knot of pain. The sailors had no reason to lie. With her pride stung to the quick, she furiously turned her emotions inward.

"Miss Raeburn, isn't it?" said Mr. Hudson breathlessly as he hurried out to meet her, his wig askew over his shiny red face. "A great loss, your father and all. Only the good Lord in Heaven knows why some of us are taken early and others spared."

Eliza hesitated. She could still leave now and save herself the humiliation if Gardner rejected her offer. *Go on, Eliza Raeburn,* she told herself sternly.

"I'm here to see Captain Griffin," she said briskly. "Would you please show me to his room?"

Hudson only nodded. Old man Raeburn not dead a week, and already the chit was kicking up her heels, calling on bachelors in their lodgings at daybreak. Silently he led her up the twisting corner stairs to the second floor.

Down the hall in his room, Gardner once again plunged his face into the basin of water and broken ice. Swearing at the cold, he shook the droplets from his face and let the rest trickle with agonizing slowness down his bare chest and arms. Trying to forget Eliza's grief, he had drunk too much second-rate rum last night, and the letter from Sam Adams didn't help his temper. One more voyage, Sam had urged, as if dodging the British were some blasted pleasure cruise. With a groan he lowered his face back towards the water, stopping only for the knock on the door and his landlord's uncertain greeting.

"What the devil d'you want, Hudson?" Gardner demanded as he threw open the door. If the man replied, he did not hear him, for there in the hall was Eliza herself. With her head held high she neatly side-stepped the two men and swept into Gardner's room.

"Thank you, Mr. Hudson, that will be all," she said firmly, and the landlord had no choice but to leave them alone. Deliberately Eliza shut the door.

Gardner watched in disbelief. "What in blazes do you think you're doing?"

"I had to talk with you today, before you left." Eliza was too nervous to meet his eyes, yet when she let her gaze drop, all she saw was the water glistening in the dark whorls of hair on his bare chest. She lowered her gaze still further, to where the path of dark hair narrowed and disappeared in to the top of his canvas breeches. Though the breeches were all he wore, he hadn't even bothered buttoning those completely, and they hung perilously low on his narrow hips. The only safe place to look seemed to be his feet. Damn him, she thought crossly, I'm James Raeburn's daughter and I won't be made to talk to any man's feet. Her cheeks flaming, she forced herself to look into his eyes, cold and blue and without welcome.

"What kind of lady comes calling to a place like this?" demanded Gardner. Why hadn't her father warned her of the dangers that lay between men and women in rented rooms?

"What kind of gentleman lodges in one?" she retorted. Faith, why didn't he have the decency to at least put on his shirt? She'd seen her share of half-naked men, especially in the tropics, but never had she found one man's body so fascinating. She wanted to touch and explore the muscles of Gardner's chest, to feel the texture of the hair against his sun-browned skin and discover if his heart had quickened the way hers had. But harshly she reminded herself that he belonged to another woman, and in her confusion her words turned sharp. "With what Mr. Brown pays his shipmasters, you could well afford someplace better. That is, if you'd know the difference."

"What I do with my money is my affair." He watched as her breasts beneath her gown rose and fell more rapidly, and from nervousness she kept biting her lower lip, leaving it invitingly moist.

"From the stench of this room, and you, too, I'd say a good deal of your money went down your throat last night."

"Is that what you're here to talk about?"

Faith, she'd almost forgotten herself. "No, it's business I want to discuss, and not your personal habits."

"Business, Miss Raeburn?" he asked sarcastically. "You're likely the first woman up those stairs who didn't settle her price before the door was shut behind her." He stepped closer and lowered his voice to a raspy whisper. "Don't you realize the danger you're in? I could toss you on that bed right now, take my pleasure any way I wanted, and no matter how you screamed or cried, no one would rescue you. Just sport, they'd think, because you came here on your own free will.''

He was so near to her now that Eliza could feel the breath behind each word on her cheeks and the tension of his body next to hers.

"No," she whispered hoarsely. "No, you won't do that. I trust you."

"Don't." He swept down on her in an instant, his mouth fierce and demanding as he caught hers half-open with surprise, his tongue sliding hot between her parted lips. He had meant to kiss her only briefly, just long enough to teach her a lesson. But his blood burned with a mixture of anger and desire more volatile than he'd realized, and when he felt Eliza begin to answer him, her tongue tentatively meeting and exploring his in return, he felt the tension rushing through his entire body and the growing hardness in his breeches. He knew he should stop, now, but instead his hands reached for her and pulled her closer.

With a little shudder, Eliza felt herself slipping under the spell of Gardner's touch. The prickly brush of his unshaven face against hers and his lips, at once both hard and soft, sent little chills of pleasure through her body. Her hands reached to the back of his neck, cradling his face close to hers, and her fingers combed through his glossy, untied hair.

Numbed by grief and mourning, she felt her senses reawaken. She was vaguely aware of him unfastening her cloak as it slipped from her shoulders, and of a half-seen blur of white as he deftly untied her neckerchief and dropped it, too, to the floor. She felt his heat as his arms pulled her closer. Her half-bare breasts crushed against his chest, and without realizing it, her hands crept around his waist to meet across the shallow valley of his spine. She was intrigued by how different his body was from her own.

She turned slightly in his arms, into his chest, and he groaned as the full length of her pressed against him. Her stays pushed her breasts into full, enticing curves above her bodice. With one finger he slowly traced their roundness, and she shivered in response. Gently he slipped his hand lower, beneath her shift to the velvety softness of her skin. He cupped and caressed one breast, marveling at its perfection, until he felt the peak rise and tighten against his palm. A sigh of pleasure escaped her lips as she arched like a cat beneath his touch.

No other man could make her feel like this, thought Eliza rapturously. He would always be the only one. *But she was not the only one for him.* With shattering force, Eliza suddenly remembered the Frenchwoman. No matter how much Eliza cared for him, she could not change that. With a cry of mingled pain and shame she pulled herself away from him. "I won't do it, Gardner," she said in a half-choked whisper. "I won't be another—another—"

Gardner cursed himself. What had come over him? He was no green boy struggling for self-control, and yet that was exactly how he had behaved. She was too inexperienced to realize the effect she had on him, and he should have been the one to stop, not her. "Forgive me, lass, I—"

"No, it's me, not you. There's nothing for you to be forgiven." She could feel her throat constrict with tears. What must he think of her? He had as much as called her a harlot, and then she'd gone on to behave exactly like one. Her face burned as she remembered how shamelessly she'd kissed him and touched him and, worst of all, how much she'd enjoyed it. How could he possibly take her offer seriously after that? She could scarcely bear to look at him, standing there with his hands now empty at his sides, his face, with one lock of dark hair tossed across his forehead, as bereft and confused as her own must be. She ducked her chin and tried to compose herself.

"I came here to talk business with you, and I swear I had no plans, no wish, for what just happened."

"Eliza, please." He reached a hand out towards her, and she backed away.

"Hear me out first, Gardner, I beg you!" She took a long breath to steady herself, then began the speech she'd carefully rehearsed. "It was my father's wish that I continue his trade, and I intend to do so. The Raeburn name has always been respected and honored and our credit good. I want to keep it that way."

Gardner was intrigued by how her assurance grew with every word. She had marshalled that confidence with surprising speed. But what in blazes was she getting at?

"Of course I'll keep up our shares in other ventures," she continued. "But the *Peacock* was our biggest investment. My fath—I mean, I had her insured for her full value. The cargo, too. I'm going to replace her, Gardner. And I'd like you to be the captain."

Gardner narrowed his eyes. "Why me?"

"Because you've outrun the British three times, at least that I know of, when no one else in Providence has been able to." Her voice caught for a moment. "Including my father. You've got skill and luck, and I'll need both."

"There's no guarantee on luck, lass," he said wryly. He plucked his shirt from the chair and pulled it over his head, watching with amusement as Eliza retrieved her neckerchief from the floor and self-consciously tucked it back in place. "You'll be building from scratch, then?"

She shook her head. "That could take a year or more, and I can't wait. I have my father's—my last order of rum waiting, and I don't think the distiller will hold it much longer. I need someone I can trust to help me choose the *Peacock*'s replacement."

"What makes you think you can trust me?" Gardner himself could name a dozen reasons, not the least of which was what had happened earlier when she'd said the same thing about trusting him.

"Because I have to," she said truthfully. "I'll match whatever Mr. Brown paid you, but not a penny more. I won't meddle with your crew or how you run the vessel. That's your affair. Mine's your cargo, and seeing you turn a profit."

Her smile was shaky, but her golden eyes were bright with determination. "Oh, likely there's not a man on Main Street who's not laughing at me. But I know I can do it. At least I can if you say yes." There, she thought, I've done all I can. But his face was expressionless, his eyes cool and introspective, and her hopes sank. He was going to refuse.

For his own good, Gardner knew he should say no. Yet nagging him was the belief that he owed the girl something for her father's death. He could risk one more run south for her sake, and call it even between them. After smuggling rifles and gunpowder, sugar and rum would be child's play. And he owed Josiah Buck something, too. Unconsciously Gardner's features hardened at the thought of the man. Free from John Brown's interference, he could find a way to trap Buck. He liked a challenge, damn it! He would bring back Eliza's vessel unharmed and her profit with it, and end Buck's reports to the British. He might even find a way to finish that last bit of business for Sam.

The hard part, of course, would be keeping his hands and the rest of him off Eliza. When he looked down at her now, her lips parted slightly with anticipation, and remembered how eagerly she'd responded before, he felt himself grow hard all over again. *No, lad, she's not for you.* She was too young, too vulnerable, for there to be any more dawdling of that sort. Their relationship would be strictly business.

"There is a pretty little schooner in Newport that would suit you, if you don't mind buying her back from the British," he said finally. "The same coaster that chased your father brought her in as a prize last month, and we might get her cheap, if you can move fast."

Eliza gasped. "Does this mean you'll do it?"

"We wouldn't still be talking if it were otherwise, now, would we?" he answered drily. "Can you be ready to go to Newport tomorrow?"

"But tomorrow's Christmas!"

Gardner sighed. "Then the next day. But mind, no later than that. We may already be off on a fool's errand."

"The Newport packet sails on the morning tide, and you'll see, I'll be there waiting for you!" Eliza was almost dancing with excitement, and she had to fight back the urge to throw her arms around his neck and hug him. "I swear I'll make sure you don't regret this!"

But Gardner knew he already did.

Chapter Thirteen

"There's Newport now," shouted Gardner over the wind.

Beside him, Eliza only nodded and clung to the rail of the little sloop. She was sure she had never been as cold and wet as she was this afternoon, soaked with a mixture of sleet and sea spray that had managed to penetrate her cloak and gown and a quilted flannel petticoat besides. Her hands in their mittens felt permanently curled around the railing, and she doubted she'd ever be able to melt the grimace frozen to her face. She longed for warm, dry clothes, a fire and an enormous cup of cocoa, and yet as the sloop skipped unsteadily through the choppy water, she knew miserably that such comforts were still far away.

"We'll have plenty of time to find the schooner before supper," continued Gardner. "Pray she hasn't already been sold."

Again Eliza only nodded, although these three sentences were more than he'd said since they'd left Providence before daybreak. With his hat tied low over his brow and his long coat flapping in the wind, he seemed oblivious to the weather, and to her, too.

Feeling thoroughly sorry for herself, she huddled her shoulders even lower into her cloak. If he could stand the weather, so could she. The exuberance she had felt earlier after he had agreed to sail for her had been replaced by a reality as cold as this day. When she had gone to Philip Deane to write and witness the bank draft for the new schooner, the lawyer had been stern, very stern. He could not forbid her to do what she chose with her money, but he clearly wasn't pleased to be helping her. Because the *Peacock*'s insurance claim would take months to arrive from London and her father's estate was still unsettled, the draft had to be pledged against her house. She had already borrowed against the warehouse to pay for the rum, and Eliza knew all too well how precariously close she was to losing everything. Her father had taught her risk taking was the only path to success, but faith, he'd never had to gamble so much at once. She stole a glance up at Gardner, lost again in his own thoughts, and hoped she was right to trust him.

Gardner caught the reproach in her eyes and knew it was meant for him. Well, so be it. He hadn't made her stand up here on the deck. It was her own choice to be wet and bedraggled. He wasn't happy, either, not with Newport in spitting distance. The town was full of Tories and navy men, and it would take only one to recognize him. He could not decide which disgusted him more: that he had let himself be swayed by the forlorn creature beside him, or that he was cocksure enough to believe he could dance his way in and out of

Newport, unscathed. Bad rum and a red-haired virgin, the two sorriest excuses a man could offer. Sweet Jesus, he deserved to be caught and hung!

As the sloop finally nudged into the wharf, Eliza tried to rub the cold and stiffness from her fingers. "Before we go looking at this famous schooner of yours, I want to know where we'll be staying tonight," she said to Gardner. "Let's try Mr. Brewster's first. I've stayed there before with Father, and they should remember me."

"So Brewster's it's to be, is it?" Gardner raised his eyebrows in mock surprise. "Bedding down with the gentry on Thames Street, shall we?"

"Oh, hush," said Eliza crossly. "You wouldn't know gentry if you tripped across them. Unlike the bedbugs and fleas that usually share your sleep."

"What, no strumpets and rum bottles?"

"You won't find those at Brewster's, either," she said.

"Ah, more's the pity, Mistress Raeburn. I always heard the gentry knew how to enjoy themselves, but I see I've been wrong about that, too." Effortlessly he swung Eliza's small trunk across his shoulder. "But whatever your fancy, let's stop lollygagging. Without hope of strumpets, I've no mind to linger in Newport any longer than I must."

"Nor do I, Captain Griffin," she answered stiffly, and in uncomfortable silence they walked to the inn.

The common room at Brewster's was noisy and crowded, filled with guests who sought the warmth of the fire on this cold afternoon. Eliza soon spotted Mr.

Brewster's lanky figure and was glad to see his face light with recognition in return.

"Miss Raeburn, I'm honored!" he said cheerfully as he took her hand in both of his. Then his expression grew sober. "I heard about your father. Sad news, that. What brings you back to Newport?"

"Business," she said proudly, liking the sound of it. "I'll need two rooms, one for myself and one for—for—" She looked around for Gardner, who had wandered off to join a group of seamen near the fire. It irritated her, even as she realized she should expect no better of him. He had never yet behaved like a gentleman around her. Why should he start now?

"A room for my associate," she finally finished.

Mr. Brewster pursed his lips and shook his head. "We're short of rooms, we are, Miss Raeburn. If only you'd given me some warning! It's the commission beginning, y'see, called to settle the *Gaspee* business! Now I know you're from Providence, and might see things different, but there's still no excuse for what those rascals did. Looting and burning, and then practically murdering the poor lieutenant!" He sniffed loudly. "A shameful night's work that was, shameful to the whole colony."

"But there are no witnesses, are there?" she asked, hoping her voice sounded more normal to Brewster than it did to her own ears. "I'd heard no one has come out to claim the reward yet."

"Ah, Miss Raeburn, do you think they'd bring two fine judges clear from New York if they didn't have some evidence? They'll catch the rogues, catch 'em and string 'em up proper."

He smiled with satisfaction and stood upright. "But that all don't go far towards a room for you, does it? I can find something for you, miss, though not as nice as I'd like for a lady. But your—ah—associate will have to share, if he don't—ah, sir, welcome!"

Brewster held his hand out to Gardner, now standing beside Eliza. Swiftly, before he could speak, she introduced him to the innkeeper.

"This is Captain Chandler, Jacob Chandler," she said, using the first name to come to her. "He's helping me with my father's trade."

Instinct told Gardner to take Brewster's hand without surprise. "Where I sleep's no matter to me," he said, "As long as Miss Raeburn rests easy."

"Oh, yes, Captain, I can assure you—"

"Good." Gardner cut him off. He wanted to get Eliza out of here, where they could talk, and learn what in blazes was happening. "We'll be back at seven, and we'll want our dinner waiting." He took Eliza's arm and led her quickly through the crowded room to the door and the street.

"We can't stay here," declared Eliza as soon as she and Gardner were out the inn's door. "We must leave Newport as soon as we can."

"Hush now, lass, can't you hold your peace for two minutes' time?" growled Gardner as he quickened his pace. "Whatever you've got to say can keep until we're clear of this place and somewhere more private."

"But Gar—"

"Captain Chandler to you, mind? If you had reason enough for calling me that before, you'd best keep using it."

Chagrined, Eliza clamped her mouth shut. She walked swiftly beside him, lengthening her stride to match his pace; she refused to give him the satisfaction of thinking she couldn't keep up. But her irritation vanished when, several blocks before them, two men in British uniforms stepped into the street and headed their way. She grabbed Gardner's sleeve.

"For God's sake, don't let them see you!" she hissed.

"They already have," he replied curtly, "and how you're hanging onto me like you're drowning." He had spotted the men as soon as they'd appeared, and their uniforms didn't make sense. They were both officers, a lieutenant with three years' seniority and a captain, and both held ranks too high to command the only navy vessel he'd seen in Newport, a little coaster anchored in the bay. Their presence here made him wary, and he wished now he'd taken the time to listen to Eliza. The pair had so far glanced at him without recognition, but he didn't want to gamble on offering them a closer look. To suddenly run off like a frightened rabbit would only draw their attention, with the street nearly empty, and he couldn't move fast enough anyway, not with Eliza hanging on his arm. Yet his options were narrowing as every step brought them closer.

"Please, Jacob, at least pull your hat down lower," begged Eliza, and she was startled to see him turn and grin.

As long as she still had the presence of mind to call him Jacob, he was willing to risk another way out. He curled his arm around her waist and pulled her back with him, into the brick archway of the nearest warehouse. Deftly he drew her closer, curving her body across his arm and purposely leaving only his back in the nondescript coat to face the street.

"What in God's name are you doing?" she sputtered, pushing back against his chest.

"Put your arms around me, damn it," he whispered hoarsely. "At least try to make 'em believe you're willing."

He kissed her hard, and even through her fear and embarrassment, she felt her own mouth and body begin to warm and respond to him almost automatically. She only half heard the two officers pass by, the lewd remark of one and their laughter. When Gardner at last released her, she did not move, only looking at him questioningly.

"Well done, lass," he said with a slow smile. "You learn fast, I'll grant you that." His hand reached to brush back her hair from her face, lingering to caress the soft place between her ear and the top of her throat, and she almost shivered with pleasure. He had saved his own skin a score of different ways over the years, but none of the others, he decided, had been anywhere near as enjoyable. "I'd wager that those two thought no better of us than we deserve."

His laugh was a throaty chuckle, and she looked away and blushed as she realized what he meant. Near the wharves of any seaport, there were few more unremarkable sights than a man and woman pressed together in any convenient doorway or alley. She should be angry to have been made to look so common, but instead she began to laugh, too, both from amusement and relief.

Then her eyes clouded with concern, and she told him briefly what she had learned at the inn. "We shouldn't have come here. Newport isn't Providence, and every Tory in town knows your name."

"They know my name, aye, but not the face that goes with it."

"But those two officers are likely here to testify at the hearing, and you don't know what evidence they might have!"

"Ah, the devil take 'em," he said lazily. Sea lawyers and a commission of periwigs didn't worry him in the slightest, not after he'd been imagining an admiral's flagship and a frigate or two lurking offshore in the mist. Relieved, he could turn his thoughts to how Eliza's body was still entwined with his, and he wondered what she'd do if he kissed her again. Lord, it was easy to forget his vow to leave her alone! His hand again strayed towards her cheek, but this time she brushed it away impatiently.

"Gardner, this is serious."

"Jacob, you mean." He was enjoying the intimacy of teasing her.

"All right, then, *Jacob*." It was hard to think clearly when he still had her pinned against the wall, but somehow she didn't have the inclination to disengage herself just yet, and besides, the two officers might come back. "This is serious. If we hire horses, we can be in East Greenwich tonight, and catch the packet back to Providence tomorrow."

"We could, but we won't. I don't turn tail that easy. Nor do you, I'd guess."

"But you'll hang if you're caught!" she cried.

"They have to catch me first. Think it through, Eliza. They've had six months since we scuttled the *Gaspee*. They've offered rewards enough for a prince of the realm, and not one man's come for'ard to claim it." Beneath the brim of his hat, his pale eyes glinted mischievously. "Now I myself don't have much faith in New York magistrates finding truth where gold has failed, do you?"

"No," admitted Eliza reluctantly. "Not really."

"No, not at all," he declared. "We came here to buy that schooner, and that's how we'll leave. Not yelping with our tails between our legs." His voice dropped lower, the rasp Eliza associated so strongly with him becoming more pronounced. "Sometimes, sweetheart, the best place to hide is in plain sight."

"Then you don't take a step without me, understand?" said Eliza urgently. Her own words had fallen to a husky whisper, more seductive than she realized, and for emphasis she rested her hands on his chest. "As long as you're with me, no one will question you. My father's name still carries good will enough for us both. I've brought you into this, and I'll see you're safely out of it."

Gardner felt curiously off balance, and not only because of her nearness. She was, of course, right—he would be safe as long as she was with him—but he found it almost impossible to accept. He should be protecting her, not the other way around. Unconsciously he drew away from her and stuffed his hands into his pockets. "Ah, well," he said gruffly. "Don't go worrying overmuch about me."

Eliza jerked her hands away. When would she learn, she thought with despair. He had kissed her to save himself, not because he wanted to, and it was her own fault if she believed otherwise. "If you're still sailing for me, I have a right to worry," she said defensively. "You'd be hard to replace."

He didn't answer, and she fussed with her mittens to avoid meeting his eyes. "Now if you please, Jacob, I'd like to find this fine schooner of yours before I have to see her by moonlight."

"Aye, aye, ma'am," answered Gardner softly, and they headed towards the waterfront.

The captured schooner was easy to find, and the minute Eliza saw her, she understood why Gardner wanted this particular vessel so badly. The *Liberty* was a sailor's dream. She was longer than the *Peacock,* but narrower in the keel and more elegant, her two masts raking sharply aft and her deck low to the water. Every line had been refined for speed, and she stood out like a thoroughbred among her sturdier sisters.

"She's everything I've heard and more," said Gardner happily as they walked along the wharf beside the schooner. "She'll outrun anything this side of lightning."

"Then why were the British able to catch her?" asked Eliza doubtfully. True, the *Liberty* was the most beautiful ship she'd ever seen, and she was tempted, sorely tempted, but she felt she needed more persuading before she invested all her fortune.

"The way I heard it, she caught herself," said Gardner scornfully. "Her master was a landsman, green as grass, but the owner's son. Playing at sailor, that boy was, and drinking his way through his cargo, too. Fairly handed this schooner to the customs men without a whimper. I hate to say it, but the British did you and me a service by sending that lad back home to his pa for a paddling and keeping the *Liberty* all nice and snug for us here."

Eliza pointed to the figurehead, a blond woman in a dark red dress. "Who was that? The owner's daughter, or his wife?"

"His mistress, I'd venture," said Gardner, suspiciously straight-faced. "Why else d'you think he'd call her *Liberty?*"

Eliza groaned and shoved him, and Gardner laughed and pretended to shield himself from her attack.

"Good day to you, mistress, sir," said a man's voice behind them. "That's the *Liberty* schooner you're admiring, and no better bargain to be found in Newport."

The man watched them eagerly as he wiped his nose with a dingy bandanna. His right sleeve hung empty and was pinned to the shoulder of his worn coat. At once Gardner read the story of that missing arm: maimed in the king's service, the former sailor now eked out his meager pension by acting as a sales agent for navy prizes.

"A bargain's what we're looking for," said Gardner. "She's Chesapeake-built, isn't she?"

"Aye, sir, you've a good eye. Baltimore-built, she is, and fresh from the yards this year. All cedar and live oak, her canvas and fittings first-rate."

With dismay Eliza sensed the schooner's price rising by the minute. "If she's all you say, then why didn't the navy keep her?"

"Ah, miss, the sorry truth is that they're scared of her," said the agent sadly, shaking his head. "She don't look safe to English eyes. They'd build up her sides and cut back her canvas, and still plow her nose-first into the waves. Admiral's orders, she be sold instead."

"Unsafe, you say?" said Eliza uncertainly, and pressed her hand to her breast in what she hoped was the very picture of feminine uncertainty. She wanted the schooner, and meant to have it, but she wouldn't pay a farthing more than she had to, and she wasn't above a little playacting to help lower the price. Gingerly she touched Gardner's arm. "I don't know, Captain Chandler. Perhaps we should continue looking."

Immediately Gardner understood, and patted her hand with the proper show of reassurance. Sweet Jesus, but the girl was full of tricks! "Now, Miss Raeburn, you know I can sail anything created by man or devil. You leave that to me."

"Oh, I have faith in you, Captain Chandler, but after the *Peacock*—it's all still so fresh," she said. She didn't have to feign the grief in her tone.

Protectively Gardner slipped his arm around her shoulder and, over her head, nodded solemnly at the agent. "Her father," he explained. "Lost this month on Nantucket Shoals."

The agent heard his sale and his commission slipping away. "Ah, miss, in the right hands the *Liberty* will sail like a dream," he said heartily. "This gentleman here, Captain Chandler, why, he strikes me as just that sort."

"I don't know," said Eliza, wavering. "She's probably too dear for me anyway, being so new and fancy. I'm no wealthy Baltimore shipbuilder. This year's been so hard for us, then losing Father with the *Peacock*..." She trailed off forlornly.

"Don't be putting a price on the *Liberty* before talking to me," said the agent promptly. "Times ain't been good for me, neither, miss. I'm willing to have a little talk about this, and I'll wager we'll come out seeing more the same way than otherwise."

"Slowly now, don't go counting your money before we've even seen how she sails," said Gardner so sternly that the agent stepped back. "Lines can deceive as much as words. I've got to see how she takes to deep water before you start wagering this and that."

"Oh, aye, Cap'n, if that's what suits ye," agreed the agent hastily. "But as for a crew they won't amount to much. Just who I can catch together in the morning."

Eliza smiled delightedly at the man. "Oh, how generous of you! That way, if the schooner pleases Captain Chandler, then the same men can sail her back to Providence! You're quite right, we are seeing the same way in this!"

The agent gulped. That wasn't what he had intended at all, but somehow, when the young lady smiled, he found himself paying day wages to a dozen seamen. With his left hand, he gestured towards the warehouse at the end of the wharf where he kept his office. "Perhaps you'd like to come inside by the fire, miss, where we can talk more comfortable?"

As he turned to lead the way, Gardner held Eliza back just long enough to smile wickedly and wink. "That poor sot didn't know what hit him, did he, lass?" he whispered. "Sweet Jesus, what a rare team we make!"

He looked almost boyish, with the wind off the water ruffling his hair beneath his hat brim, and the cocky charm that lightened his face. Oh Lord, help me, thought Eliza dismally. It would be so much easier not to love the man if she didn't plain like him so much.

Chapter Fourteen

Once again Eliza glanced up from the columns of figures she was totalling and out the warehouse window to where the *Liberty* lay tied at the end of her wharf. The *Liberty* was not only the most beautiful vessel she'd ever seen, but also one of the fastest, as Gardner never tired of reminding her, and Eliza was happier now than she had been in months, maybe even years. She told herself it was the excitement of planning the *Liberty*'s first voyage, and pretended that the time spent with Gardner, sharing that same excitement as they worked towards outfitting the schooner, had nothing to do with it.

She could see him now, his dark coat swirling around him as he came striding up the wharf towards the warehouse. Hurriedly she closed her books and checked her reflection in the polished brass of the inkwell, and slipped down from the tall stool just as he slammed the door behind himself.

"We need more paint," Gardner stated flatly without any other greeting. His brows were drawn together in a single line across his face, an expression

Eliza had come to recognize was sure to cost her money. "There's no help for it. Those Baltimore rascals put no more than a breath of wash on her, and I won't risk barnacles and rot for a pennysworth of paint."

"Your pennysworth's my guinea," Eliza grumbled, frowning herself. She did not want him to know how close she was coming to the end of both guineas and pennies, from fear he would desert her. "That schooner was sold to me with the understanding that she was only one cruise out of the yard, and that everything on her was new and first-rate. I can't believe she needs more of anything."

"And I believed you were going to keep your fine little nose in your ledgers and out of my schooner's affairs." Gardner knew he had picked this fight with her, but the truth was that anger was the only real emotion he allowed himself around her now. Working close to her each day, knowing he couldn't touch her, kiss her, love her, had almost driven him mad. "To my mind, those were our terms."

"So they are. But when *your* running of *my* schooner—" she spoke with an extra emphasis he couldn't overlook "—threatens to make *me* a pauper, then it becomes my concern, too."

"Then come see for yourself, Mistress Raeburn."

"Let me get my cloak, and I will." She hated it when he called her that. The mocking formality of it grated on her nerves. Her heels made sharp, belligerent clicks across the pine floor as she went to the other office. When she returned, she found him bent over her desk and ledger book.

"What the devil do you think you're doing?" she demanded.

He wheeled around to face her, his earlier anger replaced by a kind of guilty wonder that completely confounded her. Behind him she saw her books still shut on the desk where she'd left them, but in his hand was the blue-checkered napkin that had held her supper.

"It's gingerbread, isn't it?" he asked, holding out the napkin with a square of uneaten cake still in it. "How did you come by it?"

Eliza almost laughed, both from relief and the silliness of his question. "Of course it's gingerbread, and I came by it from my own oven. Go on, it's yours if you want it."

"Sweet Jesus, but I haven't had gingerbread since I was a lad." He sat on the stool with his long legs sprawled before him and devoured the cake with such complete dedication that this time Eliza did laugh.

"Per cents and tallies and gingerbread, too," he teased. "What other wonders can you perform, lass?"

It was easy for Eliza to picture Gardner as a boy, waiting eagerly by his mother's oven. "I'll wager your mother couldn't bake fast enough to suit you."

"My mother?" he repeated warily. "Nay, it was a neighbor-lady who fed me sweets along with her own brood."

"But surely there was some special treat your mother made for you alone?" persisted Eliza. Short though her time with her own mother had been, it was crowded with happy memories of cookie baking and candy making.

"Nay, there wasn't," answered Gardner tersely. "Eggs and sugar cost money we didn't have. Such niceties were for better folk than we."

His bitterness surprised Eliza, as did the obvious pain behind it. "There's no sin to poverty," she said quietly.

"Aye, no sin perhaps, but shame aplenty." Working together, Eliza made it easy to forget the differences that lay like an ocean between them. As a child, she had never gone to sleep cold and hungry, or been kicked and spat upon. She would never understand why he saved almost every penny he earned, putting it aside against the day he would buy the house and security he had so sorely missed. Cherished and protected as Eliza had been, how could she understand the misery of his own childhood?

Eliza watched his hand tense into a fist around the checkered cloth as his expression darkened and turned inward, and she knew he was wrestling with a past she could only guess at. "My father always judged men by what they'd made of themselves," she said carefully, "not what luck had given them at birth."

"Even if that's a canting, two-faced whoremonger for a father and his own servant as a mother, a poor besotted creature in love with the rascal who ruined her?" he demanded hoarsely. "What then, Mistress Raeburn?"

He steeled himself for her reaction. How would Eliza treat him now? Would it be the contempt he received from Abby so long ago, or perhaps worse, the bemused pity of Athenais?

But Eliza instead only offered a sad half smile. "Oh, Gardner, is that how little you think of me, then, that you believe I'd care?"

Gardner almost forgot to breathe. There had been many women in his life that he had wanted, and he seldom wanted for long. But Eliza was the first woman he needed as much as he desired her. What he felt was love; but because he had locked away the vulnerable part of himself for so long, he failed to recognize the feeling for what it was. Instead, all he could identify was the pain of longing for something he couldn't have and the sensation of being somehow incomplete.

Eliza saw the turmoil written across his face, and in the way his shoulders tensed beneath the weight of his private anguish. She saw how much that one confidence had cost him, and she wanted nothing more than to offer him the comfort of her love and her embrace, to try to ease his pain as best she could. Yet she hung back, uncertain. Would he let himself find solace with her, the woman he did not love? She could not bear to offer and be rejected. How could she, when she must see him tomorrow, and the next day and the next, until the *Liberty* sailed? Her heart refused to let her risk it, and instead she only let her fingers lightly brush his sleeve.

"Come, show me this faulty paint," she said softly, "else we'll miss the daylight, and I'll have only your word on it."

Gardner sighed wearily and rose to his feet. He'd forgotten all about the paint, and now that he was in no mood for teasing, the whole idea struck him as childish. "Nay, Eliza, it's not important."

"Oh, yes, it is, if it was enough to bring you in here huffing and puffing, fit to burst," she replied. "If there's something amiss with the paint, I'll just have to find a way to pay for it, that's all."

She held the door open, and he realized he had no choice but to go. Ah, well, he thought philosophically, the painter and the *Liberty*'s crew were still waiting for their fun, and he wouldn't disappoint them.

There *was* something not quite right about the schooner, thought Eliza uneasily. It was the crew, that was it. Every one of them seemed to be on deck. Most were making a poor attempt at looking busy, while some just stood idle at the rail with foolish grins on their faces. She frowned, knowing she'd have to speak to Gardner about that, too. The crew was his responsibility, but she didn't want to lose the *Liberty* because her men were undisciplined.

"If you look towards the bowsprit, there, you'll see the problem," said Gardner. Eliza followed his gesture, then froze. The figurehead of the blond woman from Baltimore had been repainted. Her hair was now coppery red, her eyes golden brown, and her gown exactly matched the teal blue of the dress Eliza had worn to the party at Sabine's Tavern. There was even the lightest dusting of freckles across the figurehead's elegant wooden nose.

"I'll pay for the paint from my own pocket, lass," said Gardner quickly. "But it didn't seem right, somehow, sailing your schooner behind another lady's face. She's all yours, Eliza, with your spirit and your independence, and you'll do each other proud."

When Eliza turned towards him, Gardner saw her eyes were bright with unshed tears he knew no reason for. But there was no mistaking the quick kiss she gave to his cheek, nor the impish smile of conspiracy that followed.

"You were wrong to do that without my approval," she said with mock severity, "and as your employer, I'll see that the cost of the paint's charged to your wages. But plain Eliza Raeburn thanks you anyway."

Seeing her smile, the men along the rail cheered and whistled, and Eliza, laughing, sank before them in a curtsy as gracefully as any duchess. She was laughing still as she skipped back to lock her office for the night. In these short winter days, it would be dark soon, and Gardner would walk her back to her house as he did every evening. She whistled to herself as she gathered her papers to take home.

"I'll only be a moment more, Gardner," she called as she heard the door open and close behind her.

"And will that welcome hold for me as well?" asked Josiah, and with a little gasp of surprise Eliza spun round to face him, clutching her ledger to her chest. He walked towards her slowly, leaning on his cane. He was tired, and after this long a day, the perpetual ache in his knee was almost intolerable. But he had been determined to talk to Eliza tonight, and if he had to hunt her down in a musty warehouse reeking of tar and stale molasses, he would do it. She could not continue avoiding him when there was so much left to be said between them. "I realize these aren't the proper circumstances to call upon a lady, but you, dear Eliza, are one lady who is seldom at home to callers.''

"I have a business to run, Josiah," she said defensively.

He snorted derisively. "Business? Is that what you call that disgusting performance I just had the misfortune to witness?" He had been shocked to see the woman he loved behaving so wantonly, just as the sight of the newly repainted figurehead had appalled him with its vulgarity. "I never thought I'd see the day when Eliza Raeburn would bow and scrape like some common actress for the entertainment of a pack of hooting sailors!"

"It wasn't like that, Josiah, not at all!"

"Oh, yes, it was all in perfect innocence, wasn't it?" he sneered. "Just as innocent as your relationship with Griffin, I'd fancy!"

"There is nothing beyond business between Captain Griffin and myself," she answered hotly. Unconsciously she had backed away as he approached, and now found herself cornered against her desk. She remembered how he had hurt her before, and she tried to recall what on the desk she might grab as a weapon if necessary.

"You ran off to Newport with him, didn't you? There are probably few secrets left about the man that I could tell you now, are there?"

He was so close to her now that she saw the little beads of perspiration that clustered on his upper lip, and she could smell the sticky sweet pomade he used to dress his hair. "I don't have to defend myself to you, Josiah," she said, fighting to keep her voice calm. "All that has been between you and me has been friendship, and even that you seem determined to destroy."

Somehow her words penetrated his anger, and he struggled to regain his self-control. This was how he had driven her away before, and if he wasn't careful, he would do so again. He took a deep breath and weighed each word with care before he spoke. "Forgive me, Eliza, if in my passion I grow headstrong. If I say things that may sound distasteful to you, it is my devotion that forces me to speak. I love you, Eliza. I offer you my heart, my hand, my unending respect and affection."

"No, Josiah." Eliza closed her eyes and shook her head. "I told you before. I don't love you."

But his voice rose to blot out her denial. "Eliza, my dearest, my own, you must be mine! Can't you know I've always loved you, and always will?"

He grabbed both her wrists and his cane fell clattering to the floor between them. With a low noise like a growl, he forced her arms back against the desk, and Eliza twisted and fought like a wildcat in his grasp. If she could only bring the heavy ledger down across his face, it would give her the chance she needed to break free. But he was stronger than she had guessed, and inexorably his advantage grew. Trapped by Josiah's body, Eliza did not see the door open, but there was no ignoring the way Gardner's order reverberated through the little room.

"Let her go, Buck," he said coldly, "or so help me, I'll kill you." He stood with his legs widespread, in his raised hand the long-barrelled pistol cocked and aimed at Josiah.

Startled, Josiah glanced back over his shoulder. His balance wobbled without the cane, and Eliza jerked free and ran to Gardner. He pulled her close with his free arm, his eyes never leaving Josiah's face, the pistol's aim never faltering.

But Josiah held his ground. He leaned against the desk for support and watched how Eliza clung to Gardner in a way she never would to him. In that single moment, in how their bodies touched, their intimacy was unmistakable. It was all Griffin's fault that he had lost Eliza, thought Josiah savagely, and the hatred flooded his veins like a poison. "For God's sake, Griffin, put the gun down," he snarled. "You have my word that it's not necessary."

"Isn't it now?" Gardner's expression remained unchanged. When he had found Eliza struggling with Josiah, only the risk of hurting her as well had kept Gardner from shooting Josiah at once. "Somehow I feel a good deal more comfortable with a bullet between your word and my life."

"In Providence, gentlemen don't carry firearms."

"Ah, Buck, but you're forgetting I've never pretended to be a gentleman, nor anything else I wasn't. Unlike yourself."

Josiah's lips compressed. How much did Griffin really know, and how much was bluff? He began to reach for his cane, then stopped as the gun barrel echoed his movement. "Can't you trust a cripple with his own crutch?" he demanded.

"I wouldn't trust you sound asleep and snoring," replied Gardner, but motioned for Buck to pick up the cane. "You've claimed at least three of my lives so far, and I'm mighty attached to the few I've got left. How many do you have left yourself, I wonder?"

Josiah laughed humorlessly. "You could shoot me and discover for yourself."

"I'd be more interested in who came to mourn you. Newport men, for certain. Aye, and Boston men, too. How much gold braid could you call up from the grave, eh, Buck?"

Confused, Eliza looked from one man to the other. She didn't understand their conversation, and the hostility filling the office convinced her that, if she was gone, each would gladly try to kill the other.

Josiah twitched at the ruffles on his cuffs, and Eliza noticed how his fingers shook. "So my life dangles in the balance of your curiosity, Griffin?"

"Nay, that time's not yet come," said Gardner, his raspy voice deceptively soft though the threat behind it was obvious. Reluctantly he uncocked the gun and brought the barrel back to rest against his shoulder. "The score's too long between us to settle so quickly. But mark this well—if I hear you've brought your long nose sniffing around Eliza again, you'll answer to me, and I won't be as generous a second time."

With as much dignity as was possible, Josiah stalked past them, his eyes straight ahead, and disappeared into the street. To Eliza, it seemed his limp was more pronounced, and in that moment she felt her dislike and fear tempered with pity and regret for the friendship he had destroyed.

As Gardner slowly began to relax, he let himself hold Eliza just a little longer. He could still feel her heart beating too quickly, and her very quietness told him how shaken she was. As fiercely independent as she liked to be, she was still at times, heartbreakingly vulnerable. "He didn't hurt you, did he, lass?"

Eliza shook her head, preoccupied by all that had just passed.

"Mind, you tell me if he comes near you again."

She sighed, then turned her face to look directly up at him. "Tell me true, Gardner," she asked seriously. "I'm no fool, and I can see there was more behind that quarrel than me."

Gardner squeezed her shoulder fondly, wishing she hadn't seen and heard quite so much. "'Tis nothing, lass," he said lightly. "An old story. Buck and I disagreed while I sailed for John Brown, and we're both slow to forget."

Eliza knew he was lying. His evasiveness stung more than any truth she could imagine, but her pride kept her from asking more. She shrugged free of his arm and gathered her lantern. When, if ever, would he come to trust her?

Josiah walked the length of the waterfront and back again, ignoring the cold of the January evening. By the time he finally returned to his lodgings, his leg was so stiff that he could barely hobble. Yet he welcomed the familiar pain the old wound caused. It pierced the numbness of his loss and humiliation and forced him to think clearly again. When at last he sat at his desk, the letter to Colonel Osborne nearly wrote itself.

Be advised that Griffin will sail in *Liberty* schooner from Providence 1 February. Take or destroy the vessel. You have Fair warning this time, do not fail again.

Yr. Obt. Srvt.—J.B.

There, Josiah thought triumphantly as he scattered sand across the wet ink. With a handful of words he would accomplish more than that entire fat-bottomed commission combined. They would have their traitor for a spring hanging, and he would have Eliza. With Griffin and the schooner gone, and her father's business bankrupt, she would have no choice but to come to him.

He smiled to himself as he folded the letter, methodically pressing each edge with his fingertips. It was a shame, really, that she would never learn exactly how much his love had done for her.

The last day of January dawned cold and still, the clouds a flat, leaden gray that buried the sun. The river lay calm, without a ripple, and the gulls had ceased their usual raucous wheeling and rode the water instead in subdued groups that faced southeast, towards the ocean. The air itself seemed too quiet, with voices and street sounds echoing oddly. Anxiously Eliza watched the sky for change, for a sign of the wind that would bring the storm she feared was imminent. The weather was the one thing she couldn't control for the *Liberty*'s sailing in the morning. A winter gale and high seas had claimed her father and the *Peacock*, and the memory was too fresh to be forgotten. While there was still a chance that this storm could miss Providence, she clung to the possibility with stubborn optimism.

"We could get no more than flurries and high tides," she said to Gardner as she watched him re-check the *Liberty*'s lashings. He had ordered all her sails taken in to provide as little resistance to gale winds as possible, and he wouldn't be content until he surveyed each tight bundle of canvas and line for himself. "We might see nothing at all."

Gardner scanned the clouds overhead, blowing on his cupped fingers to warm them. "If we don't see snow tonight, and a good deal of it, then I'm as great a fool as you're pretending to be."

"You know as well as I do that it's bad luck to put off a sailing."

"Better that than seeing the *Liberty*'s first cruise be her last," he replied patiently. As eager as he was to be under way, he was reluctant to leave her and end the time they had shared together this past month. "I can't predict what we'll meet at sea, but I can wait in Providence as long as I must to give myself a good chance of fair weather."

His very calmness, so different from her own agitation, irritated her into sharpness. "I thought I'd hired a shipmaster who wasn't afraid of anything."

"And here I thought you'd hired me to see your ship, cargo and crew to the Caribbees and back," he said, one noncommittal eyebrow cocked. "Not to mention I'd hoped for a little concern for my own sorry hide in the bargain."

Eliza looked at him closely, hands on her hips. Despite all the time they'd spent together, she still couldn't always tell whether he was teasing or not. "I'll see you here in the morning, Captain Griffin," she said stiffly, and marched down the gangway and wharf towards home.

Yet with each step, her irritation faded, and she cursed the pride that had made her leave so abruptly. She had been anticipating that last walk with Gardner from the *Liberty* to her house. Not that she expected anything like a farewell kiss, not this time. Oh, he still flirted with her and said things calculated to make her blush, but since they had pretended to be lovers to evade the officers in Newport, he had not strayed towards her once. And for that she was sorry, far sorrier than she'd ever confess.

In her kitchen, she carefully wrapped the gingerbread she had baked earlier, and set it in the basket with the other food and drink she had prepared to give to Gardner tomorrow. She had done many such tasks for him, adding small comforts to his cabin, like a new mirror for shaving and an extra-long quilt for his bunk. Not one of which, of course, he'd noticed. But oh, she thought sadly, how much she would miss the man!

Carefully she banked the kitchen fire as she did every night, and carried her dinner upstairs to eat. In the winter the big house was too much to heat, and she spent almost all her time in her own room. Not that she minded: the room was her haven, cheerful and inviting. The walls were a creamy yellow, the woodwork painted rose to match the parrots embroidered

on her curtains and bed hangings. Above the mantelpiece hung a large map marked with blue crosses to
show all the places she had visited. On the carpet before the fireplace was a large table piled high with letters, books and old newspapers, and now her plate and
teacup, as well.

She ate quickly, then washed her hair in the water,
scented with dried lavender, that she had heated over
the fire. Wrapped up in a quilt over her nightgown, she
sat on the carpet and brushed her hair over and over
to dry it by the fire's heat.

The knock at the back door startled her, echoing
through the empty house. Only Beckah would call this
late, and only Beckah came to the back of the house.
Quickly Eliza lit a candlestick, and sheltering the
flame from drafts with her hand, she skipped barefoot down the stairs to the kitchen door. She drew the
heavy iron latch and threw open the door.

On the bottom step stood Gardner, his arms outstretched with his hat in one hand. His hair and coat
were frosted with white, and his mouth curled in the
most disarming smile Eliza had ever seen.

"It's snowing, Mistress Raeburn," he said. "It's
snowing!"

Chapter Fifteen

Gardner would not have been surprised if Eliza had slammed the door shut outright, and, in fact, he almost expected it. He certainly hadn't counted on being invited inside and upstairs to her room with the innocent explanation that the rest of the house was too cold. All he had intended was to apologize for his earlier teasing and be on his way. Instead he found himself sitting in her bedchamber, eating gingerbread from a china plate while his coat and boots dried, steaming, by the fire. It would be downright domestic if Eliza weren't curled up in the chair across from him wearing, it seemed, next to nothing. His eyes kept straying to the shadowy cleft between her breasts as his imagination strayed a bit further south, and he couldn't decide whether he felt more like a guest in her house or a thief.

Hugging her knees, Eliza watched Gardner eat the last of the gingerbread. On impulse she had invited him inside, hoping happily for the conversation she'd missed this afternoon. But her bedchamber wasn't

Main Street, and she was quick to see he knew the difference, too.

He leaned back in his chair, stretching his arms overhead. "I want you to know, lass, you've done a grand job outfitting the *Liberty*. You've readied that vessel in half the time most owners would take, and without skimping or making do, either. And as the *Liberty*'s master, I thank you."

Automatically she smiled at the compliment, then bit her lower lip with dismay. How could he make praise for her business acumen sound so seductive? She was in deep water without a clue of how to save herself, short of asking him to leave. And perversely, she knew she'd never do that. To avoid his gaze she left her chair and went to stand before the fire. Inviting him here had been both wrong and right, and she wasn't certain any longer if she could tell the difference.

She brushed her hand across his old, worn hat where it hung off one corner of the mantelpiece. "I should have spared a bit more to outfit the *Liberty*'s captain as well," she said as she shaped the brim with her fingers. "This poor thing's old as Methuselah."

"Older," agreed Gardner. The firelight silhouetted her legs through the insubstantial linen with a clarity he was sure she hadn't intended. And they were lovely legs indeed, long as a colt's and a thousand times more shapely. Sweet Jesus, how could he banter about his hat with her within arm's reach? "But we're attached, that hat and I, and I expect the sorry thing will serve me until the waves claim both it and the head beneath it."

She sucked in her breath sharply, and at once he cursed himself for the unthinking cruelty of his words. How could he make jests like that with her father scarcely a month drowned?

She heard the chair scrape across the floor and the three steps it took him to reach her. Gently he took her by the shoulders and turned her to face him. "Eliza, sweetheart, I'm sorry. I spoke without a thought for the pain I'd cause you. I'm a thick-witted—"

"I'd give my own life to keep yours safe, Gardner Griffin," she blurted out. In frustration she struck her balled fists on his chest. "Don't you know that? You and your blasted hat both!"

"I'm not right for you, Eliza," he said seriously. "We're from different worlds, you and I. You have so much to give, and I have nothing to offer in return. I've no past and less of a future. What you don't know about me could fill this room."

"It doesn't matter, Gardner, none of it," she answered stubbornly.

With a swift pang of guilt he thought of Sam Adams's shipment of rifles waiting in Martinique for him to smuggle back, without her knowledge, in her precious schooner. Now that, for sure, would be something that mattered very much. "Find someone else to fall in love with, Eliza. Some fine gentleman who can take care of you the way you deserve."

"Someone like Josiah Buck?" she fired back, but he refused to be distracted.

"There must be others. A house and a husband and babies—that's what every woman wants." Lord, he sounded like an ass, even to his own ears.

"You're preaching claptrap and humbug, like every other man," she snapped, tossing her hair back defiantly. "You *don't* know what I want."

"Oh, yes, I do." Slowly, on their own, it seemed, his hands began to massage her shoulders, and he felt the defiance sliding out of her muscles. "And I'll have you know I'm not like other men."

"Oh, damn you, Gardner," she muttered. Her gaze lowered from his eyes to his mouth while her own lips parted expectantly. With that one look, he gave up fighting. He buried his hands deep in her hair and lifted her mouth to his. All the emotion he had forced back these past weeks burst free with the first touch of her lips, and he kissed her with a fierce intensity that left his whole body demanding more.

Eliza met his desire, opening her lips and her soul to share the heat that swelled in them both. The quilt dropped to the floor as her arms curled around his waist, pulling him closer. Unencumbered by layers of petticoats and stays, she was for the first time almost painfully aware of how soft her body was next to his, how her curves melted into his hardness. Only two thin layers of linen stood between them, and as his chest crushed against her breasts, she felt the tips tighten and a curious ache spread through her body. With shaking fingers she tugged his shirt free from his breeches and ran her hands up his back. But even to her inexperienced fingers, the skin there seemed different, puckered and ridged with old scars, and she pulled back, questioning.

He smiled wryly and replaced her hands. "I told you there was much you didn't know about me, lass."

"But your back." She knew of only one way for a man to be scarred like that, and men who had been flogged did not rise to become shipmasters. "How—"

"Hush, now. It's an old, old story, of no importance," he said softly. "Someday, if you wish, I'll tell it to you. But not now." When he kissed her, she willingly forgot the scars, forgot everything except how he tasted. He was right, old stories could wait longer than she could herself. Their tongues met and danced together sinuously only to separate and meet again.

Lifting her easily from her feet, he carried her cradled in his arms to the bed and then stretched out beside her. She gazed up at him expectantly, the firelight reflected in her golden eyes. This was all so new to her, so strange and wonderful at the same time. Tomorrow he would be gone, but tonight, if she dared, he could belong to her alone.

Carefully he untied the ribbon at the top of her gown and eased the garment from her shoulders until her breasts were uncovered before him. They were so beautiful, so perfect, and with first his lips and then his tongue he caressed one velvety peak until it tightened and rose to meet him. Eliza twined her arms around his head, combing her fingers through the silky gloss of his hair. His eyes fluttered shut, and she arched against his mouth, marvelling at the unfamiliar sensations now racing through her body. There was a growing warmth, odd but very pleasurable, centered far lower than the breasts he was kissing. Unconsciously she pressed her thighs together, and Gardner chuckled. He shifted his attentions to her other breast while his hand continued the delicious torment he'd begun on the first.

She was so perfectly made for a man's delight. No, rather, for *his* delight, realized Gardner with growing wonder. From the way she was clinging to him, her shaky little sighs, he was certain he was the first to stir her so. He must take care to go slowly, to give her time to follow his lead. He wanted this to be as unforgettable as he could make it. Yet when she twisted beneath him, pressing herself against his tongue, he felt another spark added to his own urgency.

"Oh, Gardner, please, no, that's too much," she whispered, her protest scarcely more than a sigh.

"Nay, sweetheart, 'tis only the beginning," he said tenderly.

"You—you just think you know everything," she managed to stammer.

"For now, Mistress Raeburn, I'd say I do. But mind, you're learning fast." With tantalizing slowness he slipped her gown over her hips and legs, his lips tracing a lazy trail as the linen left her body. He paused and sat back to gaze at her, revelling in the sight.

"You're so beautiful, Eliza," he breathed, one hand gently following her curves. Her waist was small, as he'd known it would be, her hips pleasingly flared. Set against the burnished copper of her hair, her skin was as flawless as new cream. To his delight she was dusted all over with the same golden freckles that crossed her nose, and he promised himself he would not stop until he had counted—and kissed—every one. He saw her expression change as his fingers strayed lower to the triangle of chestnut curls at the juncture of her thighs.

"Gardner, I've not been with a man before." She watched him touching her, his hands so large and brown against her pale skin, and her heart raced. She wasn't afraid of him, but of herself, that somehow she'd displease him with her ignorance. She thought of the faraway Frenchwoman, who doubtless knew a thousand ways to delight a man. Why hadn't she asked Beckah more questions about what men and women did together? "Not in bed," she continued lamely. "Not like this, I mean."

"Oh, I guessed as much," he said easily. He'd heard enough women protest that they were virgins when they weren't, but Eliza was the first to apologize for inexperience, and he found it touchingly endearing.

"It's just—I don't want you to be disappointed."

"There's scant danger of that, Eliza. Let me please you, and I'll be pleased." Suddenly she caught her breath as, against her will, her hips raised up to meet his touch. He smiled. "You just tell me what you want."

Her hands came up to his chest and twisted in the fabric of his shirt. "Then take this off," she ordered, her breathing ragged. "I want to touch you, too."

His lips crossed hers again briefly. Then, standing, he quickly drew off his shirt and socks. Eliza leaned up on her elbows to watch. The firelight danced across his body, highlighting the play of muscles in his arms and chest. Her eyes widened as at last he shed his breeches, and her cheeks flushed at the sight of his arousal as he returned to the bed.

"Eliza, I swear, I'll try not to hurt you," he said quietly. "But if I do, I promise it will only be this once, and never again."

"I'm not scared," she said, and she wasn't. Tentatively she placed her hands on his chest and began to explore the fascinating interplay of curling hair over bronzed skin, the flesh and muscle and sinews that made a man. Beneath it all, she could feel the rapidity of his heartbeat. It was, in a way, as exciting to touch him as to be touched. Her hands grew bolder, and he groaned under his breath.

"Ah, sweetheart, that's good," he said. "That's very, very good."

The mere sound of his voice was incredibly seductive. Shyly she raised her fingers to trace the curving outline of his lips, and he smiled.

Once again he had begun caressing her, but more insistently, and their kisses now were marked with a rising urgency that made her shudder with anticipation. His fingers slipped deeper into her softest places and she gasped. She was warm and wet and ready for him, and Gardner realized she wanted him as much as he did her. Gently he laid his whole length upon her, parting her legs and pressing her down into the feather mattress. With a little sigh Eliza welcomed him, her hands sliding around his waist. The silky touch of her skin against his was almost too much for him. As she kissed him, her mouth searched his hungrily with a fury that he knew would pale only beside what would come next. Yet as much as he ached for fulfillment, he held back, determined to give her the first taste of pleasure.

Carefully, oh so carefully, he eased himself into her heat. Her breath caught as her fingers dug into his shoulders. He moved as slowly as he could, mustering all his self-control, and with each stroke he was further inside her until at last they were complete as one. He slipped one hand between their bodies and found her and began the rhythm of touching again. With a little shiver, she called his name, as instinctively her hips rocked up to meet his thrusts. He let himself move faster now, measuring himself again and again within her. Her legs snaked around his as she tried to pull him deeper, and the cries torn from her were raw and wild. She had lost all sense of herself, of reality. All that existed now was him, and these unimaginable sensations that she never wanted to stop.

He pressed his face into the tangled cloud of her hair. His own cry came with a harshness born of desperate frustration and the incredible longing to become part of her. He had never wanted any woman as much as he now needed Eliza. And he could not wait any longer.

She twisted beneath him, her cheeks and breasts flushed and feverish, her skin filmed with moisture, as he took her higher and higher towards her release. With a groan he slipped her knees over his arms and lifted her legs, plunging finally to her core, and they met at last, lost in each other for one unbearably perfect moment.

Afterwards he held her tight, unwilling to ever let her go. Gently he rolled over onto his back, bringing her to lie atop him, their bodies still intimately joined.

"I love you, Eliza," he said simply. He had never offered the words to a woman before, and he was glad now that he hadn't and was able to give them new to Eliza. From this night on, his life was inextricably bound to hers. He, who had always been alone, would now always have her.

"I love you, too." She sighed softly. As he brushed the curls back from her face, he found her cheek wet with tears.

"Oh, sweetheart, I did not mean to hurt you," he said with remorse.

"You didn't, at least not much." She raised herself up on her elbows to look at him and smiled tremulously. How could she put it into words? He had given her everything that was himself, a gift so precious she still could not quite believe it was hers. He had showed her things she'd never known existed, stirred her passions and emotions in impossibly beautiful ways. "Is it always like this, Gardner?"

"Nay, between most men and women it seldom is," he answered truthfully. Her lips were swollen from kissing and he couldn't resist pulling her down to taste her yet again. "But for me, with you, it was special. *You're* special, Eliza. God, I've never known another woman like you."

Her smile widened. "Then I pleased you, too?"

"Lass, that's a question you shouldn't have to ask."

She laughed, deep in her throat. Her hips shifted against his and he groaned.

"Now you keep doing that, and I'll have to demonstrate my satisfaction instead of just telling it." He couldn't believe how much he wanted her so soon again.

"The tide won't turn in the river until morning," she whispered. He caught the poignancy in her tone, and he shared her regret. For the first time he would sail feeling the pull of love left behind on shore. "That's still hours and hours."

"If you're willing, I'm sure we'll find a way to spin out every one of them." As she kissed him hungrily, tenderness dissolving into passion, he realized how rapidly the boundaries between teacher and student were already blurring. And he didn't mind at all.

Eliza woke slowly, drifting in and out of drowsy sleep with a wonderful sense of well-being. With the coverlet pulled high, she lay curled into Gardner's body, his arm draped protectively across her waist. She had never felt more blissfully contented in her life.

He stirred in his sleep, and she snuggled back closer to him. She loved him, and he loved her. *He loved her!* She whispered the words to herself as if to make them more real. Until last night, love had brought her nothing but unhappiness, but now she understood how perfect and full of joy love could be. And how full of passion, she decided, remembering the many ways she and Gardner had passed the night. No wonder they'd both slept past dawn.

Or was it? Her senses sharpened as she listened for the familiar sounds of morning: the meetinghouse bell, the rumble of wagons headed for market, the one-eyed rooster next door saluting the sunrise. But there was nothing beyond the peaceful rhythm of Gardner's breathing beside her.

Carefully she slipped free of his arm and slid out of the covers and through the bed curtains. She had no idea what had happened to her nightgown, and shivering, she hurried naked to the window. The fire had long since died down and, outside of the warm island of her bed, her room was freezing, the water in her washbowl glazed with ice. In addition to Gardner's other qualities, thought Eliza, making love had been a highly satisfactory way to keep warm through a Rhode Island winter's night. She drew the curtains on one window and slid back the upper shutters. What she saw made her whistle low under her breath. The whole world was shrouded and muffled in white, and the snow was falling still.

It was the squeak of the shutter's hinges, followed by Eliza's whistle, that woke Gardner, and he rolled over to reach for Eliza, only to find no more than her warm imprint in the soft mattress. Her special fragrance still clung to the sheets, and that was enough to arouse him again. Would he never get enough of her?

He saw her by the window and, with his head comfortably pillowed, he treated himself to the sight of her dressed only in the storm's pearly light. She stood balanced on her toes with her elbows propped up on the sill to better see out the window. Poised there with her back arched and her hair tumbling uncombed down her shoulders to her waist, her breasts raised and their nipples taut from the cold, she was the most inviting woman he had ever seen. And best of all, she was his.

"Snowed, did it?" he said at last, and she smiled over her shoulder.

"Still is," she admitted. "You were right. Nothing will leave the river today, if you could even find the water."

"Seems like we're stranded, then. Trapped. Marooned."

"Seems so." She loved to see him there, his dark body lounging in her muslin sheets. He was grinning wickedly at her, his teeth startlingly white in his unshaven face. "You must be hungry. I'll go down to the kitchen and fetch us some breakfast."

"Ah, the devil take your kitchen," he said lazily. "You'll be my breakfast, lass, and my supper and dinner, too."

She laughed and clambered back into bed. Another day and night of loving Gardner: that would be heaven. But it also meant another day and night to make her plans. Because now she knew, though he did not, that when the *Liberty* sailed, she would be going with him.

"I won't be coming to the dock today," Eliza said as Gardner pulled on his boots. "We'll say goodbye here, now."

He froze, and if Eliza needed any further confirmation of his feelings for her, she had only to see the stricken expression on his face. He wasn't ready to leave her now, not quite yet. They had not been apart for a moment these past three days and nights, and he simply refused to believe she wouldn't want to be with him these final few hours.

"Why?" he demanded. "You're the *Liberty*'s owner. You should be there."

"If I were only the owner, I wouldn't care. I'd wave as gaily as everyone else, and wish you fare-thee-well. But things are different now." She hated herself for lying, even if it was for a good reason. She was positive he wouldn't invite her along, but if she could get aboard the *Liberty* and stay hidden until it was too late to turn back, then she felt sure he'd be glad she'd stowed away.

"Aye, things *are* different between us. I love you, and I've made love to you, and damn it, Eliza, that's reason enough for you to be there to see me off."

She shook her head. "I hate goodbyes, Gardner. Especially public ones."

"You've never worried overmuch before about what others said." He paused, not wanting to face the painfully obvious conclusion. "Unless you're ashamed of me, Eliza. Is that it? I'm fine enough to sail your blessed ship and to take to your bed, but not to be seen with? Not Captain Griffin, that black bastard!"

"Stop it, Gardner! I never want to hear you say such things again, do you understand? I love you for who you are, and that is all I will ever care about. You're a better man than any other in this whole town, and I won't listen to you or anyone else say otherwise!"

Angrily he tugged on his boot. "Then why in blazes won't you come to the wharf with me?"

"Oh, Gardner, this time, for once, let's not quarrel." She slipped her arms around his neck and sat wearily across his knees. "When I was a little girl, my mother always took me with her to see my father sail. She was very good at hiding from my father how frightened she was that he wouldn't come back. But once he was gone and we were alone, she'd cry and cry."

Tenderly he brushed his fingers across her cheek. "Are you like your mother, then?"

"Oh, no. No one ever said that!" She smiled wistfully. "Mama was kind and gentle and quiet, all the things I'm not, and she was so beautiful that men would turn and stare. She and Father loved each other so much, and I know he hated leaving her, too."

"No more than I'll hate leaving you behind."

Eliza's smile turned small and sad. "Way back then, I swore I'd never watch a man I loved sail away, and I won't do it now, not even for you."

His blue eyes were so full of love and trust that she almost risked asking him outright if she could sail with him. "I love you, Gardner, and I always will. Remember that when you're away. When we're together again, we'll decide what comes next."

He put his arms around her waist and held her, just held her. She was so sure he would return, when he knew the odds were always against him. Although he was certain she wasn't going to cry, he almost wished she would. It would be easier to focus on her tears, to comfort her, than to accept the raw emptiness he felt inside. Love was still too new to him to trust it, the way Eliza did. He would marry her today if she'd take him. But there were so many things he must do before he could even ask her, and he must be very careful that none of it touched Eliza. Her father's death weighed heavily enough on his conscience as it was.

Gently he stroked her hair, still loose and untied to please him. He realized, of course, that he might have already harmed her during these past two nights, that he might have gotten her with child. He wondered if Eliza had even considered the possibility. He would leave now, if that was how she wanted it, though God knows he didn't.

When he finally walked away from her house, his boots crunching in the frozen snow and his shoulders hunched against the cold and his own misery, he knew he left behind not only his happiness, but his heart, as well.

Chapter Sixteen

Eliza found it easy enough to board the *Liberty* in the last-minute bustle before the schooner sailed. Dressed in the same cast-offs she'd worn on the *Gaspee*, she had simply walked up the gangplank with a small trunk holding her belongings and headed down into the captain's cabin with plenty of time to hide in the empty locker beneath Gardner's bunk. She wriggled in and slid the paneled doors nearly shut.

Wrapped up in her coat, Eliza felt pleasantly cozy in the darkened space. The woodwork was still new enough to smell sweetly of hewn pine, and the *Liberty*'s motion under sail was lulling and rhythmic as the schooner made her way down the river towards the open water. After two nights of little rest, Eliza was soon fast asleep.

It was the gunshot that woke her. Disoriented, Eliza listened to the footsteps running across the deck above and Gardner's voice calling out orders. He sounded calm enough, but the other men were chattering with excitement. There, that was another shot, and this time Eliza recognized it at once for what it was.

Quickly she rolled out from her hiding place and ran to the stern window. They were just past Newport, but from the window she could see nothing of who, or what, was firing at them.

"Miss Raeburn, ma'am!" Stunned, Davis, the second mate, stood frozen in the doorway, whatever errand Captain Griffin had sent him on forgotten at the sight of her bending over at the window in a pair of breeches.

But Eliza was too excited to notice his reaction. "Oh, Davis, I know I heard gunfire, but I can't see a blasted thing!"

"Not from here, maybe, ma'am, but on deck's all clear as day. The Britishers—"

"The British! Since when do they have the right to fire at merchant vessels?" She didn't wait for an answer but pushed by Davis and up the gangway to the deck.

Her eyes swept the wide horizon and immediately found the source of the shots: two sloops, the larger to the north of them, and the other to the northwest. Both were bearing down on the *Liberty*, and even at this distance, Eliza could see that both were armed and carried the flags of King George's navy. As she watched, there was another bright flash and a puff of smoke from a cannon on the larger sloop, followed by the column of sea spray where the ball landed in the water. The shot had fallen short, and the *Liberty* was still out of range. But to Eliza, any guns trained on them were a threat, and she couldn't fathom why they had picked on her schooner.

Two strong hands grabbed her shoulders and turned her roughly about. Gardner's face was tight with barely controlled anger, his eyes cold and icy blue. "What the devil are you doing here?"

"Why are those two firing on us?" demanded Eliza in return.

"All that nonsense about you hating goodbyes and your poor weeping mama," he said bitterly. "I should have known you'd pull some blasted fool trick like this."

"Answer me now, Gardner. I'm the owner of this vessel, and you owe me that much."

"I don't owe you a damned thing." He practically spat out the words. "We'll talk, Eliza. We'll talk plenty. But not now."

Abruptly he returned to his place near the wheel, leaving Eliza to simmer in her own anger and disbelief. She glanced back to the two sloops, still too near to suit her and, it seemed, drawing closer. The *Liberty* should easily be able to outrun them, and yet she was barely poking along.

Eliza caught the coat sleeve of a sailor near her also watching. "Carter, you'll tell me. Why are those two after us?"

Carter tugged his knit cap lower across his brow. "I 'spect it's just 'cause we're Yankees, and they're Britishers. Ben there says they be the same two what chased your pa. They be trying the same trick anyways, trying to catch us on our lee shore. That means run us aground, miss."

Eliza glanced up at the pennant that flickered in the wind from the schooner's huge mainmast. "The wind's not right for us to run to deep water today."

"Aye, miss, that's true. And a passel of trouble it would bring us besides, going that far off course. We're set for the Caribbees, not Glasgow. But I 'spect Cap'n Griffin has other plans." Carter shrugged, unconcerned. "He'll try something we can't even think of, ourselves. I've been with him five years now, an' he's always tryin' new tricks. Cap'n Griffin, that's how he sails, but he'll pull us through safe."

Against his will, Gardner's eyes kept straying back to Eliza. He hated seeing her in the bulky men's clothing that hid her curves, hated her glorious mane braided so primly. He remembered how she looked last night instead, her hair loose and her body nestled against his in her feather bed. . . .

With an oath, he jerked his thoughts back to the two sloops chasing him. Why the devil had she done this to him? He couldn't very well take her back to Providence now, not with the navy after him. From now on, every decision he made on this entire voyage would have to be made with her safety in mind. He frowned as he watched her talking to Carter, and, without thinking, Gardner barked an order that sent Carter scurrying away.

Eliza stood alone near the rail watching the British trap tighten around them. The two sloops were angling closer to them, driving the *Liberty* towards the shallow water and the coast. The first sloop, the larger one, slowly drew ahead, her captain planning to cut off the schooner's last path of escape. Yet Gardner held steady on the same leisurely path and Eliza wanted to scream at him to change course, to tack, to do anything to avoid capture. She glanced back at Gardner, standing with his legs widespread as he intently gauged both the wind and the larger sloop's progress, and Eliza felt the fear, fear for him, tighten within her chest.

Then, suddenly, the *Liberty* came alive. With a handful of orders, Gardner sent the crew scrambling to change course, and Eliza felt the schooner swing around abruptly. Making the most of the speed that Gardner had hidden before, the *Liberty* shot between the two sloops and away from the coast. Now the British were the ones being pushed by the wind and waves towards the rocks. Their gunports on the starboard sides were still lashed shut, the guns behind them unmanned and useless as the *Liberty* glided past. The schooner's men jeered as the British struggled to turn the awkward sloops around into the wind, and Eliza's voice jubilantly joined with the others as the *Liberty* raced on ahead, and the British flags were soon no more than pinpricks in the distance.

It had been dangerous, a high-risk gamble, and yet wonderful because it had worked. Eliza was proud of Gardner and wanted to tell him so. But as he now came across the deck towards her, his face was dark as thunder and she felt her congratulations fading on her lips.

"Come below with me, Eliza," he said curtly, the hand he held out to her anything but chivalrous. "We've a great deal to discuss, you and I."

Eliza pointedly ignored his hand and, with her head high, led the way to the cabin. While he fastened the door behind them, she stood uneasily with her arms folded across her chest. "You shouldn't have risked the schooner that way, showing off with your fancy sailing," she began. "They were firing at us."

"Warning shots, that's all they were."

"You don't know that for certain," she scoffed. "What if they'd called your bluff, anyway? Why didn't you turn back when you had the chance?"

He jerked his hat off and flung it onto the bunk. "You should be damned glad I didn't, lass. Like it or not, I saved you and your precious schooner today."

" 'Saved'!" she repeated scornfully. "What do you know about safety?"

"The only safe place you'll find now is with me, because you're in this all the way up to your pretty neck. Which, this moment, I'd like to throttle."

His eyes were cold, his face taut, and there was a quiet ruthlessness in his manner that startled her. This was the man who had coolly led the *Gaspee* raid, watching with disinterest while the British lieutenant had nearly died, and she found it hard to believe it was the same man who had loved her so tenderly not twelve hours before.

"The English want me, Eliza, and do you know why? Because I dare to dream of this country without their boiled British faces hanging over my shoulder, without their acts and laws and tariffs to rob me, without their idiot German king ruling my life from the other side of the ocean. They've bloodied my back but they couldn't touch my soul, so now they'd like nothing better than hanging me to finish the job."

"The scars on your back—the British did that?"

"Aye, that they did," he answered grimly. "The press-gang took me when I was scarce seventeen, and I spent six years in the hell they call their navy."

His smile was dark and humorless. "I'm one of the Sons of Liberty, Eliza, and damned proud of it. I've friends in Boston who can put their gold behind freedom. Me, I give my seamanship. For them I'm a smuggler, lass, bringing in rifles and gunpowder and bullets against the day we can drive the beggars back across the ocean. I'm not afraid of taking chances, nor killing, if I must, and my luck's held these past four years."

Eliza frowned. "Not all that time. You sailed for Mr. Brown."

"I did both. Your Mr. Brown's as fine a patriot as there is, if a bit puffed up with his own importance, and he didn't want to be left behind his Massachusetts brothers in the cause of liberty. With his blessing, the *Three Brothers* carried more than molasses. I'd be with Brown still if he'd been a better judge of men."

"Josiah," she said softly. "It couldn't be anyone else. And it was you who had Nathaniel freed, wasn't it?"

"Ah, 'twas no matter." Gardner shrugged uncomfortably. "But Buck's as loyal a Tory as German George himself. I told Brown that Buck sold my name to the British over the *Gaspee,* but he didn't believe me. Even after they chased the *Peacock* instead of the *Three Brothers,* he said I had the wrong man.''

"Then Josiah had my father killed," whispered Eliza. Her head was spinning, all the questions now answered, and it sickened her to remember Josiah's solicitude and his desire to help settle her father's estate. "Why didn't you tell me this before?"

"How could I? Buck told me himself you were betrothed."

"Betrothed!" she exclaimed. "I don't love him, and I never did!"

"You didn't tell me that, did you? Not that it matters, not after I've seen those two sloops waiting for us like they had invitations. Which, I'd wager, they did."

"So that's why you agreed to sail for me, is it?" asked Eliza slowly. "You needed to learn if it was the *Three Brothers* the British recognized, or whether it was you they were after. I could have lost everything, just so you could prove Josiah was a spy."

Her voice rose uncontrollably. "You used me, Gardner. So you've outrun the British, and you've found out what you needed about Josiah. Now what? Will you sell my rum, keep the money and fill the *Liberty* with whatever you please? Why, you're probably not even bound for Saint Eustatius!"

"Aye, you're right," he agreed with infuriating calm. "With this wind, we should make Martinique in a fortnight."

"*Martinique!* All the time you were making love to me you were thinking of Martinique!" With a shriek she flew at him, pounding on his chest with her fists, but easily he caught her by the arms and held her fast, his expression unchanging. For another moment she twisted and plunged in his grasp, and then, suddenly, the fight went out of her. She dropped her head to her hands with a sob and let the tears flow. As Gardner gently drew her close, she buried her face in his shirt. It didn't matter what he said. She simply loved him too much to argue.

Gardner stroked her hair to calm her. Perhaps he had gone too far, telling her so much at once, but he knew he had no choice.

"I never planned to cheat you, Eliza, and that's God's own truth. Whatever else I am, I'm not a thief," he said softly. "I promise you'll see a larger profit than you ever dreamed on this voyage, and I'll see that my Boston friends cover any difference. I'll stake my Martinique merchants against your Dutchmen on 'Statia any day."

"And what about your Martinique mistress?" Eliza asked, her voice breaking.

Gardner sighed, wishing he'd been more discreet about Athenais. "Eliza, I can't tell you there haven't been other women in my life before you. But I swear you'll be the last, if you'll let me."

She turned her tearstained face up towards his. "I love you more than I've ever loved anyone, but I can't go through each day wondering how much you have or haven't told me. Don't I have reason enough to hate the British, too? They captured my cousin and held him prisoner. They killed my father and two of his men, and they want to hang you. They'd hang me, too, if they knew I'd been on the *Gaspee* with you. I want you to use the *Liberty* however you and your

Boston men think best. You won't owe me anything. It's time I paid these Tories back myself." She raised her chin higher. "Not to mention Josiah."

Gardner frowned, raking his fingers back through his hair. "I can't let you do it, Eliza. It's too dangerous. You're not like John Brown or the others. You can't afford another loss."

She shook her head. "No, take the schooner. I don't shy away from risks, either. Or else I wouldn't be here now, would I?"

Her face was flushed from the cold and wind, her hair tangled and her boy's clothes were grimy and dishevelled, yet Gardner had never loved her more than he did at that moment. "I've always been my own man, Eliza. Likely that's why I'm still alive. Depending on others—well, that's not my way. But you and I, we're already partners after a fashion, aren't we?"

He smiled to himself. She could have no idea of the changes she'd wrought in him. The image of her beside him, always fighting and loving, was now irresistible. He thought of the money he had saved in Boston, and of the house he dreamed of near the water. Perhaps that house was meant to be a twin-masted schooner, and its mistress a freckle-faced redhead in boy's breeches.

"If you're foolish enough to follow my course, then I'll take on half your risk in return. You have my word on it for now, but in Fort Royal, we'll make it all formal with the lawyers."

"Not the schooner herself," she said slowly. "I know it sounds foolish, but she's my only connection to the *Peacock*."

"The cargo, then. There's no attachment to a hold full o' rum, is there? Contrary to how you judge me, not everything I've earned these last years has gone to barkeeps and strumpets. You won't be accepting the pledge of a pauper."

"It's a great deal of money."

"So it is," he agreed. "More, I'd wager, than you have to your name. I've got eyes and ears, Eliza, and I know full well how close to the edge this schooner's pushed you." Gently he ran his thumb across her lower lip. "Come, sweetheart, I've no mind to quarrel over who's making the bigger sacrifice."

"It's not that, not exactly." She stepped away from him, knowing there'd be no way to think clearly otherwise. There was, after all, so very much at stake. She glanced back at him, and saw, for a brief moment, her own uncertainty mirrored in his weathered features, and it stunned her to realize that he might need her as much as she did him. Not all the risks for either of them were financial. They had come this far together, and she swiftly decided to trust him the rest of the way.

She extended her hand. "I accept," she said, her voice husky. Her fingers were swallowed up in his grasp, and she felt the warmth of his touch surge through her like a current. "Let your handshake be your bond for now, and you'll be half owner in this venture. Maybe that will keep you from more reckless displays like the one earlier."

He laughed. "I'll do whatever's necessary to keep you happy, Eliza, but beyond that I'll swear to nothing." The watch on deck would not change for another hour, and they'd call him anyway if he were needed. Time enough, he decided, to seal their partnership with more than a handshake.

One by one, he unfastened the buttons on her coat, then the waistcoat beneath, until he could slip his hands beneath her shirt to her waist. True to her masculine clothing, he discovered pleasantly that she wore neither stays nor a woman's shift beneath the shirt, and he smiled as his fingers found her soft, warm skin. There were, after all, advantages to her dressing like a boy.

Eliza's heartbeat quickened in anticipation, and she curled her own hands over his shoulders. "Partners," she mused. "Then you're glad I came along?"

"Aye, lass." His breath was warm on her throat, his words little more than a growl that made her shiver. "Because here at least I can be partner to your mischief."

Chapter Seventeen

Three weeks later they rode together in a hired carriage to the Governor's House at Fort Royal. Eliza sat stiffly upright in uncharacteristic silence, her head lifted with grim determination, for all the world, decided Gardner with amusement, like a woman headed to her own execution.

"It won't be all that bad, Eliza, I swear," he said. "The French may eat frogs and snails, but not red-haired ladies from Rhode Island."

Eliza's stern facade crumbled, and self-consciously she fingered the neck of her new gown, wishing now, as she headed towards a roomful of strangers, that it weren't quite so revealing. "I just don't want to shame you by acting foolish, that's all."

"The way you look tonight, sweetheart, you could dance a jig on the tabletops and not shame me a bit." He squeezed her fingers fondly, and she gave him a brief, grateful smile. Nervous or not, thought Gardner proudly, she would still be the most striking woman there tonight.

Wisely Eliza had rejected the dressmaker's suggestions for a lacy ruffle here or an extra flounce there, and her new gown was almost plain by fashionable tastes. But its simple, fitted lines accentuated the grace of her figure and displayed to advantage the swell of her breasts above the low, wide neckline. Cut from silk lutestring of the palest shade of peach, the shimmering color brightened the copper in her hair and the tawny gold of her eyes. Her sunburn had faded to a warm glow, and the only ornament she wore was a cluster of fresh orange blossoms tucked into her hair.

She leaned against his shoulder and sighed. "Tell me again why we're going tonight."

"For trade, mainly. To keep the governor happy to see our faces."

"But my rum—"

"*Our* rum."

"All right, *our* rum has already been sold—"

"And for a better price than even I expected," he drawled lazily. "You had the luck of the market with you, I'll grant you that."

"Stop interrupting me!" Eliza ordered crossly, and Gardner chuckled. Annoyed with him she might be, but she'd forgotten her nervousness. "The *Liberty*'s hold is empty, except for two score kegs of molasses, and tomorrow you're meeting the agent about the— whatever else we're carrying back. So why do we have to go for trade if our trading's all done?"

"Because we're trading more than rum and molasses, sweetheart," he said, lowering his voice so the driver wouldn't hear. "I'll ask you to keep your ears open and your wits about you, too, and remember any scraps of gossip you hear. My friends in Boston are eager for whatever news we can send them."

Eliza nodded, pleased that he included her in his plans. Piecing together stray talk and overheard conversations had been something she'd done for her father for years, only now it would be for a nobler purpose than outwitting the next shipmaster. Perhaps tonight wouldn't be so bad after all.

She twined her fingers into Gardner's, and smiled up at him. He could talk all he wanted about her attracting Frenchmen, but she was convinced it would be the women instead who'd be clamoring for his attention. At her insistence he had bought himself new clothes as well, a suit of royal-blue broadcloth that fit across his broad shoulders and lean hips to perfection, and Eliza doubted that any man in Fort Royal could rival him.

Although it was still light when they arrived at the Governor's House, the lanterns out front were already lit, and through the tall windows of the assembly room glowed a half dozen chandeliers. Two slaves in green velvet coats, their black faces startling below white wigs, ushered them inside and up the longest staircase Eliza had ever seen. There, at the top, stood a short, stout man with a bored expression that brightened as soon as he saw Gardner and Eliza approach.

"Ah, *Monsieur le Capitaine,* you have brought *la belle Américaine* to meet me!" Gallantly he bent over Eliza's hand as she remembered to curtsy. While she dipped low, Gardner introduced her to the governor, and she caught the glitter of diamonds from the medallions on his chest as powder from his hair drifted down onto her fingers. "Enjoy your visit to my little island, *mademoiselle,* but promise me you won't leave too many broken hearts, eh?"

Tongue-tied, Eliza began to curtsy again, but Gardner was already guiding her towards the governor's wife and daughters. Here the introductions were even briefer. The Frenchwomen spoke no English, but they understood readily enough that their dashing Captain Griffin was no longer unattached, and their manner to Eliza was frosty.

"I told you the ladies wouldn't like me," Eliza whispered as they headed towards the assembly room. The elegant room with its crystal chandeliers and gilt chairs filled with beautifully dressed men and women left her feeling plain and provincial, even in her new gown. "Ladies never do."

"The worst is over, sweetheart," said Gardner lightly. "You've weathered the queen dragon with nary a scratch."

He plucked a glass from a passing servant's tray and handed it to Eliza. "Jealousy, lass, that's all it is. Now enjoy yourself, but don't forget that to me you're always the loveliest creature God ever made."

Eliza smiled over the glass and took a sip. It was wine, but sweet, and filled with bubbles that so obviously took her by surprise that Gardner laughed.

"Champagne," he explained. "Not to my taste, but now you can boast to your friend Beckah that you've drunk the finest wine in a marquis' cellar."

A small, dark man with bright eyes appeared beside Gardner and eagerly seized Eliza's free hand.

"Charming, Gardner, charming!" he exclaimed. "I will take to the ocean myself if there are more like you, *mademoiselle,* waiting there to be captured! I am Laurant des Plessis, his excellency's attaché, but you must call me only Laurant, *ma belle.*"

Gardner snorted. "Laurant is full of more claptrap and humbug than any other man in Martinique, Eliza. Though likely you've figured that out yourself." He poked the little man good-naturedly in the ribs.

Laurant sighed dramatically and rested his hand across his breast. "Only a friend such as your Captain Griffin would dare speak so of poor Laurant. But come, you must be Laurant's friend, too, eh, *mademoiselle?* I will show you the beauties, the delights, of my little island, while Gardner tends to his big boat."

"Claptrap and humbug, Eliza. Don't be fooled into thinking otherwise," said Gardner drily. "Laurant knows every 'big boat' in the Caribbean, and every man on them. Now every woman, too, counting you."

Laurant merely shrugged, and Eliza could not help laughing. The little attaché reminded her of the bright-eyed monkeys for sale in the island's markets, and despite his drollery, Eliza agreed with Gardner that he wasn't half the fool he pretended.

"Promise you will come visit me, *mademoiselle,*" he continued winningly. "Honor me with your company!"

Eliza looked to Gardner for guidance, but he was frowning at a scrap of paper while a servant waited for a reply. He stuffed the message into his pocket and turned back to Eliza with a forced smile. "I must leave you for a moment, sweetheart. I'll be back in an instant."

Before she could protest, he was following the servant through the crowd. Eliza watched him uneasily, deaf now to Laurant's continuing chatter. What could take Gardner away? she wondered uneasily. An emergency on the *Liberty*, a private request from the governor?

Then she saw the blond woman gliding towards him, the welcoming smile on her flawless face as they embraced, and how she kissed him passionately, possessively. And from where Eliza stood, Gardner didn't seem to mind at all as the woman led him by both hands through the open door.

The balcony overlooking the harbor ran the length of the Governor's House, and from experience Athenais knew it would offer the most privacy she and Gardner could hope to find tonight. That the moonlight would also be more flattering and seductive was a consideration only slightly less important.

"Once again, *mon cher capitaine,*" chided Athenais as she leaned gracefully against the railing, "you have been avoiding me."

Gardner watched her warily. "We had arranged to meet tomorrow, Athenais. I didn't expect to see you here tonight."

Her laughter trilled out across the palm trees. "True enough, *mon ami!* Your face tells all, *non?* But I would not wait. I would see your *amourette,* but, oh, Gardner I am so disappointed! Her hair, *mon Dieu!* It is a crime! And her complexion is all over brown and spotty. Surely all your Yankee ladies are not so common?"

"More common than your tongue, Athenais? Or is that just growing sharper with the rest of you as the years go by?" From the way she snapped her fan open, he knew he'd struck a tender spot.

"Your interest in this homely child, it cannot be serious?" she persisted. "I am certain from how she gazes at you that you have already seduced her. You gentlemen and your foolish virgins!"

It took all of Gardner's self-control to keep his temper in check. "I haven't come here to discuss Miss Raeburn with you. I thought we had business, you and I. Something you were willing to sell, and I'm willing to buy."

Angrily Athenais swirled away from him with a rustle of petticoats. She had thought she was done with him, cured, after the last time he had turned her down. But to see him again, now so obviously in love with another, infuriated her beyond reason. She had planned to sell him more rifles if he had been willing to return to her, but not now. Now she would burden that lovely new schooner with gunpowder instead, like a floating tinderbox, or send him home empty-handed. He must not expect favors from her again. The decision made it easier to smile sweetly over her fan. "The guns you wished to buy are no longer for sale."

"The devil they're not, Athenais! We had an agreement."

"The last I heard, *mon cher,* you were no longer in this trade, hmm? I could not wait for you to decide.

All that I have at my disposal at present is gunpowder. For rifles, for cannons, a most useful item.''

Unconsciously Gardner looked past her to the *Liberty*, moored in the harbor. A hold full of gunpowder would be welcomed, but it would be the most dangerous cargo he'd ever carried. A stray spark from a pipe, an untrimmed wick in a lantern, and the *Liberty* and everyone in her would be gone in an instant.

"You hesitate, *mon capitaine*," observed Athenais archly. "Perhaps you should ask your *petite amourette*. She seems to have no trouble with her choices." With her fan she motioned through the open window to where Eliza stood, laughing, her arm looped through Laurant's, and with satisfaction Athenais noted how Gardner's whole body tensed with anger. Without another word to Athenais, he returned swiftly to Eliza.

"Come along now, lass, we're leaving," he said with more harshness than he realized. He blamed himself for bringing her here, for succumbing to his own pride and the temptation to show her off. "I'll take you back to the *Liberty*."

Glassy eyed, Eliza swayed on her feet. Not only did champagne taste better than any other wine she'd ever tried, but it seemed to have the amazing ability to make her happy, almost giddy, even though Gardner had vanished with another woman. "Why so early?"

"Because our business here is done." When her legs wobbled, he half carried her from the crowded room and down the long staircase. Outside they waited as a slave called their carriage.

"Now breathe deep," ordered Gardner as he held her upright. "Go on, fill your lungs. Sweet Jesus, but you've a sorry head for spirits, considering you're a rum-runner's daughter."

In the cool evening air the fuzziness began to clear from Eliza's head, and with it too went the numb good humor. "That blond lady," she said uncertainly. "She's the one, isn't she? Your mistress?"

"My relationship with Athenais de Neuville is more complicated than that."

"But you swore to me you were done with her!"

"I've no mind to discuss her with you, any more than I'll talk about you to her." Unintentionally his anger at Athenais spilled over to Eliza. "Especially not now."

To his surprise, her eyes swam with tears. The champagne, he thought with exasperation: wine often made women weepy with no reason. All the more reason to postpone explanations until morning. That would give him the rest of the night to ask questions, to listen and discover as much as he could about Athenais's motives.

The carriage stopped before them, and after Gardner helped Eliza climb inside, he shut the door. "Take Miss Raeburn back to the *Liberty*'s boat," he told the driver. "Tell my men not to wait for me."

Eliza's pale face appeared at the window. "Aren't you coming now, too?"

"Later, Eliza. I'll be back as soon as I can." He nodded curtly to the driver, and the carriage rolled away, the wheels crunching on the crushed stone. Unsteadily Eliza leaned out the window. Her last glimpse of Gardner was of him climbing the tall steps again, returning to the governor's party and to the blonde woman on the balcony.

It was one of the most miserable nights of Eliza's life. The short ride in the boat to the *Liberty* cost her the last of the champagne in her stomach, and even when she was safely back in the cabin, the schooner herself seemed to roll and pitch at anchor more wildly than in any hurricane. Curled up on the bunk, she slipped in and out of queasy, nightmarish dreams that always ended with Gardner and the Frenchwoman in each other's arms. When at last dawn filtered through the stern windows, he still had not returned, but Eliza's head at least was clear. She rose, washed her face and changed her clothes. Although she wasn't sure what to do next, nothing would be gained by self-pity.

The breeze off the water felt good as she joined the few crew members on deck. "Has there been any word yet from Captain Griffin?" she asked Wilson, still in charge.

Sorrowfully Wilson shook his head. Every man aboard knew how their captain had abandoned Miss Raeburn last night, and all agreed it was a sad, shameful business. "But I reckon now that sun's up, he'll be back soon."

"He's done this before? Stayed ashore overnight?"

Wilson squirmed. "Aye, miss, I fear he has. Leastways when we come to Fort Royal."

Eliza's heart couldn't bear to hear any more, and she turned to stare out at the water. There, suddenly, she noticed a difference in the harbor, a change in the scene that had grown familiar this past week. "Wilson, when did that ship join us?"

"Last evening, miss." He handed her the spyglass. "A sixty-four-gun English frigate, miss. Name o' *Hercules,* as far as we can make out. Mighty cheeky o' them English to show their colors here, but what with them an' the Frogs at peace now, I guess they got as much right t'be here as us."

"Is the frigate alone, or part of a squadron?" asked Eliza excitedly. "Has she come fresh from England or the colonies?"

"Ah, Miss Raeburn, how could I know that?"

"Then I'm going to find out. Please have the men meet me in the boat in five minutes." She might have lost Gardner, if she ever had him in the first place, but the schooner was hers, and she'd do what she could to keep it that way.

"But, miss, you can't just go off like that alone!" protested Wilson, scandalized. "You bein' a lady an' all! What if Captain Griffin returns?"

"Then he'll find me gone ashore," she replied, her eyes flashing, "same as he is now."

Eliza had learned from her experience in Boston, and this time she spent five *sous* on a hired pony cart to take her to the office of Laurant des Plessis. The attaché shared quarters with the governor within the walls of the fort, high on the cliff overlooking the mouth of the harbor. Although Eliza wished to see the attaché and not the governor himself, Laurant des Plessis was the last step between visitors and the governor, and she was forced to wait in an antechamber with other petitioners while morning stretched into afternoon. When at last the servant read her name, she almost flew off the bench from impatience.

The attaché's office was spacious and decorated far more lavishly than his position alone could afford. Clearly the man augmented his income with bribes, and Eliza hoped the price he extracted wouldn't be too steep for her dwindling resources.

"Mademoiselle Raeburn, I must confess, I did not expect to meet you again quite so soon!" Laurant exclaimed as he rose from behind the desk. With practiced ease, he kissed the air above Eliza's hand and led her to a cushioned armchair.

But Eliza was too excited to notice his gallantry. "Monsieur des Plessis, Gardner said you knew everything that happens in Fort Royal."

"As I recall, he spoke in less flattering terms. *Mais oui,* I do hear and see much on this little island. And please, I beg of you, call me Laurant."

"Well then, Monsieur—I mean Laurant, I hope you can tell me about the British frigate that arrived last night. If she's part of the Caribbean fleet, or here from the colonies." Eliza inched a little closer to the edge of her chair, wishing she knew how much to confide to the man. "I'm willing to pay for the information."

As Laurant waved his hand through the air, the sunlight danced off the topaz ring on his little finger. "Ah, *mademoiselle,* please, do not insult me! For you, for Captain Griffin, for the man who burned the *Gaspee,* I share my humble knowledge freely!"

Eliza caught her breath. The little Frenchman smiled shrewdly and dropped his frivolous tone.

"*Mais oui*, I know of your friend's past, and of his present, too. I know what brings him to our island, and what he takes away with him from the de Neuville plantation. And I suspect that Gardner is unaware that you are here with me now, *oui?*"

He drew a lace-trimmed handkerchief from his cuff and delicately dabbed at his forehead while Eliza stared at her hands in confusion. "You see, Mademoiselle Raeburn, that there truly are few things that I do not know," he continued kindly. "But while your brave captain is a hero among my countrymen, and quite safe with us, you are wise to fear the newcomers in the harbor. The *Hercules* comes from Boston, and Captain Peters has already presented his compliments to the governor with letters from Admiral Graves. That is not good news for you, *non, non!* While Captain Peters does not yet associate Gardner with your schooner, he would find our friend a fine prize to claim, eh? Gardner must sail this day, before he is noticed."

Eliza tried to smile. "I shall always remember your kindness, Laurant, and I—"

But the Frenchman's attention had shifted to a rising clamor from the antechamber, a heated torrent of voices in French and English. Then suddenly the door flew open with a crash, and in several swift strides Gardner was in the room with two frightened servants at his heels.

"Where the devil have you been, Eliza?" he demanded. Finding her here, safe, the sense of relief he felt was almost immediately overwhelmed by anger.

But his anger was matched by Eliza's own temper. "Where have *I* been? I could well ask you the same question!"

"Why can't you follow the simplest orders! For your own good, I told you to wait for me, but then I find you've gone God knows where, without a word or by-your-leave to anyone. You keep behaving like a disobedient child and I've a mind to punish you like one, to turn you over my knee and paddle some sense into you!"

"Oh, I'd like to see you try it!" declared Eliza, defiantly circling the armchair between them.

"Don't tempt me." She would try the patience of a saint. "You push me, and you'll find yourself with a whole pack of trouble you didn't bargain for."

Forgotten, Laurant had gathered his hat and gloves and a sheaf of papers and retreated to the safety of the doorway. *"Au revoir, mes enfants!"* he called cheerfully. "Since my supper calls, I surrender the battlefield to you with pleasure."

Yet before the door had closed, Eliza had begun again. "At least one of us has the sense to look after my schooner's welfare instead of running off like a stray mongrel after some bitch in heat!"

"A pretty turn of phrase, that." He should have guessed that it would all be Athenais's fault.

"She kissed you like she'd done it a thousand times before. Not that you seemed to mind."

If he didn't know how much Eliza valued her pride, he might have swept her into his arms at once. How far from the truth her guessing had led her! "Kissing or no, that lady is also the agent we came to this island to meet."

Eliza sniffed incredulously and folded her arms across her chest.

"Sweet Jesus, Eliza, why d'you think I hauled you out of there so smartly last night?"

"Because that woman asked you to," she answered promptly. "Because you wanted to be with her instead of me."

He shook his head and swore under his breath. With his hands on the back of the chair between them, he leaned across it towards her until their faces were only inches apart. "That's a neat enough tale, Eliza, excepting one thing. I don't love her, and I do love you. Or have you forgotten that already?"

Eliza ducked her chin to avoid the powerful pull of his gaze and dug her front teeth into her lower lip. She wished he would not stand so close, but she refused to retreat even one step back.

"Athenais can be a bitter, spiteful woman, Eliza. I've traded with her for years, and aye, I've shared her bed, too, but I don't trust her, and never have. She's got some mischief in her mind now, and you're the reason. I sent you back to the *Liberty* where I knew you'd be safe until I could ask some questions around the town and sort out her double-dealing for myself."

Troubled, Eliza raised her eyes to meet his. "Damn you, Gardner," she said softly. "I want so much to believe you!"

"Then marry me, Eliza," he whispered. "Today, here. Marry me."

Chapter Eighteen

Stunned, Eliza stood very still, scarcely daring to breathe. She was certain she loved Gardner, loved him with all her heart and being. But he had made it clear enough from the beginning that he was too rootless to want any permanent ties, and to protect herself she had refused to hope he might change. She had instead found happiness in spinning out each day and night with him as if no others would follow. But here he was offering her more, much more, and the promise of a future together with him seemed almost unreal.

Uneasily Gardner waited. Why the devil was she silent? Surely she would not refuse, not after all they'd shared together. Didn't she understand how much he loved her? Savagely he shoved the chair to one side. He took the last step that separated him from Eliza, and his hands enveloped her slender shoulders.

"God knows I'm no bargain, Eliza, and I've little enough to offer you besides my own sorry self." He swallowed hard. The fragrance that rose from her hair and skin in the warm room could drive him mad. "But

I swear I love you more than any mortal man should, and I will, so help me, for the rest of my days.''

Slowly she raised her face to him. Now he saw the joy that lit her eyes, and as the first tremulous beginnings of a smile flickered across her lips, he knew her answer, even before the word itself was lost in their kiss.

They were married that afternoon by the one protestant minister on the island. Eliza wore the same gown she'd chosen hastily that morning, a pale yellow lawn with a leaf-green sash, and her bouquet was plucked from the minister's rosebushes. Whenever, as a girl, Eliza had dreamed about the wedding she'd have, she never imagined herself in a stranger's garden amid wild orchids on Martinique, with an elderly servant for a witness and a cageful of pet macaws as the only guests. Yet as she stood beside Gardner, she felt as happy, and nervous, as any bride. He was, she thought with wonder, so strong and beautiful and solemn, and she loved him so very much.

A hundred thoughts crowded into Gardner's head as he took Eliza's hand. The sun caught her hair like a halo, and he thought he'd never seen a lovelier sight. But she was more than just a beautiful woman; she was a friend who could make him laugh one moment and be thoughtful the next. She shared both his passions and his dreams in a way that no one else ever had. She was the best thing that fortune had ever cast in his path, and he still couldn't believe that she would be his wife.

As the serious words of the service rolled over her head, Eliza stole a glance up at Gardner. To her simultaneous horror and delight, he winked, and it was all she could do to keep from giggling. No, it certainly wasn't the wedding she'd always dreamed of. But she wouldn't change one thing about it.

With the new husband's arm comfortably around his bride's waist, Eliza and Gardner walked slowly back towards the waterfront. Near the wharves, a small mulatto boy called Gardner's name, and Eliza waited as he bent down to take the slim package the boy brought from Laurant. It was from the corner of her eye that Eliza spotted the bright red patch of uniforms in the crowded street. Reflexively she turned and caught her breath. The British lieutenant was still young enough to have pimples on his upturned nose, but his expression was grim as he drew closer, and the marines with him were armed, the late afternoon sun glittering off the steel of their bayonets. Gardner was still crouched down, talking in French with the boy. What was it he had said in Newport?—"Sometimes the best place to hide was in plain sight." With great effort, she forced herself to be calm and smile as warmly as she could at the officer.

"Good day, Captain," she said, praying he'd be flattered by even that obvious foolishness. She tried to mimic the silly way ladies pretended ignorance to make men feel important. "That must be your big ship out there. My, how much safer I feel already, knowing there are good, true Englishmen in the harbor!"

The brilliance of her smile almost blinded the young man. She had to be the prettiest girl he'd ever spoken to, or at least tried to speak to, for his mouth had gone so dry that the words seemed stuck inside. "Thank you, miss, but no, miss, I'm not the captain of the *Hercules*. Lieutenant Andrew Fothergill, at your service, miss."

Gardner stood silently behind Eliza, his posture deceptively relaxed. What in blazes had attracted this meddling officer's attention? The boy, that's what it had to be; the boy had used his name. To himself, Gardner cursed their luck. Five minutes more, and he and Eliza would have been safely in the boat on their way back to the *Liberty*. So far she was handling this pup of an officer well enough, but he could hear the tremor in her voice, and he wondered how long she would be able to continue without blundering. "Good day to you, Lieutenant," he said with more heartiness than he felt.

Fothergill's disappointment was keen. Of course a girl like this would have a husband. They always did. "I didn't catch your name, sir."

"Chandler, Griffin Chandler," Gardner replied, and he was pleased to see the younger man's discomfiture. "We're visiting here at Fort Royal as the guests of Monsieur des Plessis. You've known Laurant since you were a girl, haven't you, Mariah?"

He rested his hand on Eliza's waist with affectionate possessiveness, but also to prompt her to respond to the unfamiliar name. But Eliza needed no prompting. Now that she was getting accustomed to this sort of playacting, she was actually beginning to enjoy herself. "Laurant, and of course the dear governor, have been most kind to us, haven't they?" she said brightly. "Perhaps, Lieutenant, while you are here, I could ask him to invite you and your friends to the Governor's House as well."

"Ah—thank you, ma'am." The chances that Mr. and Mrs. Chandler were the Yankee traitors he'd heard so much about in Boston seemed increasingly slim. The governor of the island would not be entertaining them if they were, nor could Fothergill honestly imagine the well-bred Mariah Chandler as some wild creature dressed in men's clothing. He could hear the men behind him growing restless, no doubt wondering why he was wasting so much time with these civilians. Another question or two to satisfy his conscience, and that should be enough.

"You've never been to the northern colonies, ma'am, to New England?"

Eliza felt Gardner's fingers tighten at her waist. "Why ever should I want to? I've always hoped to visit London and the continent of course, but New England? Snow and ice and savages!"

"Now why would his majesty's officers be so curious about my wife's whereabouts?" demanded Gardner, and his sharpness was only half-acting. It was he they wanted most for treason, not Eliza, and this pimple-faced jackanapes had no grounds for badgering her.

Fothergill's face grew warm. He'd stood unflinching in cannon fire, but his experience with irate husbands, particularly such large ones, was nonexistent. "Oh, sir, you'll think me a very fool," he said sheepishly. "Last summer one of his majesty's vessels was destroyed in New England waters by a group of rebels. The leader was a man named Griffin, Captain

Griffin, and with him he had his—had a woman. Scuttlebutt says she had red hair. Your Christian name, sir, and your wife's hair—it was a hasty conclusion, I know, but one must be careful."

The halting explanation struck Gardner like a blow. So after all he had done to keep Eliza safe, it was, ironically, together that they were in the most danger. Thank God this boy was so green!

"Not that your wife in any other way resembles that woman, or you yourself a pirate," Fothergill stumbled on miserably. Gardner's expression had become so ominously cold that the poor lieutenant was convinced he'd find himself standing on some lonely Martinique bluff at dawn tomorrow with a dueling pistol in his hand. "You have my word that I intended no slander—"

"Now what you intended, sir, wasn't what I heard. Tell your captain I'll be calling on him tomorrow. Come along, Mariah."

As Gardner took Eliza by the arm, the crestfallen lieutenant meekly stepped to one side, and they were free to sweep grandly past. Grandly, at least, until they turned the corner past a warehouse and were out of sight. Then they unceremoniously ran to the safety of the waiting boat.

In less than two hours, the *Liberty* was swiftly cutting among the other vessels in the harbor on her way to open water. Although they were able to steer far from the *Hercules*, Eliza had changed back into her boy's clothes for good measure and tied her hair back under a scarf. If Gardner could have devised a way, the schooner's figurehead, too, would have hidden her carved red curls.

"It must have been Josiah," said Eliza glumly as they passed beneath the fort's silent cannons. "When I told him I wouldn't marry him, he must have sold my name like he did yours."

But Gardner, at the wheel beside her, shook his head. "No, sweetheart, this time I don't think he's to blame. Too many pieces don't fit. They don't know your name, only that you've got red hair and aren't a lady. Buck would have given them more. And besides, you've always sworn to me that he didn't know."

"Well, I never told him. But how else would the whole fleet in Boston know!"

"Lieutenant Dudingston. The *Gaspee*'s master. He saw you with me in his cabin, and that was likely enough to start the tongues wagging."

"Faith, who would've guessed," she muttered, disgusted at her own bad luck. "I never meant to bring you so much trouble."

"Nor I you, Mrs. Griffin, or Chandler, or whoever you are." His smile was more of a grimace. "This is hardly the wedding day you deserve, lass."

Eliza touched the slender band of beaded gold, still shining and unscratched on her left hand. She liked the sound of that "Mrs. Griffin," and smiled shyly. "Just don't tell Mariah what I've done. She'd swoon dead away."

In spite of himself he laughed. "Oh, aye, I think that secret's safe enough from her." The schooner was clearing the harbor and before them lay the deepening blue of the Caribbean. "So what's our course now, lass? We've an empty hold to fill, and pockets lined with French gold. Do you still favor 'Statia?"

"What about the guns we came for in the first place?" Eliza asked, surprised. "Aren't we going to meet your Athe—Athe—"

"Athenais. No. I didn't like her terms. We'll have to be honest traders instead for once."

"Tell me her terms, Gardner. We're partners, remember, and it's my decision, too."

"Then tell me if you're willing to see the *Liberty* and you and me and every other man blown skyward to the Almighty," he said, exasperated by her insistence. "Athenais won't sell me any more of the rifles, leastways as long as I'm with you. All she's offering now is gunpowder."

Eliza stood with her hands on her hips, considering. "Then gunpowder's what we'll have to take. The stuff's no more dangerous than a hold filled with rum. Both will go off like a firecracker if you're not watchful. And I'm sure you'll be very, very careful."

She was daring him to do it, and Gardner didn't like that. But before she could change her mind, he called out the order that would send them up the island's western coast. Angrily he pulled the wheel to the starboard. "It's your decision, isn't it? Your schooner, your money, your life."

Eliza looked away, refusing to accept the challenge in his words, and touched her new ring again for reassurance. As far as she was concerned, she'd chosen her own fate when she'd married him that afternoon, and not even sixty tons of gunpowder could change it.

Shortly after sunset, the *Liberty* reached the cove that curved into the de Neuville plantation. In the pale moonlight the plantation's main house had an unreal, fairy-tale quality. Twin balconies trimmed with lacy iron railings ran the length of the facade and flowering vines curled up the supporting columns, and the long drive that led to the beach was flanked by formal rows of orange and palmetto trees. Eliza had no difficulty imagining the elegant woman in green at home here; she wished, though, it wasn't quite so easy to picture Gardner here with her, too.

"Are you sure she'll see you this late?" asked Eliza doubtfully as the *Liberty*'s boat was lowered. "The house looks dark. Perhaps she's gone to sleep."

"*She* is still in Fort Royal. *She* is seldom asleep at this hour. Abed, aye, but not asleep," said Gardner pointedly. "I'll deal with the overseer instead. Anyways, I don't think Athenais wants much to do with me right now, even if we were expected."

Unconvinced, Eliza scowled at her feet.

"Don't you trust me, lass?" asked Gardner drily.

The wistful look she turned his way made him instantly regret his ill humor. "It's not you. It's her. Why would she give you up without a fight if she loves you?"

"I don't think Athenais has ever loved anyone except herself, Eliza. I don't think it's in her heart."

"Ah, well, you just don't know how easy you are to love." She looked back down at her feet. "I wish you'd let me come, too."

"I would, Eliza, if there were something for you to do, but this time I need to give your place in the boat to someone with a strong back."

"You took me on the *Gaspee*."

"Aye, and a peck of trouble that's brought to the both of us, hasn't it?" He circled his arm around Eliza's waist and pulled her close. She felt the pistol's butt beneath his coat as they embraced, and prayed he wouldn't need to use it.

"I haven't forgotten you're my bride, love," he whispered, his breath suggestively warm below her ear. "Though tonight may be lost, we've a whole lifetime ahead of us to make up the difference."

He kissed her quickly and hurried over the side with the others. Eliza sighed and hugged her arms around herself.

"He'll do just fine, miss," said Wilson as he joined her by the rail to watch the boat push off. "Capt'n Griffin, he's done this more often'n most landsmen shave. He'll be back in no time, you'll see, miss—or I guess it's Mrs. Griffin, now, ain't it? The capt'n, he couldn't've picked a fairer maid in all Providence."

"Thank you, Wilson," Eliza answered shyly, glad that in the dusky light the man couldn't see her blush. Through some mysterious male way, every man on board had immediately heard of their marriage, and though Wilson was the first to congratulate her, she'd overheard several decidedly bawdy if well-intentioned remarks directed to Gardner.

"You'd best go below and catch some rest while you can, miss," he said with gruff kindness. "When they come back, we'll all be set to work like African slaves.

Capt'n Griffin, he'll jus' forget what sleep is until the task is done."

Eliza shook her head, her eyes focused on the dark shadow of the boat as it skimmed across the water towards the beach. "I'll wait here. I wouldn't sleep, anyway."

But by noon the next day, Eliza wished she'd rested when she'd had the chance. It was, as Wilson promised, back-breaking labor. Because the plantation had no wharf, the heavy barrels had to be loaded into the boat, rowed out to the schooner and carefully hoisted one by one into the hold. Eliza's job was to supervise the three seamen stowing the barrels below. She stenciled each barrel with the Raeburn mark and labeled them falsely as molasses. Because she was nimble, she was the one who clambered over the stacked, curved sides to check for any cracked staves or a trickle of loose powder, and to make sure each was securely in place. Finally, on the outside of each row went a barrel that was actually filled with molasses, in case they were boarded by a particularly zealous customs inspector. Not that Eliza expected that to happen, given the *Liberty*'s speed and Gardner's skill, but it was best to be prepared.

After fifteen hours of work, they were all exhausted, from Eliza on down to the cabin boy. Only Gardner, seemingly everywhere at once and doing the work of two wherever he was, appeared unaffected by the heat and strain. The hold where Eliza worked was airless and close, and as the day grew warmer, her clothes became plastered to her back and arms, and she envied the men who labored barefoot and shirtless. When, by late afternoon, Gardner came below to tell her the last barrels were coming on board, she was almost too weary to care.

Gardner's heart went out to her at once. She was coated with dirt and sweat, her hair damp and tangled and her clothes streaked with the red marking paint. The grime on her flushed cheeks couldn't conceal the dark circles of exhaustion that ringed her eyes. Yet although she had worked as hard as any of the men, she had not complained once. Gently he pried the paintbrush from her fingers. "Go on to the cabin, lass. I'll finish for you here."

He took her by the shoulders, using the firm strength of his hands to find and knead the soreness in her muscles. With a little moan, Eliza arched her head back and twisted beneath his touch. Gardner's pulse quickened. If it wasn't for the three grinning sailors pretending not to watch, Gardner would have made love to her there among the barrels in the murky twilight of the hold. Instead he merely kissed her on the forehead and steered her towards the narrow gangway. "Off with you now, Mrs. Griffin. I'll join you as soon as I can."

Eliza pressed her fingertips against his lips. "Don't keep me waiting," she whispered, her voice thick with longing. The way he'd touched just her shoulders made her forget her weariness.

In the cabin she quickly shed her filthy clothes. The small washtub that Gardner had ordered filled for her was almost an unspeakable luxury. Over and over she ladled the cool, clean water over her hair and body, and scrubbed away every trace of the grime and paint with French-milled soap she'd bought in Fort Royal. The fragrance of lilies and roses mingled with the salty tang of the sea through the open stern window. Instead of dressing again, Eliza pulled on one of Gardner's shirts and stretched out in the center of the bunk.

The sun had set with a burst of tropical exuberance, and the moon was rising in its place, silvery streaks reflected on the water. As the tide changed, the *Liberty* had gradually swung round in her moorings, and now she was tugging impatiently against her cable as she felt the pull of the open sea. Overhead Eliza heard one of the crew begin singing a ballad of thwarted love, his voice ringing sweet and true across the quiet cove, and before the song's heroine had reached her inevitable fate, Eliza had reached hers and was fast asleep.

"Gardner?"

Eliza shifted drowsily on the coverlet, her consciousness still caught halfway in her dreams. Her body, however, was wide-awake and tingling with pleasurable sensations. Her shirt was gone and the cool breeze tickled across her bare skin, while another tickle, this one warm and more tantalizing, played across her belly. "Gardner, love, is that you?"

"Now that's a fine question to ask a new husband." Gardner's hands spread around the curve between her waist and hips, steadying her as they explored the satiny smoothness of her skin. With his lips he feathered a little trail of butterfly-light kisses along her body and she shivered with delight. "Who else might you be expecting in your bed this night?"

"Only the man who taught me this." She pulled his head up towards hers, cradling his face in her hands. Her mouth met his halfway, tasting, teasing, first with her lips and then her tongue, until, impatiently, his mouth crushed down on her soft, yielding lips. Even as their tongues circled each other, he could feel, more than hear, the vibration of the laugh in her throat that his kiss had smothered. She looped her arms fondly around his neck.

"You've been swimming," she said enviously. His hair was still wet and as sleek as a seal's.

"Aye, and what of it? I thought you'd thank me for taking the trouble to wash."

"Hmm, you know I like the way you smell, and taste, and feel." His skin was cool and salty, like the water he'd just left. "This way you're like a—like a—what would you call a mermaid that's a man?"

"Sweet Jesus, not another question!" Sweeping back her hair, he found the sensitive place below her ear and nuzzled it. "I have no idea, excepting that a mermaid only lives in the tales of tosspots, while I, sweetheart, am very much flesh and blood."

He knelt between her legs as his hands continued to travel across her hips, her belly, her thighs, caressing and kneading. Eliza abandoned herself to the pleasure he was giving her, scarcely aware of the little moans of delight that escaped from her throat. She wondered how he always knew exactly what her body craved and how to satisfy the craving.

He eased his full length onto her, relishing the feel of her breasts pressing into his chest, her hips against his. He held her arms over her head, and beginning with her wrists, he slowly traced the lines of her veins to her heart. With his lips he found first one nipple, then the other as she sucked in her breath. In response she curled one leg up over his flanks, languorously pressing her calf against his buttocks, and he felt himself drawn closer against the depths of her heat. He was hard and throbbing from wanting her, and he entered her with a single thrust that made her gasp.

"Put your legs around me, lass," he ordered hoarsely, and Eliza obeyed without thinking, wrapping them high around his waist. Magically she matched his rhythm and his need, and he groaned her name. He could not imagine a woman more perfect for him, this woman who was now miraculously his wife.

Effortlessly he rolled onto his back and took Eliza with him, and he was now so deep within her he could go no further. His fingers dug into her hips as she worked against him, rocking back and forth as their urgency increased.

"Oh, Gardner, oh, please!" Eliza murmured raggedly.

He grinned up at her wickedly. "Please stop, or please don't?"

She smiled but couldn't answer. Her hair fell around them like a red-gold curtain as she bent forward to kiss him, and her taut nipples grazed his chest provocatively. He caught her breasts, and she felt the deliciously unbearable tension growing as his hands stroked lower to where their bodies joined. She plunged wildly against him, his name a tattered cry of passion torn from her throat. He couldn't take his eyes from her, the way her head arched back and her breasts thrust forward, the way her hair tumbled like wildfire across her shoulders. Then his own release came powerfully, and she welcomed him, both wishing it would never end.

Long afterwards Eliza still lay across Gardner's body, spent and contented as she listened to his now-quiet heartbeat beneath her cheek.

"I love you so very much," she said softly, "and I think I always have. Do you know that each night when you were away with the *Three Brothers,* I would look for the North Star before I went to bed. Because I knew the same star was guiding you wherever you were, I didn't miss you quite as much."

His arms tightened around her as he kissed her temple. "You're my guiding star now, Eliza. I've no need of another, for I'll never let you go."

Chapter Nineteen

Eliza lay in the bunk with the sheets wrapped high, watching Gardner, bare chested, shave by the half-light of a single candle lantern in the dusk before sunrise. Watching him perform such a distinctly male ritual was something she usually enjoyed, for she liked the cozy intimacy of it. But this morning she felt impossibly tired and her head ached too much to focus on the lantern light. The past few days, and nights, too, must have finally caught up with her, and all she could think of was pulling the coverlet higher, closing her eyes and sinking blissfully back to sleep.

"You're quiet this morning, love," said Gardner as he dried his face. "Don't tell me I wore my little bride out last night?"

He was practically swaggering with pride, and if Eliza had had more energy, she would have deflated him at once with a well-aimed pillow. "I'll remember to remind you of that the next time you're so enthusiastic," he continued. "But Jemmy should be here any minute with breakfast. That should help."

"I don't want any, not right now." Just the thought of food made her suddenly nauseous. "I only want to go back to sleep."

"Then do whatever you please, sweetheart," he replied with more tenderness. "Lord knows you've earned it these last days."

He finished dressing and came to stand beside her. She did look tired, he thought with concern, her face uncharacteristically pale against her hair. Gently he tucked the covers around her bare shoulders and kissed her.

Eliza managed to smile just as her eyes closed from weariness. By the time she opened them again, the cabin was filled with sunlight and the schooner had left Martinique far behind. But Eliza's headache had only worsened, the pain sharpening like an iron band around her forehead. With an effort she forced herself to rise and dress. She threw open the stern windows as widely as she could and let the cool air play across her face. That was better; all she needed now was something to distract herself.

On Gardner's desk she found the canvas packet from Laurant. Inside was a letter filled with information gleaned from the *Hercules* captain, news about British shipping for Gardner to pass on to his Boston contacts. As Eliza scanned the contents, she realized that this single sheet of paper was every bit as dangerous as the gunpowder in the hold, and after carefully refolding it, she hid it for now in the bottom of her trunk for safekeeping. There was another letter, too, addressed, surprisingly, to Eliza herself. The brief note from Laurant beneath her name— "For you, *ma chère,* by the *Hercules, au revoir,* L." —only confused her more. Who would write to her by way of a British frigate? She had only to reach the end of the first sentence to realize it was from Josiah.

> My Dearest Eliza: If this finds you at all, it will remind you of he you have left Shamed by your impetuous Actions. If you return now, I promise to forgive you, and Preserve you from the gallows. But if you persist in this Dishonorable Alliance with Griffin, I swear to God I will see you both hunted down and hung as Traitors to your King.
>
> Yr. Devoted Srvt. —Jos. Buck

Eliza knew Josiah would act upon his threat, and fear settled over her, not for herself but for Gardner. She had to show this letter to Gardner now, before they were any closer to New England.

Replacing the sheet of paper in the packet, she climbed down from the stool. Her legs trembled beneath her and she clung to the desk to steady herself. It was exhaustion that made her so weak, she told herself firmly, that and the blasted headache. Slowly she inched her way from the cabin and up the narrow steps of the companionway to the deck.

Gardner was startled by the way Eliza was dressed. The thin muslin was far too light for the blustery day, and her feet were bare. Then he saw how she staggered across the deck. He rushed towards her as she pitched forward and caught her in his arms just before she fell. Her lips soundlessly formed his name, then her eyes closed and she went limp. He brushed her hair back from her forehead and his fingers were filmed with moisture. She felt warm, too warm, and her skin was not just pale, but more parchment colored. Gardner's heart grew chill as the wind. He knew, even before Wilson joined him and put his dread into words.

The man touched Eliza's cheek and drew back sharply. "It's the fever, ain't it, Cap'n," he said fearfully. "Yellow fever. God help us all!"

Gardner carried Eliza below, undressed her and put her back in the bunk himself. No one else must come near her now from fear of spreading the infection throughout the crew, and the men who had worked with her yesterday would have to be carefully watched for any symptoms, as well. He dipped a cloth into the bucket of cool seawater he'd had brought to the cabin, and gently drew it across Eliza's brow. She sighed and turned away into the pillow. In this early stage, she seemed to be more asleep than ill, but he knew from hard experience how deceptive this fever could be.

Long ago, one of the first navy ships on which he'd served had been anchored off Nevis when first one man had been stricken like Eliza, then another, and another. Gardner himself had suffered from only the headaches and a passing fever, but he was one of the fortunate few; out of a ship's company of two hundred, only sixty men survived. Although he himself was now immune, yellow fever on the *Liberty* could leave him without a crew. What the fever would do to Eliza he refused to consider.

By dusk the next day the fever had tightened its hold on Eliza. Drifting in and out of wakeful sleep, she was repeatedly sick to her stomach as the heat rose in her blood. She whimpered from the blinding pain of the headaches and cried out each time Gardner changed the cloth on her forehead. In the morning she seemed limp and spent, and her eyes, when they opened, were red rimmed and confused.

"The letter," she whispered weakly through cracked lips. "Read Josiah's letter. If I die—"

"You're not going to die!" he said fiercely. That she was ill, very ill, he could accept, but losing her forever was unthinkable. "I won't let you, understand?"

"We've had so little time together, haven't we?" The pressure of her fingers was barely perceptible. "If I die—"

"Damn it, no, Eliza!" he cried, but she had once again drifted off beyond his reach. Asleep, he hoped, though he couldn't be certain. Her breathing was shallow but constant. Perhaps her bout would be like his had been, and tomorrow she'd begin to improve. He stared down at her face, her cheeks a jaundiced yellow, and tried to swallow the pain that nearly choked him.

"If I die..." If she died, he would be lost. After sharing her love, there was no way under heaven he could return to the bleak loneliness that had been his only other companion. If the power of love and the strength of his will meant anything in this world, she would not, *must not,* die.

Reluctantly he rose from her bedside. She was quiet now, and there was nothing more he could do for her. He needed air, the familiar solace of the sky and stars.

He only half heard Wilson's report on the schooner's course and bearings, but Eliza's name on the older man's lips caught his ear. "Mrs. Griffin, I mean, sir. How's she farin'?"

"Too soon to say for sure. The next twelve hours will tell. Any fever among the men?"

"No, sir, nary a touch, though they're all afeared and looking for signs. Though it's queer, ain't it, how Miss Eliza's the only one took," mused Wilson with unusual familiarity. "Almost like she's been singled out, somehow. Most all them Raeburns died young, and none of 'em in their own beds. Ain't lucky that way."

Bleakly Gardner stared out over the dark sea. He heard the *shush* of the waves, the wind singing through the rigging and the joshing laughter of two men on watch. All the sounds of a contented, well-run ship, yet tonight he found no comfort in it. Abruptly he left Wilson and returned to the cabin.

He drew back the coverlet and bathed Eliza again, drawing the wet cloth across the familiar curves of her breasts and belly, down the length of her arms and legs. She was already growing wasted from the fever, the outline of her ribs now sharp beneath the skin. Gently he rested his palm on her forehead and swore under his breath. She was warmer, no mistake, and rapidly he bathed her again. This time, she did not lie still, but moaned and twisted away.

"Take me with you, Papa," she cried, wild-eyed. "It's me, Eliza, your Miss Monkey! Oh, please, Papa, don't leave me behind!"

"You're mine, Eliza, y'hear?" he argued fiercely without caring that she couldn't understand. "You're mine, and so help me, I won't let you go!"

With unexpected strength she tried to break free, writhing and kicking. Rapidly Gardner ladled the seawater onto her, ignoring the soaked sheets and puddles. He had to break her fever, now, or she would die. He had no concept of time or how long he fought for her life, but it was daylight again when her struggles finally faded.

"Too cold," she murmured. "I'm so cold."

Yet her skin remained as hot as coals, and this new stillness was more terrifyingly final than the delirium. He had fought for her, and he had lost. Numbly he lay down on the bunk and curled himself around her for the last time. He would hold her in his arms until the final spark of life had slipped away. So little time together, she'd said. So little time left.

Eliza woke to the comfortable rhythm of Gardner's breathing behind her ear. That he should be there beside her seemed right, but little else did. Why was he dressed, for one thing, all the way down to his boots? And why were they here abed in broad daylight, when there were likely a million things to be done on deck? The mattress was soaked, and so were the sheets and quilt. She tried to lift his arm from across her body, but she felt weak as a kitten.

"Gardner?" Her mouth was dry as sand. "Gardner, wake up."

He jerked awake in an instant and leaned over her. She was shocked by how haggard he looked, and the beard on his jaw meant he hadn't bothered shaving for days.

"Sweet Jesus, Eliza," he said with awe. "You're alive."

And there above her was the strangest sight of all: the tears that glittered in Gardner's eyes.

The fog was thick from Point Judith onward, but even so, through the window, Eliza recognized every landfall and rocky outcrop from its ghostly outline alone. Even the fog itself seemed familiar, and she knew, at last, she was almost home. She buttoned the worn boy's coat over her woolen gown and layered a shawl over that. Since the fever, she felt any chill more keenly, and late March on Narragansett Bay was still more winter than spring. But today she was determined to go on deck, where she belonged, beside Gardner. She paused for a moment before the mirror and wrinkled her nose. Although excitement had put some color back into her cheeks, she still looked sallow and far too thin.

Gardner couldn't help but smile. Eliza had less vanity than most women, but even so she still believed the worst part of yellow fever was how it had temporarily affected her complexion.

"Happy to be almost home, aren't you?" he asked, and Eliza smiled back. Odd how in these past ten weeks, home for him had come to mean this little cabin, and her in it. He opened his hand to show the ring in his palm. "You lost this when you were sick."

Eliza sighed with obvious relief. "So you had it all along. I swore I'd never take it off, and then to go and lose it so soon..."

She held out her left hand expectantly, but to her surprise he made no move to return the ring to her finger, and instead she finally took it back herself. But as she began to slip the gold band over her knuckle, Gardner reached out quickly to stop her.

"You don't have to do that, Eliza. God knows I won't blame you if you've changed your mind."

Eliza stared at him, stunned. "Nothing will ever change the way I love you."

"Damn it, Eliza, I love you more today than when we wed. But things are different now, aren't they?" He raked his hand back through his hair in frustration. "There's half the world out to see you hung beside me."

He had meant not to touch her again, but somehow his hands were cradling her face, turning it up towards his. "You must believe me, Eliza. I'd do anything to keep you safe, anything at all. Even if it means giving you up."

"But you don't have to!" cried Eliza as she caught his hands in hers. How many times would she have to say this before he accepted it? "Why can't you understand—"

He broke free and frowned, and Eliza realized he was listening not to her but to something overhead. Then she heard it, too: the excited hail from the lookout. Gardner was already halfway down the companionway, and as she ran after him, she slid the ring back onto her finger.

The men on deck were oddly quiet, all staring in the same direction. There was another ship out there in the fog, her identity still hidden but her bell and the creaking of her spars and lines clear enough. Gardner had already silenced the *Liberty*'s bell, gambling that they might slip by the other vessel unseen. If that other captain had reason to hide in the fog, then so did he. Beside him, Eliza twisted her hands in her shawl against the cold and fear.

Suddenly the fog seemed to tear apart like a curtain, and there, not a hundred yards away, was a British frigate with ten open gunports and ten guns trained on the *Liberty*. No one moved, but Wilson let out a long, low whistle under his breath.

"We don't have space to run, do we?" asked Eliza softly.

The tightening of Gardner's jaw was the only outward sign of concern as he allowed himself. "Not with a hold full of gunpowder, we don't. We'd best let 'em come aboard and try to bluff it out."

"That's not likely this time. I guess Josiah wasn't bluffing, either."

"Aye, but I didn't expect a twenty-gun frigate."

Eliza heard the little note of desperation in his tone. She herself felt surprisingly calm, or maybe it was only resignation as she linked her hand with his. "They must want us very badly."

The frigate's lieutenant led the party of marines that boarded the *Liberty,* and when his head cleared the side, with a shock Eliza recognized him as the *Gas-*

pee's commander Dudingston, his mouth curled with unconcealed triumph and hatred.

"You are the master of this vessel?" he demanded bluntly of Gardner, and Eliza noticed the intentional absence of "sir."

Gardner dropped Eliza's hand, and his own curled into fists at his side as he nodded curtly.

"And is your name Gardner Griffin, of Boston, in the colony of Massachusetts Bay?"

Again Gardner merely nodded.

"Then I hereby arrest you in the name of the King on charges of piracy, grievous assault and attempted murder of a royal officer, treason, smuggling and desertion." Two burly marines stepped forward and seized Gardner. At once the larger one struck Gardner across the mouth with his fist, and Eliza gasped as her husband's head snapped back from the blow.

"You have no right to treat any colonist like this, you who fancy yourself a British gentleman!" she cried as she pushed her way forward. "You're behaving no better than a common tavern bully, with these trained swine to do your dirty work!"

The Englishman stared down his long nose at her. He'd been so pleased to find Griffin that he hadn't noticed the woman before, and the corners of his mouth curled upwards. "And what courtesy did you show me on the *Gaspee*, you ginger-haired bitch?" he sneered. "What a catch I've made this day, to land the pirate and his whore in one net!"

"I'm Captain Griffin's wife." Eliza folded her arms across her chest and raised her chin defiantly. "I am also the owner of this vessel, which you, sir, have seen fit to board without reason or warrant. You may be sure I'll report your actions to both Governor Wanton and Admiral Graves as soon as I can."

Gardner listened to her with mounting unhappiness. *Oh, Eliza, hush now, don't do this to yourself! Save your own neck, lass!*

"It's me you want, not her—" he began, but the guard struck him again.

Dudingston reached out to stroke Eliza's cheek. She jerked away, her eyes full of sparks, and he chuckled. "Tell me, hussy, would a gentleman's gold piece make you spread your legs faster than this rogue's treasonous prattle?"

Gardner lunged forward and threw himself at Dudingston. The lieutenant tumbled backwards to the deck beneath Gardner's weight and the onslaught of his fists. Dudingston represented everything that Gardner hated most, and he made sure each blow drove savagely into the Englishman's face and chest. It took four men to pull Gardner back, and a rifle butt in his ribs to knock the wind out of him.

As Dudingston unsteadily regained his feet, he shrugged off the assistance from his crewmen. "Get this cur into the boat, and the woman, too," he sputtered angrily. "A spell in irons will take the fight out of them both. And I want this schooner searched for contraband and her crew put below."

Eliza's thoughts raced ahead. If both she and Gardner were imprisoned on the *Rose,* there would be virtually no way to escape. She called out to Dudingston as a sailor's hand tightened on her arm.

"Look at me closely, Lieutenant. When we cleared Martinique a fortnight ago, I was near death from yellow fever. Do you really want me in your precious ship?"

Dudingston squinted at her, noting for the first time the unmistakable yellow tinge to her skin. Damn the wench, and he'd touched her, too! "Very well, then, you shall remain here, confined to the cabin. But Griffin comes with me."

As the British seamen led Gardner towards the side, Eliza noticed that, in their cockiness, they hadn't bothered to bind his hands. There was a hope, albeit tenuous, that he might escape if he had the chance, a chance perhaps she could give him. She rushed forward from her own guard and threw her arms around Gardner's neck.

"Take care, my love!" she said loud enough for all to hear. Then pressing closer, she whispered urgently into Gardner's ear. "When I act like a fool, jump, and may God keep you safe!"

Strong hands jerked Eliza back. Her eyes met Gardner's, and a lifetime of unspoken promises passed between them. He tried to smile to reassure her, but the bruises were already swelling across his cheek, and blood flowed from a gash in his lip. Then roughly he was shoved over the side and into the waiting boat.

The tears Eliza now shed were genuine, but because they served her purpose, she made no effort to hide them. When the longboat pulled away from the *Liberty,* she hurled herself at the side. With one hand on the ratlines, she climbed onto the narrow railing and tottered there dizzily, shrieking Gardner's name.

Every face in the boat except the one that mattered turned up towards her. As the sailors finally pulled her back, she heard the splash and the outcry from the longboat and realized joyfully that Gardner had seized the opportunity she'd given him.

But later, locked alone in the cabin where they'd spent so much time together, Eliza struggled to fight back her panic and fear. All she knew for certain was that she had spared Gardner from dying on the gallows. And that, in her despair, was little comfort indeed.

Chapter Twenty

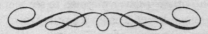

On the fourth night, Eliza sat alone in the cabin, picking at the supper the guard had dropped onto the table before her. The knock at the door startled her, and she gasped at the visitor who now entered.

"Josiah!" She rose from her chair, the napkin clutched in her hand.

He bowed slightly and smiled. "Good evening, my dear, I hope—"

"No, Josiah, don't even start! I have nothing to say to you, and you'll say nothing I want to hear," said Eliza hotly. "Guard!"

Josiah leaned on his stick, unperturbed. He hadn't expected her to see him willingly, but he could be generous, knowing tonight he held the winning hand. "Spare yourself, Eliza. I sent the man away. I'm here with the blessings of Lieutenant Dudingston, who is, incidentally, an old associate of mine. A business associate, shall we say."

"Another Tory villain like yourself, I'd say! You're a vile, despicable Judas!"

"I wouldn't be so quick to brand me a traitor, Eliza, considering you're the one who's held for treason."

"You should be the one in gaol, there for murdering my father and two others!"

Josiah sighed. "You must believe that Captain Raeburn's death was a lamentable accident. For your sake, if no other, I never planned to see him harmed."

Eliza remembered Josiah's empty words of condolence, and bitterness swept over her. "How could I believe anything you say?"

"Perhaps because despite all you've done, I still love you, and always have," he declared. "How much longer do you think Dudingston's patience will last before he sends you to London? He's eager to make an example of you, to see your 'pretty rebel neck stretched,' is how he indelicately phrased it. But I can offer you a choice, Eliza. Marry me, and Dudingston will release you."

Eliza thrust out her hand with Gardner's ring. "I'm already married, Josiah."

"Already widowed, from what I hear. I've made inquiries. No one in the colony has seen your *husband*—" he sneered at the word "—since he foolishly jumped from the boat. I'll grant you Griffin was strong as a bull, but not even he could survive for long in these waters. Your own father could tell you that."

Eliza sucked in her breath as if she'd been hit, wounded by his casual cruelty.

Josiah stepped closer, reaching for the hand that Eliza jerked back. "I would have preferred to be your first husband, true, but I'll soon make you forget Griffin. I can offer you so much more, Eliza. The crown is generous to loyal subjects. We'll have a grand house in Newport, away from that rabble in Providence. You shall have whatever you please—gowns, jewels, servants—whatever will make you happy as my wife."

"I'd rather hang than marry you, Josiah."

"Don't be so hasty, my dear. Hanging isn't a pretty death."

Only a little table remained between them. Eliza felt suffocated by his presence, by the triumph that lit his eyes. He could not force her to marry him, but there were things he could do to her that would be worse. She remembered too well that her strength was no match for Josiah's, but Gardner's guns and knife had been confiscated, along with anything else she could use as a weapon. She forced herself to stay calm, to look for a way to save herself. Her gaze darted past Josiah and around the cabin, and for the first time, she noticed that he had left the cabin door unlatched.

"Come with me, Eliza," coaxed Josiah. "Come, and be my wife."

Eliza hooked her hands under the edge of the table and flipped it towards Josiah. Boiled peas and greasy salt pork splattered across his clothes, and he cursed her as hot tea showered onto his face and hands.

Eliza rushed past him and through the unlatched door. The lantern had burned out since the guard had gone, and the companionway was inky black. Without hesitating, Eliza ran into the darkness and struck directly against the solid barrier of a broad, male chest. She tried to pull back, but the man had already caught her, and behind him she could hear the breathing and rustling of other men there in the dark.

"Let me go, you English pig!" she cried as she fought. "Let me go at once!"

Behind her Josiah threw open the door, and light from the cabin now flooded the companionway. Abruptly Eliza's captor shoved her away. Josiah stood silhouetted in the door, his walking stick raised like a sword.

"Eliza!" he called angrily. "Where the hell are you?"

"She's where she belongs, Buck," said Gardner. "With me."

Eliza gasped. She had pictured this moment so many times over the past days that she still half believed she was dreaming, but there was no mistaking Gardner's voice. Nor was there any mistaking the pistol he aimed at Josiah.

"Has he hurt you, sweetheart?" Gardner's eyes never strayed from Josiah. "I'll shoot him dead if he has, and be done with it."

"I'm fine." Eliza rose unsteadily. Another man stepped forward to help her to her feet, and his gap-toothed grin was familiar, too. "Nathaniel!"

"So it's an entire family reunion, is it?" snarled Josiah as Eliza went to stand behind Gardner. "So many men to defend your tawdry honor, Mistress Griffin!"

Nathaniel's grin vanished. "You shut your mouth, Buck, or I'll shut it for you!"

But Gardner held him back. "Nay, not yet, not like that," he said. As much as he would have liked to end

Josiah's life here and now, there were too many questions he would still like answered. "We haven't the time to treat him proper. Wilson, truss him up for safekeeping."

Josiah stood perfectly still as his wrists were tied behind his back, but his face was mottled with such unbridled hatred that Eliza shrank behind Gardner's shoulder. "How did you know I was here?"

"I didn't. I came for Eliza and her schooner, and an easy enough task that was. After we took the *Gaspee*, you'd think the British would do a better job of keeping watch." Gardner lowered the pistol, his eyes still hard chips of blue ice. "But then I'm not like Dudingston, with a snake like you to tell me secrets of every ship in these waters."

Josiah glowered. "Loyalty has its price."

"Aye, your kind, maybe," answered Gardner contemptuously. "I always preferred the stuff that's given for free."

"Free!" Josiah spat out the word. "I gave my leg to King George! I offered my loyalty, and became a cripple in return. Can you blame me if I ask for more now?"

"You made your choices, took your chances."

"No, not like the rest of you, damn you all!" He swung around towards Eliza. "I did it all for you, Eliza Raeburn! I did everything I could to make you mine!"

"And so because I could not love you," said Eliza slowly, "you had to send my father to his death, and Gardner, too?"

"I would do it again if I knew you'd be mine!" There was an unnatural wildness to his expression. "Yet no matter what I did, it was never enough, was it? You were always too proud for a cripple like me, weren't you?"

"I never felt that way, Josiah," she began, but he cut her off with a harsh laugh.

"Save your pity. I don't want it, and I don't want you, not now." His gaze reeled back towards Gardner. "You prattle on about loyalty, Griffin. Who can teach you more about it than a faithless woman? You're welcome to the bitch, and the devil take you both!"

"That's enough, Buck!" ordered Gardner. He refused to argue with a madman, and he had no doubt now that Buck was beyond reason. "Take him to the boat."

Eliza watched Wilson prodding Josiah towards the deck. Without his cane, he limped painfully, his chin down as he muttered into his once immaculate shirt front, now flecked with the food she'd thrown on him. He could not hurt her anymore, yet still she shook uncontrollably. "What will become of him?"

Gardner drew her into his arms. "That's not my decision, love. I'll keep him bound in the *Betsy's* hold until I can give him to John Brown. But before that, we have a little game of cat and mouse to play."

Gardner's plan was simple enough. He would sail the little sloop *Betsy* close enough to the *Rose* for the English watch to recognize him. Gardner was counting on Dudingston to then chase the *Betsy*, and give

Nathaniel and the *Liberty* the chance to escape unnoticed up the river to Providence.

Dawn found the *Betsy* dancing across the bay towards the *Rose,* Gardner at the tiller and Eliza beside him. The *Betsy* was no different from the score of other sloops, nimble and quick, that dotted Newport harbor on their way up and down the coast. The morning sky was a sharp enamel blue, the wind brisk. Eliza tugged her coat sleeves over her hands.

"If we're the mouse," she said as they drew nearer to the frigate, "then the *Rose* is the biggest cat I've ever seen."

Gardner grinned. "More like the British lion, y'think?"

"*I* think John Brown must have had one claret cup too many to lend you the *Betsy* for such a fool's errand," she declared. She was edgy from excitement and lack of sleep. Rowing from the *Liberty* to where the *Betsy* had been moored had taken most of the night, and this was the first moment she'd had to talk to Gardner alone.

"Be thankful he did, or you'd never see the *Liberty* again." He handed her the spyglass and gestured towards the schooner. "Everything peaceful there, I'd say, and no sign we went calling last night. And Sam Thomson makes a more passable lady than you ever did."

Eliza squinted through the glass. She and Sam had traded clothes, much to the boy's dismay, and now, with the hood of Eliza's cloak turned up to cover his blond hair, Sam walked back and forth across the

Liberty's deck much as Eliza had each morning. "Do you really think this will work, Gardner?"

His expression darkened, and Eliza realized his bantering has been as empty as her own. "Aye, lass, it will. Dudingston would chase me to China and back if he had to. I'm a thousand guineas in his pocket and a six-foot-four thorn in his side. He'll follow, no mistake."

"What if he fires on us?"

"He won't. There's no reward if I'm dead." He saw how she looked away from him, hugging her arms around herself. He reached out his fingers to brush her cheek. "You're not frightened, are you, love?"

"Of course not, Gardner, I'm only—" Then she stopped and bit her lower lip before she could meet his gaze again. "Yes, I am scared. How could I not be? The *Rose* is four times our size."

The poignancy in her voice made him feel unbearably selfish. "Then we'll turn back here. I shouldn't have brought you. You can wait with Nathaniel."

"No!" she cried fiercely. "I'm honest enough to admit I'm frightened, but that doesn't mean I'd wish it otherwise. It will take a good deal more than the *Rose*'s guns to scare me away from you!"

She stood before him with her chin raised defiantly, her cheeks ruddy from the cold and wisps of coppery hair trailing from under her hat, and he knew he'd never seen a more enchanting woman. How could he ever dream of protecting her when she was every bit his equal?

"There's no one under heaven that I'd want here instead." he said. "Your place is here with me, Eliza, as long as you wish it. Seems that whenever I'm watching after you, you're fussing about watching after me. We're like two dogs chasing each other's tails. Truth is, I can no more leave you behind than my right arm. You're part of me, lass, and I wouldn't have it any other way.''

Tears welled in Eliza's eyes. "I love you, Gardner," she said hoarsely. "Oh, how much I love you!"

"Beggin' your pardon, Cap'n Griffin, but look!" High above them in the rigging, Wilson was pointing excitedly at the *Rose*.

Gardner turned quickly towards the frigate. "Well, now," he drawled. "It's about time they took notice of us, isn't it?"

The *Rose* was now near enough that Eliza could see the sailors gesturing wildly to the officer of the watch, who immediately trained his glass on the *Betsy*.

"Duck your face, sweetheart," said Gardner, and Eliza quickly pulled her three-cornered hat lower. "Don't want you giving the game away just yet."

Almost at once Dudingston appeared, the sun glinting off his uniform's braid and polished buttons. He too studied the *Betsy* through the glass. With a grand, mocking flourish that brought a roar of laughter from his own crew, Gardner swept off his hat and bowed. Dudingston snapped the spyglass shut, and Eliza could feel his anger clear across the water.

"Damn your eyes, Griffin!" he bellowed through a speaking trumpet. "You're a bloody scoundrel, a pirate, and I mean to see you hung from the yardarm before sunset!"

Gardner cupped his hands around his mouth. "Brave promises, Dudingston!" he called. "But you'll have to catch me first!"

He lowered his hands and grinned wickedly at Eliza. Her golden eyes were bright with excitement, her lips parted. He wanted very much to kiss her, and would have, if Dudingston hadn't been watching. Instead Gardner had to content himself with lightly punching her shoulder with acceptable masculine camaraderie, and Eliza giggled. Stern as a preacher, he settled his hat lower on his brow, but the sparkle in his blue eyes gave him away. "Laugh now, Mrs. Griffin, but when we win this race, I'll ask for that kiss, and a great deal more, as my prize."

But as the frigate's sails caught the wind and the *Rose* came neatly around to begin the chase, Eliza saw Gardner's teasing good humor vanish, replaced by a steely concentration. He was a master mariner, his crew the best Providence could offer, and the *Betsy* the ideal vessel for the warren of islands and inlets before him. But neither could he afford to underestimate Dudingston.

Gardner steered the *Betsy* along the Eastern Passage through Narragansett Bay as far as the tip of Conanicut Island, then cut sharply to the east to the far side of Prudence Island. Eliza could imagine Dudingston's glee as he easily followed them through the channel. Anxiously she watched as the gap between the *Betsy* and the *Rose* slowly narrowed.

"I don't like this, Gardner," she finally told him. "They're too close."

"Aye, lass, too close by half," he agreed. "But I must give Nathaniel time enough to bring the *Liberty* up the other side of the island. He must be well ahead of us before we clear Warwick Neck. We can't show our speed until then."

Thoughtfully he ran the back of his thumb across his upper lip. "You've sharp eyes. Take the glass, and tell me the moment you see the *Liberty*."

Free today from petticoats, Eliza nimbly climbed the shrouds to the crosstrees. She had not been so high since childhood, when her father had let her clamber over the *Peacock*'s rigging. The sloop's motion in the waves was exaggerated this far up, and Eliza felt as if she were clinging to the top branches of a very tall tree, swaying in lazy arcs with the wind. She braced herself against the mast and levelled the glass. Far across the broad back of Prudence Island, she could see the glitter of the bay, but no sign of the *Liberty*. Now with her eyes alone, she gazed across the empty horizon. Where could Nathaniel be? The wind was in his favor, the schooner swift, and Gardner had given him plenty of time. The *Betsy* was nearly even with Warwick Neck, and if Gardner couldn't increase the distance from the *Rose* now, the frigate would surely overtake them in the open water of Providence Bay.

Then she saw the little tip of white, far ahead of them. Quickly she raised the glass again, and the white spot became the *Liberty*'s huge angled mainsail.

"Nathaniel's done it!" she crowed. "The *Liberty*'s miles ahead of us!"

Eliza felt the warmth of Gardner's smile all the way from the deck. Rapidly he shouted the commands the crew had been waiting for, and even as the men cheered, Eliza felt the *Betsy* leap forward with new speed.

Jubilant, Eliza looked back at the *Rose*. Faith, how she wished she could see Dudingston's face when he learned how they'd foxed him! But there was, she decided, no reason for him to wait for the news. Gleefully she stripped off her hat and let the wind whip her long hair outward like a pennant.

"Get down here, you brazen creature!" Gardner called up to her. "You'll give that poor lieutenant apoplexy!"

Laughing, he caught her as she reached the deck and lifted her lightly off the shrouds with both hands. "Mind, we're not home free until we reach Providence. That's still twelve miles."

"But half that to Namquit Point. You've said yourself they can't follow us beyond that."

"And there's much that can happen between here and there," cautioned Gardner. "I'll claim that kiss at Namquit Point and not before."

The little sloop almost flew across the water. Soon they would be out of the bay and into the river and safe from the *Rose*'s pursuit. But still they had not shaken the frigate; to Eliza it seemed the bigger ship was even closer now. Too slowly the *Betsy* neared the rocky point that meant safety, and Eliza's whole body was tense from willing the sloop to go faster.

"You can stop praying now, sweetheart," said Gardner at last. "They can't touch us."

Eliza stared at him so dubiously that he laughed. "Nay, it's true. Low tide's on our side today. Look at the water."

Eliza peered over the rail. The waves beneath them had changed perceptibly to a lighter blue as the water had grown more shallow. "Now set your eyes to our poor friend Dudingston. At any moment his leadsman will tell him about that sandy bottom, and you can wave farewell to the *Rose* for good."

Through the glass, Eliza watched it all as Gardner described, down to Dudingston petulantly stamping his foot at the unwelcome news. With a happy smile, Eliza slipped her arms around Gardner's neck. "You have a prize to claim, Captain Griffin."

But instead of kissing her as she expected, Gardner swore loudly and pushed her arms away. "Damn them all! They can't let me go, can they! They'll blast us out of the very water!"

Immediately Eliza looked back at the *Rose*, and what she saw left her with the same dread and foreboding that Gardner felt. Without realizing it, she curled her fingers into Gardner's for comfort. Quite gracefully, the *Rose* was swinging about to face them broadside. Already her gunports were flipped open, a long row of black squares ready to explode with fire and smoke and death. Across the water faintly came the snare drum's roll to clear the decks and call the men to action.

Wilson hurried towards them. "Will y'look at that, Cap'n? I've not seen the likes in all my years on these waters. What business can they be about?"

"The business of sending us all to the devil!" snapped Gardner.

"Nay, Cap'n, not the British. I mean all them to the larboard."

As Gardner turned to where Wilson was pointing, his expression changed from desperation to wonder. From the mouth of the Pawtuxet River came dozens of boats, smacks and sloops and cowhorns and shallops, all rushing towards the *Betsy* as fast as the wind could fill their sails. Quickly they ranged themselves around the sloop like chicks around a mother hen. As soon as Gardner realized what they were doing, he felt something curious swelling in his throat, and he wondered whether he would laugh or weep.

"I don't understand," said Eliza. "Who are they?"

To his great relief, Gardner began to laugh. He picked Eliza up and twirled her around in the air. "It doesn't matter who they are, love. They've come and saved us, they have! The *Betsy* alone Dudingston could destroy, and claim it was worth it to put an end to me. But to fire on two score vessels for the sake of catching one man—nay, not even Parliament could call that sane."

The lead smack bumped alongside the *Betsy*, and a fisherman, with black eyebrows as thick as yew bushes, hailed Gardner from the bow.

"You got your own navy, Griffin?" he called. "I stack us any day against those mewling, yellow-livered creatures the king's got servin' him."

"You may get your chance, Trask, and sooner than you think," answered Gardner. "But tell me, man, how did you know I'd be needing you?"

The fisherman winked and tapped one finger against his bulbous nose. "Your plan sounded grand as far as it went, but I be thinkin', now that lad could use a few friends, jes' to give him a welcome home." He boldly looked Eliza over from head to feet. "This be your lady-love, ain't it? Don't set much store by the way she's rigged."

Gardner introduced Eliza to the man who had rescued him after he'd jumped from the *Rose*'s boat. "I can't thank you enough for saving my husband's life," she said. "I owe you so much."

"Eh, 'tis nothing beside what we all owe the cap'n here," the man answered sheepishly. Another boat drew beside his, and Trask gratefully turned to introducing the newcomers to Gardner. Eliza watched with amusement as Gardner squirmed beneath the extravagant praise piled on her husband's broad shoulders. To merchants like John Brown, the *Gaspee*'s interference had meant the loss of a cargo or higher insurance to pay. For these men, whose lives and livelihoods depended on a single small boat, the threat had been much more. Gardner was right. When the rebellion came, it would be these men who would form the colonies' first navy.

Behind her, Eliza heard her name called, and, expecting Wilson or one of the other sailors, she turned with a smile. The smile froze when she saw Josiah, crouching beside the unconscious body of one of the seamen. He had taken the man's pistol and now clutched it tightly in his hand. He called her name again, this time almost joyfully, as he steadied the gun with both hands and carefully drew back the trigger.

In that single moment, Eliza saw the perfect vision of her future life with Gardner burst and vanish. All the children they would never have, the laughter they would never share and the love that would now be ended by the selfish act of a madman.

"No," she whispered to herself, and closed her eyes. *"No!"*

She heard the first shot but not the second, and felt herself knocked hard to the deck. With confusion she realized no bullet had found her. The impact that had sent her tumbling had come from Gardner, who still lay sprawled on top of her.

"Josiah—" she began.

"He won't be bothering you, not ever again." Wincing, Gardner lifted his weight off her onto his elbows, and Eliza saw his fingers still curled around the gun in his hand and, beyond, Josiah's lifeless body crumpled beside the hatch.

"Oh, Gardner," she murmured. She reached up to put her arms around him, to feel again the comfort and security that only came from him. Her hand brushed the side of his coat and came away wet and sticky with blood. "My God, he hit you instead of me!"

"Hush, love, it's no matter." With enormous effort, he smiled down at her. Though he didn't believe the wound was serious, it still hurt like hell. Yet to see Eliza's dear, freckled face, wide-eyed with concern but safe at last, was worth the pain.

"Kiss me, sweetheart," he ordered. "I won the blasted race, didn't I?"

But before she could, he had collapsed, unconscious, on top of her.

A week later, Eliza leaned from the open window, enjoying the first true day of spring. The sun felt warm on her upturned face, and the breeze ruffled her hair and skirts. "The roads south will be dry soon. If Dr. Mawney says you're well enough, we may be on our way to Philadelphia in a fortnight."

"Damn Dr. Mawney!" thundered Gardner from the bed. "I've a mind to leave tomorrow, even if it must be by blasted coach. How much cosseting is a man supposed to take?"

Eliza came to stand beside the bed, her hands on her hips. Even with the white bandage wrapped around his chest, Gardner looked healthier—and more impossibly handsome—than any man had a right to. "You stay put," she said sternly, "or I'll dose you with laudanum to keep you in bed."

He grinned suggestively. "I can think of far more pleasurable ways to keep me here." Before she could answer, he grabbed her around the waist and tugged her onto the bed beside him.

"You treat a bullet in the ribs as if it were no more than a scratch from a kitten," she chided gently as she nestled beside him on the quilt. "But I cannot, not when I think of how close I came to losing you forever."

"Thank the Lord that my aim was better than Josiah's."

Eliza stared up at the ceiling. Despite Gardner's flippancy, she was still haunted by the memory of the gun in Josiah's hand. "Dr. Mawney told me if his bullet had hit you but two inches higher..."

"Ah, love, it will take a great deal more than one bullet to kill me. Over and over I tell you that, and you never listen."

"I'll listen when you stop trying to prove it." Lightly she rested her head on his shoulder. "Perhaps in Philadelphia you'll be better behaved."

"Nay, lass, I've friends there who will find mischief enough for both of us, and I've no doubt Sam Adams will find me, too, once he gets that letter from Laurant," he said, and Eliza smiled at the anticipation in his voice. "When Nathaniel brings us the *Liberty,* why, we'll be back in business. It could take the British years to find us there."

"We'll need new names, then, I'll be your Mariah again if you'll be my Captain Chandler."

He laughed too loudly and grunted at the pain in his side. Eliza sat up quickly, ready to call the doctor, but Gardner shrugged off her concern.

"You'll kill me with kindness, sweetheart, and there's nothing in that for either of us." He caught her hand and lifted her fingers to his lips. With a sigh, Eliza once again curled up beside him, and together they lay in contented silence, listening to the gulls outside the window.

"You have a good life here in Providence, Eliza," said Gardner quietly. "A fine home, neighbors and friends, a family that cares mightily for you. There'll be none of that in Philadelphia, or wherever we come to roost, and when the war comes, I can't say what will happen."

He smiled crookedly. "I can't even promise you'll be called Mrs. Griffin."

"Hush, love," she said softly. "Don't you know by now that none of that matters? As long as I'm with you, none of it matters at all."

And when he kissed her, she knew it never would.

* * * * *

**Now that you've been introduced to our
March Madness authors, be sure to look for
their upcoming titles:**

From Miranda Jarrett—

COLUMBINE—Wrongly convicted for murder, Lady Diana Grey
finds herself on her way to the American Colonies as an indentured servant.

From Ana Seymour—

ANGEL OF THE LAKE—The warm-hearted story of a widower,
wracked with guilt, and the woman who teaches him to love.

From Kit Gardner—

THE DREAM—A stiff-necked boarding school teacher is defense-
less against the charm of a handsome, carefree lord who has set
his sights on her.

From Margaret Moore—

CHINA BLOSSOM—Raised as a pampered Chinese slave, a young
Englishwoman must adjust to 19th-century British society.

Four great stories that you won't want to miss!

MMANB

Take 4 bestselling love stories FREE

Plus get a FREE surprise gift!